SWORD
ARt
ONline
PROGRESSIVE
002

REKI KAWAHARA
ILLUSTRATION BY abec
DESIGN BY bee-pee

SWORD ART ONLINE

"Yes. We'll go together, the three of us."

Asuna

A player trapped inside *Sword Art Online*. Without a care for her life, she throws herself into battle against monsters.

"It wasn't the gods. Asuna and I were there of our own will. We'll stick with you until the end."

Kirito

A swordsman aiming to beat the top floor of Aincrad. He adventures as a solo player but temporarily teams up with Asuna.

Kizmel

A dark elf NPC from the third floor's campaign quest. She was scripted to die in the beta version of the game, but now...

"In that case, I will do my best to protect you. Until our paths part."

"Are you really that stupid?!"

"Oh, my serious switch is always on, partner."

Morte

A member of the Dragon Knights Brigade, currently run by Lind, one of Diavel's followers. A swordsman who wears a distinct metal coif.

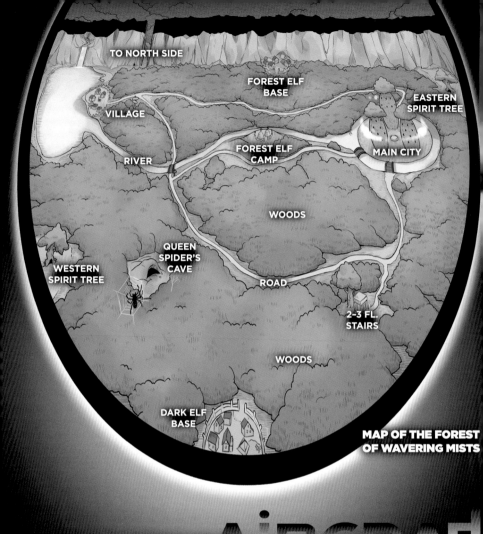

TO NORTH SIDE

FOREST ELF
BASE

EASTERN
SPIRIT TREE

VILLAGE

FOREST ELF
CAMP

MAIN CITY

RIVER

WOODS

QUEEN
SPIDER'S
CAVE

WESTERN
SPIRIT TREE

ROAD

2-3 FL.
STAIRS

WOODS

DARK ELF
BASE

**MAP OF THE FOREST
OF WAVERING MISTS**

FLOATING CASTLE AINCRAD FLOOR DATA AINCRAD

THIRD FLOOR

The design theme of this floor is "forest." Unlike the woods near Horunka on the first floor or the southern area of the second floor, the third floor is covered entirely by enormous ancient trees. The southern area of this floor is called the Forest of Wavering Mists, a baffling place choked with thick fog. The main city of the third floor, Zumfut, is built inside gigantic hollowed-out trees. There is a dark elf stronghold at the south end of the forest and a forest elf stronghold at the north end. These act as the bases for each side of the campaign quest.

The bases have tents for sleeping, eating, and even bathing, so players in the midst of the quest have no need to return to town. A field boss guards the tiny pass between the mountains, beyond which is the northern area of the floor and the labyrinth tower.

The boss of the third floor is Nerius the Evil Treant. Nerius takes the form of a giant walking tree, and like Illfang the Kobold Lord and King Asterios, its attack patterns have been changed from the beta test.

SWORD ART ONLINE PROGRESSIVE

VOLUME 2

Reki Kawahara

abec

bee-pee

YEN ON

NEW YORK

SWORD ART ONLINE PROGRESSIVE Volume 2
© REKI KAWAHARA

Translation by Stephen Paul

SWORD ART ONLINE PROGRESSIVE
© REKI KAWAHARA 2013
All rights reserved.
Edited by ASCII MEDIA WORKS
First published in Japan in 2013 by KADOKAWA CORPORATION, Tokyo.
English translation rights arranged with KADOKAWA CORPORATION, Tokyo, through Tuttle-Mori Agency, Inc., Tokyo.

English translation © 2015 by Hachette Book Group, Inc.

Yen On
Hachette Book Group
1290 Avenue of the Americas
New York, NY 10104

www.hachettebookgroup.com
www.yenpress.com

Yen On is an imprint of Hachette Book Group, Inc.
The Yen On name and logo are trademarks of Hachette Book Group, Inc.

The publisher is not responsible for websites (or their content) that are not owned by the publisher.

First Yen On edition: June 2015

ISBN: 978-0-316-34217-9

10 9 8 7 6 5 4 3 2 1

RRD-C

Printed in the United States of America

"THIS MIGHT BE A GAME, BUT IT'S NOT SOMETHING YOU PLAY."

—Akihiko Kayaba, *Sword Art Online* programmer

SWORD ART ONLINE PROGRESSIVE

CONCERTO OF BLACK AND WHITE

THIRD FLOOR OF AINCRAD, NOVEMBER 2022

1

THE FIRST FLOOR OF AINCRAD WAS AN "ANYTHING goes" floor, with no unifying design theme. The terrain was rich and varied, with fields, forests, wastelands, and canyons, not to mention numerous smaller towns and villages outside the main city. It added up to a welcoming atmosphere for new players, but now that the game was deadly, few people were in the mood to soak in the surroundings.

The second floor, however, had a very clear, unified design. The land was covered with green grazing fields and multilayered flat-topped mountains, and the monsters within were all animal types. As a nod to the effort of beating the first floor, the wilderness of the second was not very difficult, which, combined with the visual style, gave it a laid-back, "pastoral" theme. Most players called it the "cow floor," for obvious reasons.

Next up was the unconquered third floor.

As I climbed the spiral staircase from the second-floor boss chamber to the third-floor town, I clenched my fist and muttered, "In a way, this is where *SAO* really starts…"

It was meant more as a reminder to myself, but my companion heard me and asked, "Really? Why is that?"

I scratched my head and explained, "Well…the third floor is where human mobs first show up. The kobolds and tauruses from below were demihumans, so they could use simple sword skills, but they were still monsters, right? Well, some of the enemies ahead look indistinguishable from other players. You honestly wouldn't be able to tell them apart without a color cursor. Just like NPCs, they can talk and use expert sword skills. Meaning..."

I looked over my shoulder and fixed Asuna the fencer with a look. "This is where the real *Sword Art Online* begins. I read plenty of magazine interviews and articles on Akihiko Kayaba, the man who trapped us in here. He said that the term *Sword Art* refers to the light and sound of the clash of sword skill on sword skill—a concerto of life and death."

"...Oh..."

The phrase that had given me shivers of excitement a year ago did not have any noticeable effect on Asuna. We continued walking up the stairs at a measured pace. Her next comment took me by surprise.

"Does that mean he was already plotting this crime when he gave that interview?"

"Umm...well, I guess it does."

On that fateful day five weeks ago, Kayaba summoned all the players of *SAO* into the center square of the Town of Beginnings and announced, "I created the NerveGear and *SAO* precisely in order to build this world and observe it. I have now achieved that aim."

If those words were true, then from the very first line Kayaba ever drew on a NerveGear diagram, he'd been envisioning this terrible crime as his ultimate goal. All of his statements that thrilled my young mind (well, only a year younger) now held a terrible double meaning.

Asuna quietly murmured, "A concerto...of life and death. I wonder if he really meant that to refer to the sword art of player against humanoid enemies."

"Huh...? What do you mean?"

It was my turn to be confused. I'd climbed up identical sets of spiraling staircases to the next floor nearly a dozen times between the beta and the full release, so it was familiar enough that I could continue to climb while facing backward. The only thing that differed between floors was the style of carvings on the blackened walls. A closer look always revealed some kind of thematic hint at the next floor's contents, but I was concentrating on Asuna's words at the moment.

Her face serious, she whispered, "Maybe I'm overthinking this…but a concerto isn't a performance where instruments form a pair to play against each other. That would be a duet."

"So what exactly is a concerto, then?"

"The definition changes depending on the era, but at its most basic, it's an orchestra acting as the background accompaniment to a soloist or small group of independent players. So it's not one-on-one, but one-on-many, or few-on-many."

"One…against many…" I repeated and stopped myself before I asked if it could mean a player against a group of monsters.

It was almost never the case that a single player faced off against a large collection of foes—say, ten or more. Without any magic spells that could attack a large area at once, and the closest sword skills merely adding a foot or two to the weapon's reach, being surrounded by monsters in *SAO* meant certain death.

That ironclad law was reflected in the game's design, so nearly all monsters were solitary, or in groups no larger than three or four. As long as you didn't run around intentionally drawing attention or hitting alarm traps, a single player would never encounter a large mass of enemies. Even if it happened, no one would be foolish enough to stand and fight.

"In that case, there's no battle in this world that actually corresponds to a real concerto. If anything, it might refer to a boss battle…but in that case, the boss would be the lead, and the players, the accompaniment," I said with a wry chuckle. Asuna opened her mouth to respond, then shut it. After a brief pause, she grinned slightly.

"I suppose so. I'm just overthinking this. More importantly, Kirito…"

"Huh? What?"

"Never mind, too late."

As soon as she said those words, the back of my head slammed against the thick stone door at the top of the stairs.

"*Nguh!*" I grunted pitifully and lost my balance, hands waving wildly. I made sure to fall backward, sensing it would still be better than flopping forward and directly onto Asuna.

But in that brief instant, the stone door that should have propped my back up had already opened, and I fell shrieking through the doorway to land directly on my butt atop the mossy paving stones—the momentous first step into the new, uncharted floor.

The third floor of Aincrad.

Its design theme was "forest," but this was forest on a scale unlike the woods around Horunka on the first floor, or the southern area of the second floor. Even the smallest tree here had a trunk at least three feet across and towered nearly a hundred feet in the air. These vast, ancient trees stretched as far as the eye could see, and the golden beams of light that trickled through their endless branches and leaves was a magical sight.

"Wow!" Asuna marveled, walking right past me as I writhed and clutched my tailbone. I spun around halfway on my rear end to take in the sight. She stopped ahead and spun around in the narrow band of light, drinking in the panorama of thick, endless forest.

"Incredible…Just this sight was worth all of the trouble to get here!"

The hood of her familiar wool cape was pulled back, so the glint of light reflecting off her long brown hair caught my eye. With her slender build and elegant beauty, Asuna looked more like a frolicking forest dryad than a human player.

"…Yeah. It really was," I murmured and got to my feet. I straightened my leather coat and stretched. Even the air seemed to be sweeter and moister here, full of rich phytoncides…I could imagine.

I turned back to see that we'd just walked out of an ancient stone structure built into the roots of a particularly huge tree, the mouth of the staircase yawning and black. Within twenty minutes, the other frontline players would be wrapping up their tasks and coming out of this exit.

"And now," I murmured, opening my window and starting up an instant message to Argo the Rat. I told the information dealer that she should inform the public that the second floor had been conquered, and the teleport gate to the third floor would be open within an hour. She'd been present in the boss chamber but had disappeared before the fight was over, so this was just in case.

The task set to me by Lind, leader of the raid party, was complete. I closed the window and took another look around the forest.

I wanted to stand around and enjoy the feeling of satisfaction at reaching the third floor, but time was of the essence. Like any other new floor, there was shopping to be done, quests to undertake, and levels to gain. But before any of that, I had to confirm something with my temporary party member.

I steeled myself for the task, sidled up to Asuna as she continued to soak in the scenery, and coughed politely.

"Um, I hate to interrupt your leisure…"

"…What is it?"

She turned to me, a rare smile on her face. I drew her gaze north with the point of my index finger. A stone path leading away from the structure behind us split into a Y-intersection just twenty yards ahead.

"If we turn right up there, it goes to the main city. The left side takes us through the forest for a while, and eventually to the next town."

"…I see."

"Normally, we ought to go to the city and activate the portal, but I'd prefer to leave that up to Lind and Kibaou's teams, since they'll be coming right up after us."

"……I see."

"Part of it is because I don't want the attention, but the other part is that there's a task we can take care of if we go down the left path. I realize both of those reasons are my own personal rationale, so..."

The grin on her face began to fade. In fact, there was a threatening glare forming in her eyes. It finally dawned on me that if I chose my words poorly here, I would be earning myself the full and mighty wrath of one of Asuna's bad moods—I just didn't know the rules of how to avoid that.

"...And?" she prompted, her voice cool.

"Um...well...we do need to restock on supplies, so if you wanted to just go straight to the main city, I suppose we'd have to break up our party here...But of course, if you wanted to join me in tackling this quest in the forest, I wouldn't try to convince you to reconsider..."

"If you're asking me if I don't want to break up the party, then *no*, I have no problem with that. We're both solo players, unless I'm sorely mistaken?"

"Y-yes, ma'am."

"But this errand you're talking about is best if taken care of first, I assume? In that case, I'll join you—I hate being inefficient. Of course, if you'd rather kick me out of the party so you can reap the benefits all to yourself, I suppose I can't stop you."

"N-no, no, I don't want to be selfish at all. Besides, it'll be more efficient for us as a group."

"Then let's get going. I won't need to restock and repair for a little while yet."

"G-great."

She turned on her heel and strode off down the path, her boots clicking on the stones. I hurried after her, inwardly deciding that I'd just barely slid in safe, though I had no idea what I was safe *from* exactly.

If I'd known it would come to this, I would have talked to the girls in class more often, I silently rued, then snorted in denial. If I was playing a middle schooler with that kind of character build, I wouldn't have been ready to log in to the retail version of

SAO five seconds after the servers went online, and I'd never be walking through this fantastical forest with this fickle fencer in the first place. It was a pointless conjecture.

Speaking of which...

In the month that I'd been trapped in this castle, I'd been hell-bent on survival, on powering myself up through whatever means I could find. Had I ever even stopped to regret my decision to jump into *Sword Art Online*?

Regret would be the normal choice. Anyone who didn't regret getting stuck in here was insane. But no matter how far back I scrolled through my emotional event log, despite the presence of terror or homesickness, there were no hits for "regret."

So either I was insane, or the circumstances never gave me enough breathing room to even consider regretting my choice. If it was the latter, then the fencer strolling along ahead of me was part of those circumstances. I'd spent so much time catering to her whims and needs that perhaps regret and other negative emotions simply couldn't find any purchase in my brain...

No, don't you dare start to thank her! She's torn you a new one ten times more often than she's ever shown any gratitude!

I picked up my pace to draw even with my casual partner.

Based on my beta experience, I knew that for the thirty minutes or so between the previous floor's boss's being slain and the teleport gate being activated, the spawn rate of monsters was drastically decreased.

I suspected that it was a gift to those weary champions, to ensure that they didn't get wiped out by mobs before they could reach the gate of the next floor's main town. Sadly, that effect was only active around the town itself.

After five minutes of walking through the forest, I sensed a shift in the surrounding air, even before my Search skill went off. The beautiful, fairy-tale forest seemed to grow harder and more menacing with every step.

"Listen up, Asuna. The enemies here aren't any tougher than

the ones on the second floor. They're mostly animals and plants, too, so they won't use sword skills on us," I explained. She nodded silently.

"But there's one pattern all the mobs here employ: They're going to try to draw us into the forest and away from the path during battle. If you charge forward every time they give you an opening, you'll be totally lost by the time you win the fight."

"Can't you just open your map and see the places that you've walked already?"

"The thing is…" I waved my right hand to open the menu, flipped to the map, and enabled visible mode to show it to Asuna.

"Oh…It's all dim," she remarked. Indeed, while normally most of the map would be grayed out with clear little 3-D models of where we'd already been, the current map screen was dim and hazy, as if obscured by mist. Even squinting closely at it did not reveal the location of the path.

"This area has a name: the Forest of Wavering Mists. The map's hard to read, and occasionally you walk into mist so thick, you can barely see a thing. So the ironclad rule around here is, don't leave the path or your party. Keep that in mind at all times."

"Understood. So why don't you give me a demonstration?"

"Huh?"

"Something's watching us back there."

I slowly turned around. Off the path, at the very lip of the woods, stood—no, grew—a thin, withered tree. Its pale yellow trunk was only a foot and a half thick and six feet tall, far smaller than the behemoth specimens all around. But pale lights shone in two small knotholes in the bark, and the branches stretching out to the sides waved like slender claws.

The dried-out tree and I stared at each other for several seconds. Eventually it pulled a creaking root out of the ground and stepped forward. Next, the left root pulled out for a step, and it began to walk toward me. The wobbling steps soon turned to a full-speed dash. A third knothole opened beneath the other two, and the tree warbled a howl.

"*Molooo!*"

The Treant Sapling had several special abilities, one of which was that when it stood perfectly still, it wouldn't set off my Search skill. I was so absorbed in my explanation that I must have walked right past it.

Constant vigilance! I admonished myself, reaching over my shoulder to pull my beloved Anneal Blade +6 from its sheath.

Three minutes later, I'd cut off both of the arm branches, and Asuna had penetrated its mouth knothole with her Wind Fleuret +5. The treant moaned sadly and exploded into polygonal shards.

We fist-bumped in celebration and put away our swords. Despite my warning, I'd fallen for the tree's deceptive flipping of its front and rear sides, and wandered five yards into the forest. That wasn't a big problem now, but when the mists were out, even ten yards' distance could be disastrous.

As she walked down the old stone path, Asuna said, "I feel a bit...guilty about that."

"Oh?"

"Well, that tree monster was a sapling, right? It's not very eco-friendly to cut it down like that."

"M-maybe, but you wouldn't be saying that if you saw the Elder Treant that he'd grow into. You'd be saying we gotta chop that sucker down now while we got the chance!"

"...Don't talk like that. I get enough of it from Kibaou," she warned.

We returned to the path and shared a short sigh of relief. The angle of the golden light from overhead was changing already, but we had plenty of time until nightfall.

"So, it should be right around here..."

"What is? Oh, that task you said you wanted to take care of."

"Yes. We're just initiating a quest...but the starting location of the NPC is a bit random. How are your ears, Asuna?"

I gave her a glance and saw that the fencer was backing away, holding her hands over her cute little pink ears.

"...Is that what you're into, Kirito? You have an ear thing?"

"N-n-no! I was referring to your hearing, not the shape of your ears..."

"I'm just kidding. Besides, this situation has nothing to do with our hearing. We're listening with our brains, not our eardrums."

"Ah, good point. Well, let's try to find it. If only one of us had the Eavesdropping skill."

I straightened my back and cupped my palms behind my ears, knowing it was probably pointless. Asuna followed my example.

"So what sound am I listening for? Don't tell me it's a single leaf falling."

"Don't worry, it's not a natural sound. We're trying to find the clanging of sword on sword."

Asuna looked startled for a moment, then nodded her understanding.

We stood in the middle of the path, our backs pressed together, focusing in all four directions with four ears. I often ignored them, but there was actually quite a lot of atmospheric noise in the game. The whistling of the breeze and rustling of leaves, scampering critters and chirping songbirds—I shut each and every one of those sounds out of my mind, searching for the harsh, artificial clang of metal on metal.

"...!"

Asuna and I twitched together. I turned to my right, and Asuna to her left...to the southwest. There was a faint but distinct clashing of blades coming from that direction.

"Let's go," I said, striding forward. Asuna pulled my coat from behind.

"Is it safe to go into the forest?"

"Don't worry, as long as we start the quest safely, we'll be able to return to the path."

"...And what if we don't?"

"Not a problem—I have a camping set. Let's go!"

As I trotted off into the woods, I heard a skeptical "Camping?" It quickly turned to footsteps.

* * *

Away from the stone path, the ground was soft and mossy, with just enough give to be noticeable, but not uncomfortable to walk on. I wove around trunks left and right, trailing the source of the sound. Coming across any monsters here would disrupt our search, so I gave any cursors that popped up in my Search range a wide berth. The last thing I wanted to see was another treant, and fortunately we did not run across any.

After less than five minutes of jogging, the clanging of metal was much louder than before, joined by shouts and screams. Two NPC cursors appeared directly ahead, followed by the flashes of colliding swords peeking through the branches.

One more massive tree trunk, and we'd be at the battleground. I stopped before we rounded the tree and held Asuna back with an outstretched arm, holding up my index finger in a shushing motion. We leaned around the trunk to peer at the same time.

Two silhouettes were locked in fierce combat in the middle of a wide clearing.

One was a tall man wearing gleaming metal armor of gold and green. Even at a glance, it was clear that his longsword and buckler were high-level equipment. His long, platinum blond hair was tied at the back, and his face was that of a dashing Scandinavian lead actor in a Hollywood film.

The other combatant stood out in stark relief, with black-and-purple armor. The curved saber and small kite shield were dark in color but equally powerful. The fighter's hair was short and smoky purple, which combined with darkly tanned skin, was strikingly beautiful. Luscious red lips and a swelling curve on the breastplate made it clear that the dark fighter was a woman.

"*Haah!*"

The blond man let out a fierce roar and swung down his sword.

"*Shaa!*"

The purple-haired woman struck back with her saber. A fierce clang echoed throughout the clearing, and the flashing light effect lit the deep forest for an instant.

"A-are those...really NPCs...?" Asuna murmured below me, her voice filled with wonder.

I understood how she felt. Their precise movements and realistic expressions were so lifelike, it was hard to see them as soulless avatars under the control of the game system. But...

"Technically, they're classified as mobs. Look at their ears."

"Huh...? Oh! They're both pointy. Which means..."

"The man is a forest elf. The woman is a dark elf. Look above their heads."

Asuna's eyes traveled up a bit. She murmured in surprise again.

Both warriors had a golden *!* mark above their heads. That was proof that they were quest-initiating NPCs. Normally, walking up and starting a conversation would automatically open up a quest log. But in this case...

"What does it mean that they both have quest marks and are fighting each other...?"

"It's simple—you can *only accept one.* I need you to make a very important choice here, Asuna," I said. She took her eyes off the elves and looked at me.

"A choice?"

"Yeah. The quest they'll give us isn't a one-off quest, or even a series of quests. It's the first major campaign quest in the game. It lasts through several floors and won't wrap up until we get to the ninth."

"N—"

Ninth?! she was going to scream, but clamped her mouth shut in time. Her hazelnut-brown eyes were wide with shock. Secretly enjoying her surprise, I added another bombshell.

"And if you screw up along the way, there are no do-overs. No switching to the opposing side, either. The choice you make here is going to last us until the ninth floor of Aincrad."

"Excuse me...Couldn't you have told me this earlier...?" Her face went from anger to indecision. "Wait, opposing side? Does that mean those two elves...?"

"Exactly. We have to choose one to save and one to fight. Which one will it be: black or white?"

Asuna gave me a scorchingly appraising look. "This isn't a real choice, is it? Maybe if this was a regular game, but not now. We have to follow the same route you took in the beta. In fact...I'm positive that I can guess *exactly* which one you chose."

Now it was my turn to clam up uncomfortably. Her cold gaze bored into my face, and she spoke with absolute conviction.

"You chose the dark elf lady, didn't you?"

"Y-yes, I did...b-but not because she was a lady. Because she was dark."

But I knew that excuse wouldn't fly. Asuna stood up straight and turned away in a huff.

"Well, fine. I would never take the side of a man to cut down a woman, anyway. Let's help out the dark elf and defeat the forest elf. Agreed?" She hurried to pop out of our hiding spot, but I grabbed the back of her hood first.

"W-wait, wait, wait. One important thing first!"

"What?"

"Well, um...Just so you know, even if we help the dark side, there's no way we can beat the forest elf."

"Wh...what?!"

Her eyes went wide. I put a hand on her slender shoulder to calm her down. "As you can probably tell from the tough-looking gear, they're both elite mobs. You don't find Forest Elven Hallowed Knights or Dark Elven Royal Guards until the seventh floor. No matter how much of a safety margin we're working with, we only just made it to the third floor. We can't win."

"Then...what do we do? I mean...if we die in this fight..."

"Don't worry, there's no death if we lose. Once we're down half our HP, the fighter we're helping will use her secret attack to win. We just have to keep focused on defense. Don't panic when he starts chopping our HP away, just stay calm and wait for the lady to do her thing. Losing control and running around is the worst thing that can happen here—you never know when you might pull in a nearby mob by accident."

"...All right."

"Good." I patted her shoulder and let go. "Then we'll jump out on the count of three. The quest starts automatically when we get near, so just stay next to me."

She nodded in understanding, and I lined up next to her, counted to three, and said a silent apology.

There was one thing I hadn't told Asuna. When we jumped in to save the dark elf—her name was Kizmel—she would unleash her forbidden art to save us from the forest elf knight, dying in the process. If we chose the opposite route and helped the forest elf, he would do the same thing. No matter the choice, both elves would die in this clearing, and we'd be embroiled in the war of the two races. That was the start of a long, long campaign...an epic tale.

"...Two, one, go!"

We leaped out into the clearing. The battling elves looked at us momentarily, then jumped backward to keep distance between them. Each of the *!* marks turned into a *?* to indicate a quest in progress.

"What is humankind doing in this forest?" the male elf demanded.

"Do not interfere! Begone from this place!" ordered the dark elf.

We had the option of leaving, of course. But that was beside the point of being here. Asuna and I made eye contact, drew our swords—and leveled the points at the gaudy forest elf's chest.

His handsome features grew cold and furious. The yellow event-related mob cursor gained a blinking red border, a warning that the target was about to turn aggressive.

"You fools...For the crime of siding with this dark elf scum, your blood will quench my sword's thirst."

"That—"

"That's right, but it's you who will perish, you wife-abusing pig!" Asuna retorted, stealing my one-liner and adding a dubious charge of domestic abuse. The forest elf's cursor shifted from pale yellow to a menacing dark crimson. Before I could even note the foreboding tint of red, the man put on a beautiful but haughty smile.

"So be it! I will start with you, humans."

"Remember, just focus on defense!" I called out to Asuna, focusing on his longsword.

Of course, we'll only last three minutes at best, I silently added. But when I glanced over at my partner's face, I felt a distinct sense of unease. Even in the short time I'd known her, I could recognize the expression she was wearing now: the one that said she was dead set on something.

"Um...focus...defense?"

"I know, I know!" she snapped, but there was a ferocious glint to the rapier clutched in her right hand.

Twenty minutes later.

"This...can't be happening..." the forest elf muttered as he collapsed to the ground.

"This...can't be happening..." I repeated, blinking in surprise as I checked to confirm that his HP bar did indeed read zero. In contrast, both Asuna and my HP bars were at half, just before we would reach the yellow zone. During the beta, I'd been in a party of four, and we'd been thrashed in just two minutes.

"...Well. He wasn't so tough, after all."

I looked over to see Asuna, back straight despite her obvious fatigue. A few feet to her left was the dark elf, dark saber and gaze pointed right at the fallen foe.

Ya shoulda died, missy, echoed a mysterious, unsourced phrase inside my head. Kizmel the dark elf knight looked up at me.

Her onyx eyes seemed to be filled with shock, bewilderment, and an unanswered question of what she should do next. But that had to be my imagination.

I prayed it was my imagination.

2

IF THIS QUEST, THE "JADE KEY," HAD DEVELOPED AS IT happened in the beta, the following should have occurred.

Whether we allied with the forest elf or the dark elf, ultimately both would end up dead. The elf we sided with would remain alive for a few seconds extra, long enough to say, "Deliver this key to such and such," before perishing. The such and such being either the forest elf base on the north end of the woods or the dark elf base to the south. Once the bodies had vanished, a small bag of sewn leaves would be left behind, containing a large and beautiful key carved of green stone.

At that point, of course, the player was to take the key to the northern or southern camp; they could sell it at an NPC shop if they wished, but that would permanently prevent them from finishing the quest. If properly delivered without falling into temptation, the commander at the elf base would part with a special reward and the initiation of the next quest.

But I had no idea there was a different branching pathway in the quest, one in which the elf ally survived the battle. If I didn't know it, no one else did—even Argo. We had to expect a totally new and unfamiliar story ahead.

A short distance away from me, Asuna, and the still-silent dark elf Kizmel, the forest elf's body disappeared with a brief crackle. We received considerable amounts of experience and col, along with a couple rare items, but I didn't have time to check that now.

A familiar bag of leaves was lying on the ground where the forest elf's body had been. Abandoned items had to be claimed soon, before they disappeared into thin air, but I wasn't even sure if I was supposed to pick this one up. What if I touched it, and that was the trigger that turned Kizmel hostile?

"Umm...gee, what's this?" I said unconvincingly. Asuna bent down to pick up the key as though nothing was out of the ordinary, so I hastily grabbed the hood of her cape, which earned me a furious glare. Finally, Kizmel reacted.

She bent over and cradled the bag carefully in her black leather gloves. An exhalation of relief left her lips as she held it to her chest.

"...At least we can protect the sanctuary now," she murmured to herself, put the bag in her waistpouch, and stood up to face us. The subtle way the ferocity returned to her eyes despite her wavering hesitation didn't seem possible for a mere simple system-controlled object.

"I must thank you," she said, her armor clanking as she bowed in salute. "The first secret key has been protected. Your assistance is appreciated. Come with me to our base, and the commander will wish to reward you for your help."

Again, a ? appeared over her head to indicate quest progress. I was inwardly relieved, though I did my best not to show it. It seemed that the quest would proceed as normal, even after we beat the forest elf ourselves.

However, my original plan was to butt into their fight, let both elves perish, get the key, and return to the main town. We hadn't taken a break to refresh and resupply since beating the second-floor boss. The elation at reaching a new floor was masking my fatigue, but exhaustion here was mental rather than physical and hit the player like a ton of bricks out of nowhere. My current partner Asuna had passed out from extreme exhaustion right after our first meeting down in the first-floor labyrinth. While it was rare to get that far, lapses of concentration led to mistakes, and controlling that fatigue safely was a vital tool for any solo player.

I peered sidelong at the fencer. She took a step forward without a glance at me and spoke to Kizmel herself.

"In that case, we'd be honored."

"..."

I wasn't the only one who held my tongue. Kizmel stared at Asuna in silence. NPCs in Aincrad—technically, the dark elf Kizmel was classified as a mob—did not respond to player comments unless they came in a clear yes or no form.

I coughed awkwardly, ready to give a simpler answer, but before I could get the words out of my mouth, the knight nodded and spun around.

"Very well. The base camp is through the south end of the woods."

My quest log updated, and the *?* over her head vanished. At the same time, a message appeared to the upper left indicating that a third party member had joined, and a fresh new HP bar was' added to the list.

Kizmel strode off coolly, and Asuna sprang after her. I stood rooted to the spot for three seconds before hurrying off to catch up.

The elf must have picked up an affirmative nuance from Asuna's reply. But as far as I knew, the NPCs in the beta test had nowhere near that kind of conversation ability.

Perhaps it was as simple as the NPCs' response database being expanded between the end of the beta and the start of the retail game. But something about Kizmel's speech and expressions felt too natural for that to explain it. She was just like any other player.

I walked at the rear of the three-man team, examining her color cursor just to be sure. It was the yellow of an NPC—technically, an event mob—and her name was listed as KIZMEL: DARK ELVEN

ROYAL GUARD. Players weren't allowed to replicate monster titles within their names, so this was proof that Kizmel was indeed nothing more than a moving object controlled by the system. If *SAO* was a normally functioning game, there might be a faint chance that she was actually being played by a member of the game staff, but that couldn't be true now that it was deadly.

...It must be my imagination.

I sped up to draw even with the two women.

Being an overpowered beater might have created a dangerously unpredictable set of circumstances in this case, but there was one way in which it was a definite improvement.

Reaching the dark elf base required venturing off the path and through the woods, increasing the chances of enemy encounters. And given the thick, obscuring mists that gave the forest its name, it was all too easy to lose sight of one's location.

But Kizmel served us valuably in more ways than one: Her saber made quick work of any foes who happened across our path, and as an elf, she seemed to know exactly which way to go through the heavy mist. As an admirer of efficiency, I considered taking this opportunity to wander around and fight more mobs with Kizmel, but I thought better of it. I didn't want to give the proud, elite elf warrior a reason to be angry with me.

So it only took fifteen minutes of hiking through the misty forest to reach the sight of many black flags rippling in the breeze.

"That didn't take very long," Asuna said next to me, and I had to reluctantly agree. Kizmel stopped marching and turned around to face us. She spoke with what I thought was a note of pride in her voice.

"A Forest-Sinking charm has been cast on the camp. You would not have found it so easily without me."

"Ooh, a charm? Is that like magic? I thought there wasn't any magic in this world," Asuna boldly remarked. I felt a chill run down my back. Aside from her overly informal tone, I wasn't sure if what Asuna said was even understandable to the NPC and her preset array of responses. It felt like Kizmel might not be able to answer it, even if she understood the meaning.

The reason magic didn't exist in *SAO* was to allow the player to experience melee combat firsthand in the VRMMO environment—they didn't want to turn it into a long-distance shooter.

"Listen, Asuna, that's not..." I started, trying to help Kizmel out by explaining the concept. But once again, my consideration was totally unnecessary.

"...Our charms are not up to the level of magic," the dark elf said, her long eyelashes low. "If anything, they are just a faint afterglow of the great magic of old. When we were cut free from the earth, the people of Lyusula lost all magic..."

The shock of what she'd said hit me five seconds later—that was as long as it took to actually process what she'd said.

We lost all magic because we were cut free from the earth.

I had a feeling that she wasn't just giving an explanation of why magic skills didn't exist in *Sword Art Online*. This might be something that corresponded directly to the existence of the floating castle, Aincrad.

Now that I thought about it, I'd never had any exposure to the background story of *SAO*. I tore through countless articles and interviews after the game was first announced, but nothing more was said about the setting other than that it was a floating castle in the sky made of a hundred floors with their own little world maps. This was strange, because whether single player or multiplayer, the background story of an RPG, of how the world came to be, was usually just as important as the concrete game system itself.

Even in the beta test, the background of the world was opaque. I completed this campaign quest back then, but I recalled the story being rather simple and unconnected to the origins of Aincrad—the forest elves and dark elves were fighting over some holy "sanctuary," whatever that actually was.

When the retail game launched and promptly trapped all of its guests inside, I felt like I understood why the background of *SAO* was such a blank slate.

The lack of story, of any kind of descriptive background, was a challenge from the developer himself. Kayaba was telling us, *The stage is set; it's up to you to create the story now.*

That was just my imagination talking, of course, but it didn't seem very farfetched at this point. In that case, the words of Kizmel the elf knight—as an extension of the *SAO* system—surpassed even Kayaba's intentions.

I was possessed by an urge to overwhelm the elven knight with questions as we walked. Whether this "Lyusula" was a continent, a kingdom, or a city. Why the dark elves were torn from their home. Why they were trapped here in this floating castle. What this castle really was, and why it had been built.

Most likely, none of that information had any bearing on our primary goal: beating the game and returning to reality. The only reason I had started this campaign quest was for the plentiful experience points and high-level rewards. There was no emotional attachment to the dark elf forces. If Asuna had insisted, I would have sided with the forest elf man against Kizmel earlier.

I stifled my sudden burst of curiosity with a deep breath and continued my silent march behind the knight.

As we approached the swirling black flags, the mists suddenly cleared away as though they'd never been there, and my field of vision returned.

We were very close to the southern end of the forest; sharp-cut rock walls extended left and right. A narrow passage barely fifteen feet wide proceeded through the rock, slim pillars on either side. Atop the poles flew the landmark black flags, adorned with crests of horns and blades.

Standing before the two poles were dark elf soldiers, proudly bearing glaives and wearing heavier armor than Kizmel's—though still light compared to the variety available to players. Our companion strode up to the guards.

When I did this quest in the beta, Kizmel had perished against the forest elf, and our party of four had to approach these guards without a go-between. But it was this situation that had me more nervous. Asuna leaned over and whispered, "I might as well ask...We're not going to have to fight in this base camp, are we?"

"We won't...We shouldn't. As long as we don't attack any of them, at least. Or maybe they just cancel your progress and kick you out..."

"You'd better not attempt to find out." She glared at me, then summoned her courage and picked up the pace.

Fortunately, the guards did nothing worse than glare suspiciously as we passed them. After a short walk through the narrow passage, it opened wide into a round space a good fifty yards across. About twenty tents of black and purple in various sizes filled the space as glamorous dark elves strode about the grounds—all in all, an impressive sight.

"Wow...the camp's a lot bigger than it was in the beta," I murmured, quiet enough so Kizmel couldn't hear. Asuna looked at me doubtfully.

"Was it in a different place before?"

"Yeah, but that's not a strange thing. Most of these locations related to the campaign are temporary instances."

"Inse...tanse?"

Asuna had brushed up furiously on her gaming lingo in the last month, but this term was unfamiliar. I explained as we walked toward the largest tent in the back of the canyon.

"It's a location that's created temporarily for each party taking on the quest, I guess you could say. See, we're going to talk to the dark elf leader to advance the quest, but if another party comes along, that makes it complicated, doesn't it? Some quests are like the 'Herbs of the Forest' quest on the first floor, and they just shut off the area from general access if someone's talking to the NPC."

"So...you're saying that you and I have temporarily vanished from the third-floor map to move to this base?"

"That's right," I said, impressed by the speed of her understanding.

She narrowed her eyes and gave me a searing look. "We can leave anytime, right?"

The proceedings had been rather irregular, but the meeting with the commander of the dark elf advance forces went smoothly. Of course, being presumably stronger than Kizmel, the commander could have slaughtered us in seconds if anything went wrong.

He was delighted at the safe return of Kizmel and the Jade Key, granting us considerable rewards and equipment. Even better, we had our choice of several items. The saber decorated like Kizmel's sword drew my eye, but my Anneal Blade +6 was stronger, so I settled on a ring that added a point to strength. Asuna made a similar decision, choosing an earring with +1 to agility.

The commander finished by initiating a new quest, the second leg of the campaign, and Asuna and I left the tent.

Back in the grassy canyon, the ceiling formed by the floor above that acted as our sky was turning the color of sunset. It had to be close to five o'clock. Now that my nerves had eased, fatigue was thudding down. It was time to rest for the day.

Kizmel stretched in a realistically natural way and turned to us, a hint of a smile on her lips.

"Warriors of humankind, allow me to thank you again for your help. I hope that you will assist in our next operation."

"W-we'd be happy to help."

"Now that I think on it, I have not heard your names yet. What are they?"

My eyes nearly bugged out of their sockets again. I'd never been asked my name by a mob before—no, I couldn't keep treating her like a monster. She was an NPC.

"Um…my name is Kirito."

"Ah, your human names are difficult to pronounce. Is it… Kirito?" Her intonation was slightly off, so I repeated myself.

"Kirito."

"Kirito."

"That's perfect."

That must have been the system sequence to fine-tune name pronunciation. Somewhat relieved that she was finally doing something recognizably NPC-like, I watched Kizmel repeat the process with Asuna.

Once she was satisfied she'd learned the way our names were said, the lady knight continued, "Kirito, Asuna, please call me Kizmel. I will leave the timing of our departure up to you. If you wish to return to your human town, I can send you nearby with another charm, or you can spend the night in one of our tents."

Finally, something going exactly as I remembered, I thought.

Back in the beta, I took a fair number of naps in the tents to save time on the travel back to town. The beds were nice, the food was good, and most importantly, both were free. It only lasted while the quest was active, but it would be a waste not to take advantage of that value.

Asuna read my mind like a book. With an exasperated shrug of her shoulders, she answered, "In that case, we will gratefully accept your hospitality."

"Perhaps you should save your thanks. After all..."

That's right, this is how it...wait, that's not right.

At this point, we'd been granted the use of an empty tent, as its owner had died at the start of the quest. In other words, it was originally Kizmel's sleeping chamber that me and my three party members (all men) had borrowed. But now the lady knight was alive. Which meant...

"...without a spare tent, you will need to share mine. It will be a tight fit for all three of us, but you are welcome."

"No, we'd be happy to—three of us?"

Asuna stopped still. Kizmel seemed to be waiting for a more definitive statement, so I picked up the slack.

"Thank you. We'd be happy to use it."

"Good. I will be here within the grounds, so call upon me if you should need anything. So long for now."

The proud dark elf bowed again and strode off toward the dining tent. Asuna was frozen in place for three whole seconds, then turned toward me, her face shifting through about three different expressions.

"Is it possible to back out and have her charm us over to the town?"

Sadly, I knew the answer already. One of our party in the beta had tried that very thing. As a beater, it was my duty to pass on the information in my pocket.

"Um...no."

As with the base camp itself, Kizmel's tent had been upgraded significantly since the beta.

The owner had described it as a "tight fit for three," but in reality, six of us could have set up beds with room to spare. Thick, luxurious pelts were spread across the ground, easily comfortable enough to sleep on until the morning.

The tent fabric that served as walls was thick and woven as well, enough to block out all sound from the outside. In front of the center pillar was an oddly shaped heater that emitted an orange glow and pleasant warmth.

I walked into the center of the pleasant, comfortable space and sat down, sighing in contentment. Lazily, I lifted a hand to open my window and slowly removed my sword and various articles of armor.

When I rolled onto my back, I accidentally met the cold glare of Asuna. The fencer took a few steps over to me and gently nudged my side with the tip of her boot.

I submitted to her silent pressure, rolling over and over until I hit the left wall of the tent, at which point Asuna removed her boot.

"That's your spot. Imagine there's a border right here." She traced an imaginary line with her boot about a third of the way into the tent.

I had to find out. "And...what happens if I attempt to invade your border?"

"This camp isn't considered a safe zone, is it?"

"I read you loud and clear," I said, nodding on the ground. She smiled back and walked to the other end of the room. The round tent was about twenty-five feet across, so there was quite a distance from wall to wall. I watched her cross, then remove her breastplate and rapier, shaking out her long hair before she sat atop the furs. She leaned her back against a pillar and mulled something over for a moment before putting her long boots in storage as well.

Asuna stretched out her long, white-socked feet, looked up at the ceiling, and let out a slow, steady sigh. When she eventually looked over toward me, I was rudely staring back. I glanced away hastily and babbled in a high voice.

"So, um, I don't mind sleeping outside, if you prefer. I've got a sleeping bag and everything..."

"It's fine, as long as you respect the border," she responded, her voice surprisingly neutral. I hazarded another glance across the tent. Asuna was rubbing the furs on the ground with her hand as she changed the topic to something that had caught her interest.

"So, about this quest series...I'm not quite sure of the point of it yet. It's not something about how either the dark elves or forest elves are good or evil, right?"

"Eh? Um...yeah, that's right. Assuming the gist of it is the same as in the beta, there's a floor above with a place called the Sanctuary, with some incredibly powerful item sealed inside of it. And the dark elves and forest elves are fighting over it."

"Hmm...So that key in the bag of leaves was to the Sanctuary?"

"Yep. If I remember correctly, there are six of them in total, hidden across all the floors, so collecting them is the main focus of the quest."

"I see...That's what I was wondering about. You said that when we first spotted Kizmel and the forest elf fighting, we could choose which side to help, right?"

"I did."

"Which means that some players could choose to side with the forest elves, and be working the other side of the story at the same time as us, right?"

"That's right," I said and finally realized what Asuna was getting at. "Oh, and you're wondering that if we come across players working on the forest elf side while we're doing the quest..."

"...maybe we'll end up competing or fighting with them," she finished, her eyebrows knitted in concern. I put on an awkward smile to reassure her.

"Don't worry, it won't come to that. It's not like those quests to kill a certain number of enemies or collect a certain amount of loot, where you have to compete with other players to reach your allotted total. These story-style quests make it so that each player or party has their own independent, um, whatchacallit..."

I tried to frame it in a way that a beginner to MMOs would understand, but Asuna had already pieced it together.

"Oh, like this base camp? So a number of different parties can be at different points in the story and reach completely different endings?"

"Yeah, that's the gist of it. So we don't have to worry about groups following the enemy camp's quest trying to take the items from us. It's not as if one side completing the quest successfully means the opposing side loses."

"Ahh..."

Asuna nodded in apparent understanding, but her expression did not clear up in a way that suggested her fears had been eliminated. She heaved herself back up to sitting position and crossed her legs, facing me directly.

"Something still bothering you?"

"Umm, I'm not sure if it's bothering me or just hard to grasp. If you're right, and this base camp...instance? If a different one exists for every party doing the quest, then that means the same number of Kizmels and commanders exist, too. That seems kind of..."

"Ah, yeah..."

I finally understood the nature of Asuna's confusion; it was the greatest contradiction of questing in an online game. Normally, an incident should only arise once. For instance, in the "Herbs of the Forest" quest from the first floor, the sickly girl Agatha required special healing herbs that could only be collected from plant-type monsters. I handily—okay, it wasn't quite that easy—collected all of the quest materials, Agatha's mother brewed a medicine from them, and the girl recovered.

But the next player who visited that house would find a sickly Agatha. As long as there were players to accept the quest, she was locked in an eternal cycle of painful disease and recovery.

The campaign quest Asuna and I had started was an expanded version of that concept. After a twenty-minute battle, we defeated the forest elf knight and saved Kizmel's life, but as more players took on the quest after us, dozens, if not hundreds of Kizmels would die, along with a similar number of handsome forest elves.

But that was unavoidable. If each quest was only playable by one player or party for the sake of story consistency, the game would lose all pretense of fairness. It might be one thing to side-step that by creating an infinite number of unique quests, but that was not realistically possible—even for a mad genius like Akihiko Kayaba.

When I finished explaining all of this to Asuna, she nodded slowly and thanked me for the information, but I suspected she'd known it all along. Like her, there was something about this that still sat wrong with me. After all, for an event-related NPC, Kizmel was all too *human*—or elvish.

A lonely, plaintive horn blew within the camp. I checked my clock and saw that it was already six o'clock. Plagued by equal parts sleepiness and hunger, I was wondering which of the two to address when the flap of the tent entrance lifted open.

It was Kizmel, the owner of the tent. She was still dressed in her gleaming metal armor and long cape. Asuna and I hastily scrambled to our feet. Kizmel looked at each of us in turn and said, "I'm afraid I cannot offer you much at this humble camp, but you are free to use this tent however much you wish. The dining tent will serve you food anytime you need it, and there is also a simple tent for bathing."

"You have a bath?" Asuna repeated instantly. Kizmel nodded and pointed off to her left.

"It is next to the dining tent. Again, it is available at your leisure."

"Thank you. I'm certainly going to take advantage of that," Asuna said without hesitation, bowing to Kizmel and heading out the tent flap without a backward glance at me.

Kizmel strode farther inside and said, "I believe I will have a rest. Just say the word if you need anything."

I was still idly contemplating whether I should prioritize food or sleep when Kizmel stopped next to the heater and put her hand on the large gemstone that acted as a clasp on her shoulder plate.

With a strange tinkling sound, her armor, cape, and saber vanished into motes of light. All that was left beneath it was a sheer undergarment that shone like silk. I was so shocked that I couldn't pull my gaze away. There was a distinctly un-elven volume to the body beneath the black fabric—perhaps that was what made her a dark elf...

Suddenly, a hand grabbed the back of my collar and an icy voice said into my ear, "You should take a bath as well. You must have gotten sweaty during that boss fight."

...Well, I'm certainly feeling a cold sweat now.

An irresistible force dragged me backward out through the entrance of the tent. Outside, the dark elf camp looked even more fantastical than usual with the transition from late afternoon to evening.

Here and there about the base were elegantly designed steel mesh cages holding silent, purplish flames. A restrained lute melody was playing from one of the tents, to which the crickets in the grass added their own ringing harmony.

Even the soldiers' laughs coming from the large dining tent and the clanging hammer of the elves' attendant blacksmith seemed like musical instruments adding to the performance. I walked behind Asuna, concentrating on the unfamiliar sounds of the nonhuman camp. Suddenly, I remembered a very important mission and called out to the back of the tunic ahead.

"Oh, Asuna."

"What?"

She slowed down so I could catch up to her side, but did not stop walking.

"The NPC blacksmith here is a really high level, so we should upgrade your weapon to its maximum while we can."

"...To the maximum? Are you sure?" she replied doubtfully. She must have been recalling the scene of her favorite sword helplessly shattered before her eyes several days ago. Of course, that was only a fake substitute switched in with the Quick Change mod, but she hadn't known that at the time. The visceral shock still remained in her memory.

I nodded vigorously to set her at ease. "You might not have a hundred-percent chance of success, but just a few materials should boost the rate to its maximum. If we can get yours to plus six, that should last you through the middle of this floor."

Asuna bought her beloved Wind Fleuret just before the strategy meeting for the first-floor boss raid. Statistically, it wasn't really cut out for the third floor, but if upgraded completely—every one of its limited upgrade attempts successful—it might serve her a little while longer.

For me, this was a rare prioritization of sentiment over efficiency, but to my surprise, Asuna looked down and mulled it over. Her fingers wandered along her waist, as though searching for the sheath of the rapier that was currently stored away in her inventory.

"...Remember what you said before? About melting down a sword to use as material for a new one?"

"Ah...yeah, that's right."

"Could I have that done here, with their blacksmith?"

"Su-sure, if you want, but…"

Asuna finally stopped walking and turned to me, causing me to realize I'd stopped already. There was a rare hint of a smile on her face.

"Thanks for the concern. But if we're going to brave the risk of attempting to upgrade for a sword I'm just going to get rid of in a few days, I'd rather have it reborn here."

"I see…" If that was how Asuna felt, it wasn't my place to tell her otherwise. "All right. I'm sure it'll make for a powerful blade. Well, let's go see that blacksmith's tent…"

I headed for the other direction and Asuna grabbed my shirt.

"The bath comes first!"

I didn't remember if the base camp had a bath during the beta. Even if it did, none of our all-male party would have bothered to use it. If we wanted to bathe back then, we could just log out and take a real one. If any of us fell asleep in the tents, it was to enjoy the camping experience, nothing more.

Even now that we were permanently trapped in here, I wasn't particularly attached to the idea of bathing, but it was clearly a top priority for my temporary partner. Perhaps if there was a magical hot spring that offered its own buff effect…but in that case, I'd just jump in fully clothed. The sensation of being wet was unpleasant and added a bit of weight, but it wore off soon after you left the water.

Since this bath was a favorite of the dark elves, perhaps it did have some magical effect of its own. Then again, it might have a negative prank effect, like causing your ears to grow pointier the longer you stayed in the water…

Asuna and I arrived at a small tent behind the dining area while I pointlessly pondered the effects of elf baths. We stopped and looked at each other—there was only one entrance to the bathing tent, and there was no marking on the swinging flap that designated male or female.

"......"

Asuna silently parted the flaps to peer inside, then pulled her head out. "There's only one bath in there."

"I see."

Even as a dweeby middle schooler, I knew enough not to joke that this meant we had to bathe together. I put on as serious a face as I could manage and stepped back.

"In that case, I'll just go next door and grab a bite while you're bathing. Take your time, and I'll come back when you're—"

"I asked this before, but are you *sure* this place is outside of the crime-prevention zone?"

I blinked a few times, baffled by this seemingly unrelated question, then nodded.

"That's right…"

"Which means it would be dangerous to remove all your equipment here."

"W-well, in a general sense, sure…"

"In which case, it makes sense for one of us to stand guard at the entrance while the other is bathing. We can flip a coin to see who goes first…"

I finally understood Asuna's concern. She wasn't truly afraid of a sudden attack by monsters or enemy players, but the possibility of the male dark elves in camp barging in while she was bathing. It seemed silly to get worked up about NPCs, but I could see her point.

Given that it was my fault that Argo the information dealer had burst into the bathroom while Asuna was bathing earlier, I ought to be accommodating here. I reached that conclusion in the span of a second and nodded to reassure her.

"Understood. I'll take the second turn; you go first."

"Thank you." Asuna grinned and disappeared into the tent with blinding speed. In the brief moment the flap was raised, I saw an elegantly carved bathtub filled to the lip with pale green water. The only thing separating the bathing area from the outside world was a simple cloth door that hung loose in the wind.

It was easy to see why a girl would feel uncertain about bathing on her own in such circumstances. If it was that bad, she probably didn't *need* to take a virtual bath, I thought, but she had her own priorities. In a world where death lurked around every corner, there had to be some way to relax and let all that accumulated stress ease away. I needed to find my own way to refresh while we were here in the safety of camp.

I sat down and leaned back against a support pillar. From beyond the simple layer of canvas, I heard two small swishing sounds. Those had to be the commands to remove all clothes, then all underwear. There was a splash, then a contented sigh.

"...How can anyone relax like this?" I growled at myself, folded my arms, and assumed a Zen sitting position.

SAO had a Meditation skill but not a specific Zen skill. I prided myself on my ability to focus my concentration, however. I might not be able to fully relax here, but I could at least dedicate my mind to my future build choices and equipment upgrade paths...

"Mmm-mm-mm, hmm-hmm" came a faint humming to my ears, obliterating all concentration.

At this point, it seemed like the only possible solution to this quandary was if the pillar failed to support my weight, sending me tumbling backward into the tent. But the thick log stayed firm, lodged concretely into the ground.

The mental assault of splashing and humming continued unabated for the next thirty minutes.

3

MY EYES OPENED AS SUDDENLY AS A BUBBLE POPPING on the water surface.

It was still night; the only sound was insects. The lute playing as I drifted off to sleep was no more, and neither were the voices and footsteps of the soldiers, or the hammering of the blacksmith's anvil.

I shut my eyes, considering going back to sleep, but within a few seconds, I was fully awake. Abandoning my attempt to rest, I sat up.

Across the tent, the fencer was fast asleep, her posture pristine. But I didn't see Kizmel in the space between us, where she should have been.

After my temporary partner had finished her bath, I had slipped in for my own and was out of the water by the count of a hundred. Fortunately, neither of us had grown pointy ears after using it. We moved over to the dining tent with the surprisingly friendly elf soldiers and dined on lightly baked bread, roast chicken, vegetable soup, and fruit. When we returned to Kizmel's tent, I felt highly satisfied.

We found the tent's owner already curled up in the blankets and sleeping peacefully. The moment I saw that, all of my fatigue from earlier came flooding back, and the two of us silently took our corners of the tent and lay down on the furs. I remembered pulling a nearby blanket up to my chin, and nothing after that.

My menu window said that it was two in the morning. No wonder I felt awake—I'd gotten a solid seven hours of sleep. Taking care not to make any noise, I closed the window and slipped out of the blankets.

When I passed through the hanging flap of the tent, the night lamps of the camp were mostly out, leaving the area lit by pale moonlight. A quick scan of the area showed no one moving except for two sentries marking the walls.

So where could Kizmel have gone? Perhaps onward to the next quest on her own? I shook my head—an NPC wouldn't be that independent, and her HP bar listed next to Asuna's and mine was still full.

I thought it over, then decided to head for the one part of the dark elf base I hadn't visited yet: behind the commander's tent at the very back of the clearing.

The moonlight in Aincrad was bright enough in any place open to the sky to make it easy to walk around. The moon itself was out of sight unless you were close to the outer perimeter, of course, so its light was reflecting off the lower side of the floor above, but that just gave the blue glow an even more unearthly beauty.

I headed east around the great command tent and stopped when the space behind it came into view. It was a tiny, grassy stretch with a single tree. I recalled it being an entirely empty, dead space in the beta.

But now there were three new objects beneath the long branches of the tree. Three simple but beautiful grave markers carved of wood.

The woman I'd been searching for was standing before the leftmost grave. She was in a tunic and tights now—not the underwear from earlier, but still without her signature armor. She was downcast, staring at the base of the grave. In the light of the moon, her smoky-purple hair was glowing lilac.

After a few seconds of hesitation, I slowly approached, stopping several feet away. The dark elf knight noticed my footsteps and looked up at me.

"...Kirito. The morrow will be difficult if you don't get your rest," she whispered.

"I slept better than I usually do. Thanks for letting us use your tent."

"I don't mind. It is too large for me alone," she responded, then looked back to the grave.

I took two more steps and examined the marker. There were small words carved into its fresh, unfinished surface. I squinted and made out the name Tilnel.

"Tilnel...?" I said aloud and noticed that it sounded very similar in rhythm to Kizmel.

She paused, then said, "My sister. She lost her life in the first battle after we descended to this floor last month."

The phrase *descended to this floor* indicated that the dark elves—and likely the forest elves as well—understood that the floating castle Aincrad was made of numerous stacked floors. Not only that, they could use their magical charms to sidestep the system of labyrinth stairs and town teleport gates. Perhaps their movement range was limited from this floor up to the ninth.

I'd had this basic knowledge of the elves since the beta, when I completed the campaign quest for the first time. But I was so preoccupied getting further into the game than anyone else at the time, it never occurred to me that the battle between the elves might tie into the game world itself.

I was struck by the sudden urge to ask Kizmel how Aincrad came to be, but I held it in with a breath of cool night air. It wasn't fair to ask such an important question while Asuna was absent, and this wasn't the time to ask, anyway.

Instead, I asked about Kizmel's late sister.

"Was Tilnel...a knight, too?"

"No. My sister was an herbalist. Her job on the battlefield was to tend to the wounded. She never carried anything larger than a dagger. She was at the rear vanguard when the forest elves' falconers ambushed us from behind..."

"......"

I grimaced and held my breath. The Forest Elven Falconers were the worst mobs on the third floor after the bosses and event enemies. The dark elves had their own Dark Elven Wolfhandlers, but the falconers were the bigger danger, given that they could attack you from ground and air simultaneously.

However she chose to interpret my silence, Kizmel's tense profile eased somewhat.

"I have no chairs or blankets, but you ought to sit. There's no need to stand around."

"Um…sure."

I sat down next to her. The thick, soft grass of this tiny graveyard supported my weight with ease.

The knight picked up a leather skin sitting next to her, pulled out the plug, and took a swig, then passed it to me. I thanked her and accepted the drink, temporarily forgetting that I was interacting with an NPC rather than another person.

When I put my lips to the skin, a thick liquid flooded between them. It was slightly sweet and sour, and when I finished, there was a burning like alcohol in the back of my throat that felt fresh and cool.

I handed back the skin. Kizmel held it out over the grave and poured the rest of the liquid onto Tilnel's grave marker.

"This was her favorite: moontear wine made of moontear herbs. I snuck some out of the castle, hoping to bring it to her. In the end, she never had a sip…"

The empty skin slipped from her hand and plopped lightly on the grass. Kizmel crouched, lining her knees together and hugging them tight.

"When I accepted the mission to retrieve the Jade Key yesterday, I was prepared to die. Part of me might have hoped for it. At best, I might have taken that forest elf down with me, otherwise I would simply have lost…But fate helped you guide me away from my death. And after I had sworn that no gods existed in this forsaken place anymore…"

Kizmel glanced over at me. I noticed that her onyx eyes were moist and was at a loss for how to react. Kizmel and her sister Tilnel were residents of this world, risking their lives for the sake of their people, and I was nothing but a temporary visitor, an outsider...

But in truth, that was not the case anymore. Asuna and I were trapped in this game now. Just like Kizmel, we had only one life to give. And yet, when we inserted ourselves into the fight between her and the forest elf knight, I'd foolishly rested on my laurels, convinced that once we were half-dead, the dark elf would sacrifice herself to let us win.

It had been wrong of me to draw my sword with that mind-set. Whether I knew what would happen or not, I should have fought with all of my ability. To protect my own life and the lives of Asuna and Kizmel.

Biting back a sudden flood of regret, I said, "It wasn't the gods. Asuna and I were there of our own will. We'll stick with you until the end. Until you get back home."

The dark elf knight grinned. "In that case, I will do my best to protect you. Until our paths part."

Thursday, December 15, 2022.

Kizmel, the level-15 dark elf knight; Kirito, the level-14 swordsman; and Asuna, the level-12 fencer and temporary party member, left the base camp for a new adventure.

The night had not broken yet. It was three in the morning, and the trees of the forest were quietly slumbering in the pale moonlight. When Kizmel and I returned from our graveyard vigil, we found Asuna not sleeping but fully packed and ready to leave.

When the fencer saw me without my weapon or armor on, she looked annoyed and wondered why I'd left if not to get prepared for the trip. When I was followed into the tent by Kizmel in her thin underclothes, Asuna's glare turned downright icy. My only choice was to claim that I'd been ready for hours.

Asuna continually threw me skeptical glares as we walked

through the camp clearing, but only until we passed through the narrow canyon out into the Forest of Wavering Mists again. The sight was even more fantastical now that the mossy trees and low, thick mists were lit by pale blue moonlight. I'd seen the exact same thing months before, but I couldn't help but gasp at its beauty. Asuna was completely bowled over. She murmured, "It's stunning," and didn't move for another thirty seconds.

Kizmel silently waited along with me, though it was hardly the first time I'd been surprised by her behavior. It would be perfectly ordinary behavior for an NPC waiting for players to react, but it seemed to me that she was choosing to take her time and respect Asuna's feeling of wonder.

When my partner came to her senses again, the knight spoke softly.

"She loved the night forest as well…Come, let us be off."

The quest given to us by the commander after completing the "Jade Key" was titled "Vanquishing the Spiders."

The forest was exploding with poisonous spider monsters who were sabotaging patrol missions, so it was our job to find the nest.

I'd done this quest before, of course, but the location of the nest was generated randomly, so my memory was of no use here. We just had to trek through the forest, fighting spiders until we narrowed down their source.

Poison would be a constant threat on this quest. Damage-causing poison was the most common status effect out of the many negative effects in *SAO*. Level-1 "weak poison" and level-2 "light poison" weren't such a big deal—as long as you were prepared to deal with them.

I made sure to check with Asuna as we hiked through the forest.

"How many antidote potions do you have?"

"Hmm…" She brought up her window with a jingle. "Three in my pouch, sixteen in the inventory."

"About the same as me. That'll be enough."

Something stuck out to me. Unlike healing crystals, potions couldn't be used on other people. So if Kizmel got afflicted with poison, she'd need to use her own potion to recover...

I turned back to the elf knight, who was bringing up the rear. "Um, Kizmel? Do you have any antidote potions...?"

"I do have a few, just in case, but I do not need them. I have this," she remarked with what I thought might be a hint of pride, showing off her right hand in its tight leather glove. There was a ring shoved directly over the glove on her index finger. The gemstone gleamed brightly despite the dim light—green, just like an antidote potion...

"What kind of ring is that?"

"I received it along with my sword from Her Majesty when I was knighted. It allows me to use a purifying charm once every ten minutes."

"...W..."

Wowzers!!

I barely kept the word from bursting out of me. In all of my time in the game, I had never seen or heard of an accessory that allowed for unlimited poison curing—even with a cooldown timer. If it actually worked on level-5 "lethal poison," this was an elite item of the highest quality.

Kizmel coughed awkwardly, sensing the desire written plain on my face.

"I cannot give it to you, much as you might like it. For one thing, this ring draws upon what little magic is left in the blood of Lyusula, so you humans would not be able to use it, I suspect."

You suspect? I nearly asked but held back. "Wh-why do you say that? I don't want your ring at all. I'm just checking to ensure that you're equipped to deal with poison," I said breezily, denying any greed on my part.

Asuna grinned. "That's right. You're a boy, so you'd never stoop to demanding a ring from a girl."

"O-of course...Wait, are you saying that the reverse would be possible?" I grumbled. Asuna's smile disappeared.

"I wasn't saying that! When did I ever beg you for a ring?"

"I-I wasn't referring to you specifically!"

We stopped walking and glared daggers at each other. The elf knight looked on, concerned.

"Kirito, Asuna. I hate to interrupt your chitchat, but—"

Grrr.

"—something is approaching. Based on the footsteps, it is neither elf, nor human, nor beast."

Grrrrr.

"There are two of them, from the front and right. I will leave the one ahead to you."

Grrr...rr?

Asuna and I stopped glaring at each other and looked in the direction of our travel. A shadow was flitting at high speed through the trees. It only came up to our waists, but it was very wide. Many thin legs skittered and scuttled, gliding it along the ground.

Within a second, a cursor popped into view, partway between pink and red. The name beneath the HP bar read THICKET SPIDER.

"Prepare for battle, Asuna!" I called, drawing my sword and bracing myself for the fight. Asuna already had her Wind Fleuret in hand. This quest was an opportunity to gather a few more materials to forge herself a new sword back at camp, meaning it was the last time to shine for the fine battle partner she'd fought with since the first floor.

"Its only direct attack is a bite, but watch out for the thread it shoots from its ass—it'll slow you down!"

"Understood!" she shouted back, then briefly shot me a dirty look. I wondered what she was mad about this time, then realized my poor choice of words.

"S-sorry! I shouldn't have said ass! It's not an ass, but more of a, um..."

"Just stop staying that word!"

Asuna neatly sidestepped the poisonous spider fangs that came lunging at us, then thrust a furious Linear into its giant eye.

The venomous fangs and sticky thread were not to be trifled with, but the Thicket Spider was one of the easier insect-type monsters until this point. It didn't fly or run away, and its hide was not protected by a hard shell. All of its attacks were simple and direct, so it was easy to time when to switch players for combos.

Asuna knocked down about 40 percent of the spider's HP with sword skills and regular attacks, then stepped back and glanced at me. I noticed her eye contact and prepared to join the fight. If this was in the open rather than the forest, Asuna could handle the spider all on her own, but the threads the spider shot from its rear would last for close to a minute, which gradually decreased the available space to fight as the battle wore on. It was always possible to move to a fresh location without webs, but there was the risk that you'd snag more mobs on the way—not to mention the treants that looked just like withered old trees.

The Thicket Spider charged forward with a very spidery hiss—at least, as far as video game spiders went. Asuna released an Oblique, a low thrust skill. Its range was lower than Linear, but with the user's weight behind it, the power was higher. Her sword hit the spider's large, gaping fangs, and both of them were knocked back with a flashy visual effect.

"Switch!" I yelled, striking the large spider on its soft butt. It was only a normal swing, but I hit it right on the weak point of its thread-producing end, and it wheeled around with a painful screech. The cluster of eyes along the front of its head glared at me, poisonous jaw working furiously.

The Thicket Spider was one of the smallest spiders of its type, but it still made for a menacing sight, several feet across from leg to leg. Anyone afraid of spiders would suffer a tremendous mental debuff, if I had to guess. I was used to spiders of all sizes from the shrine grounds near my childhood home—I'd even gotten stuck face-first in the web of a yellow spider once—so it wasn't a big enough deal to affect me in combat, but I was surprised at how well the urbane, fastidious Asuna was handling the giant arachnid.

I got so wrapped up in wonder at that last bit that I glanced away and met her waiting gaze for just a second. As though waiting for its moment, the spider struck. The eight gray, hairy legs tensed, and it bounded into the air. If its jumping attack succeeded in causing a Tumble status, I'd end up bitten several times by its poisonous fangs, so avoidance was the top priority.

"Fwah..."

Due to my late reaction, I knew I couldn't step aside or counterattack with a heavy sword skill in time, so I fell onto my back, waited a split second, then kicked with all my might. The toe of my boot glowed yellow and swung in a semicircle through the air: Crescent Moon, a martial arts kicking skill. It was meant to be used from a standing position into a backflip, but as long as the motion was correct, you could pull it off while lying down.

So the skill was convenient to throw while lying on my back, but there was a serious drawback: If I missed, I would be hit with both a Tumble status and movement delay. Fortunately, it was worth the frightening gamble, as my foot struck the airborne spider directly at the base of one of its legs. With a satisfying *thud*, the spider shot away, spinning through the air.

The follow-through of the kick flipped me back onto my feet. I turned to see the spider upside down at the base of a nearby tree, its legs scrabbling against empty air. Nonwinged insect enemies were generally slow to recover from a tumble, so I calmly and carefully held my Anneal Blade at waist height. The dark blade took on a brilliant blue glow, and my body shot forward.

"Ryaa!"

I leaped, sword flashing. The blade swung horizontally from left to right, directly across the Thicket Spider's bulging belly. As soon as it had passed, my wrists flipped over and reversed path from right to left to complete the Horizontal Arc, a flat two-part skill.

Its weak spot hit deep from two directions, the poison spider flew through the air, spewing green liquid, and landed upside down again, legs curled inward this time. Its large body exploded into countless fragments.

The attack left me leaning forward, sword held out to the left and ahead of me. I slowly stood up straight, swishing the blade left and right before returning it to the sheath on my back. When I turned around, Asuna was staring at me, so I instinctively raised my hand for a high five.

She was not expecting that reaction in the slightest and looked awkward for a moment, but was kind enough not to leave me hanging. After the high five, she wasted no time in getting after me.

"You were getting distracted during that battle, weren't you?"

"...Y-yes, ma'am."

"What were you thinking about?"

I stopped to consider my answer under her withering gaze, then recalled that I was surprised how well she handled the giant spider. However, whether to mention that out loud or not was another quandary.

"Sloppiness against even weak foes will lead to disaster, Kirito," came a voice from my right.

Kizmel was standing to the side, arms crossed, having dispatched the other Thicket Spider well before Asuna and I finished. Like Asuna, her face was hard. It felt like I was being scolded by both a classmate and a teacher at once. I had to make an excuse for myself.

"I-I wasn't being sloppy, I was just thinking..."

"And that's what I'm asking you about."

"Uhh...Umm..." Nothing convenient was coming to mind, so I had no choice but to lay the truth bare. "I was just thinking that it's surprising you don't have any issues with the spiders and wasps and such..."

"Huh?! Were you really wasting your time thinking about that nonsense?!"

"Y-yes," I admitted. Her shapely eyebrows went wide with displeasure for a moment, then she sighed.

"Once they're that big, the bugs are no different from wild animals. I can't waste my time being afraid of how monsters look."

"Ah, I see."

She shook her head in exasperation, and Kizmel chuckled softly. I turned to the dark elf in surprise and saw her looking down at the short fencer with warmth in her eyes.

"That is very reassuring. My sister Tilnel did not shy away from corporeal monsters, either, whether insects or oozes…"

She finished at no more than a whisper. Asuna and I both looked away politely. Asuna hadn't seen Tilnel's grave, but I'd secretly told her about Kizmel's sister as we trudged through the forest.

When she noticed our expressions, Kizmel apologized for bringing that up, then raised her hand to change the topic.

"What is the meaning of that gesture you just did?" she asked, waving her hand forward. I thought this over—was it right to explain to Kizmel, an NPC of the world of *SAO*, the significance of a real-world high five? Before I could come to a conclusion, Asuna spoke up.

"It's a human gesture meant to congratulate one another for their effort."

She held up her own hand and slapped Kizmel's much more thoroughly than she had bothered to with me, producing a satisfying *smack*. Kizmel looked down at her palm and squeezed it, as though savoring the sensation.

"I see. We elves do not make it a practice to touch others often… but this is not unwelcome."

She held up her hand again and looked to me this time. I gave her a hearty high five, realizing it would just be awkward to hold back now. There was another crisp *smack* and an instant of warmth on my hand.

A memory flooded back into my brain.

The very first day of this game of death—it felt like ancient history at this point. But in fact, it was before everything turned deadly. I was thinking of the afternoon of Sunday, November 6, thirty-nine days before, when my very first friend in Aincrad, Klein, lazily hunted blue boars with me outside the Town of Beginnings on the first floor.

Klein was struggling with the initiation of a sword skill, so I taught him the basics of the first motion, then slapped him five when he succeeded in killing his first boar. That was the last time I ever contacted him.

As soon as Akihiko Kayaba's cruel tutorial on the new rules of the game finished, I headed for the next village as soon as I could. I left Klein, a helpless newbie, back in the Town of Beginnings. I abandoned him.

"...Kirito?"

"What's the matter, Kirito?"

I came back to my senses with a start. My hand was still hanging up in the air, so I lowered it and said, "Er, n-nothing."

My awkward smile did nothing to remove their concerned looks, but Kizmel soon moved on.

"I see. Let's get going. If we follow the direction from which those spiders appeared, we should find the nest eventually."

"C-cool. So that means we're heading...uh..."

"This way," Asuna said exasperatedly, pointing to the northwest. We set off again, and after about thirty steps, Asuna pulled level with me to whisper into my ear. "Hey, did Kizmel just say something about 'corporeal' monsters?"

"Eh? Um, yeah."

"Which means there are monsters in this game without bodies?"

"Huh? Yeah, like ghosts and stuff?" I asked in return. She blanched briefly at the word *ghosts*.

"Like...like that."

"Hmm, I dunno...I didn't see any in the beta. Besides, I don't know how you defeat a monster without a body in a game where you can only use swords..."

"Let's hope so."

I wasn't sure what she was hoping for, but Asuna didn't bother

to elaborate. She slowed her pace to draw even with Kizmel. I continued my march in the direction of the spider nest.

After another four battles with Thicket Spiders and their larger cousins, Copse Spiders, slightly adjusting our direction after each encounter, we eventually spotted a small hill rising ahead.

Highlighted against the side of the moonlit hill was the gaping black mouth of a natural cave. I crouched in the shadow of the trees and saw about fourteen small spiders (still the size of real tarantulas) darting around the entrance. This was the spider nest we were after.

"...Do we have to get rid of those little ones, too?" asked Asuna, looking at the nest in annoyance. I shrugged.

"No, those are just critters."

"What? Do they jingle?"

"...?"

I turned upward to look at her in confusion. She spoke with the bossy tone of a teacher explaining to her students. "Didn't you just say it was a 'clitter'? Like *clitter-clatter*? Do they make lots of noise?"

"Ummm...no. 'Critters' in an MMO are like background animals that aren't monsters. You can't interact with them; they're just for show. Like butterflies or alley cats in town."

"You know what? I'm getting tired of asking about every single game term, so why don't you just create a slang glossary for me?"

"Ugh..."

If she didn't mind being ripped off, she could ask Argo for something like that. Kizmel chuckled from behind us and murmured, "Your words have not been unified yet, it seems. I suppose that is not a surprise, for there were nine nations of humankind when the Great Separation happened."

"..."

Asuna and I shared a look.

The "Separation" was a term many used to refer to an incident that arose one month before. Many players suffered sudden disconnections and were stuck in limbo for around an hour before they rejoined the game. When it became clear that every player was going to be disconnected in such a way, I stopped my breakneck leveling for a bit and waited around in an inn room so that it didn't catch me off guard. The mysterious phenomenon caused alarm and chaos at first, but the common assumption that emerged was that it was just our bodies being temporarily disconnected so they could be transferred to a proper hospital.

But this Great Separation Kizmel spoke of must be something else. She was a resident of this world, not a player diving in through the NerveGear like me and Asuna. It must have something to do with the creation of Aincrad the floating castle...

I instantly had a number of different questions to ask Kizmel on the subject, but she cut me off before I could open my mouth.

"Come, let us investigate the hole. We will need more concrete information to bring to the commander about the spiders."

According to my increasingly unhelpful beta knowledge, the spider-vanquishing quest had two stages. Part one involved finding an article from one of the dark elf scouts within the nest and bringing it back to the base. In the second part, we had to return to the cave and fight the queen spider in the second level of the nest.

So even though I knew this opening led right into the spider's nest, that alone did not fulfill the quest requirements. We'd have to delve into the clammy cave twice.

"...I don't like these natural dungeons," Asuna grumbled, stepping into a shallow puddle with her leather boots. I nodded in agreement.

"If only it was a bit brighter in there..."

The man-made dungeons, like the giant labyrinth towers, at least had oil lamps or luminescent stones on the walls to keep the interior lit. But this cave was almost pitch-black; the only source of light was very dim moss that gave off a faint glow in the dark. To counteract the darkness, Asuna and I carried torches in our off hands, but they did not cast very much light and would extinguish if dropped into water. Even worse, I normally fought with one hand free, so the difference made everything feel wrong in battle. Still, it was better than being a shield user who had to do without that valuable defense. And warriors with two-handed weapons would slap us for being spoiled—they had to find a dry spot on the ground to drop the torch before they could fight at all.

Thankfully, in this situation, we had Kizmel with her special elven ability to see in the dark. Unlike the jumping spiders out in the forest, the ones in the nest were speedy fishing spiders, and Kizmel's ability to warn us of their presence before they reached the torchlight radius gave us plenty of time to ready our blades.

We searched each room on the first level of the cave slowly but steadily, occasionally finding chests with treasure, or valuable ores that could be used to craft Asuna's next weapon. Once we had nearly finished mapping out the entire floor, Asuna raised a belated question.

"Hey, is this dungeon one of those…instance things? Or is it…?"

"I believe the antonym of an instanced dungeon would be a public dungeon. This is the public kind," I murmured quietly into Asuna's ear, afraid that if Kizmel heard she would give us another lecture about the fractured language of humankind. "The reason I know it's public is because there are other quests that use this dungeon aside from ours."

"Oh? Like what?"

"Well, there's a pet-finding quest at the next village past the forest, and another one from the main city of the…"

My mouth shut with a snap. Asuna's orange-lit face looked at me curiously, and I tore away to look behind us.

The way we'd come was almost complete darkness, without a soul in sight…but did I just hear something? A faint, brief scrape of metal?

"Hey, what's wrong?"

"…How many hours have we been on the third floor, Asuna?"

"After all the sleep we got, I think it's around fourteen hours."

"Ugh…crap, that's the exact timing."

"Exact timing of what?"

I turned to look back again and whispered quickly, "This is the location of a major quest you can start from the main city. There are a few different patterns to the quest, so it's not guaranteed, but a solid percentage of players doing that quest are going to be coming here for an item. Depending on the size of the party, it might take between ten to fifteen hours for them to get this far…"

Just then, I heard another faint clang of metal. Kizmel stopped dead still, a sign that it wasn't just a trick of my ears. She watched and waited for a tense moment, face sharp, then turned to us.

"Kirito, Asuna—it would seem there are other visitors to this nest."

"Yeah. It must be other pla…human warriors. We have reasons to avoid encountering them, Kizmel."

"I do as well," the elf knight grinned and pointed to a divot in the wall. "Let us hide there for a moment."

"Huh? How can we hide with the light of the torches all around?" Asuna asked, wide-eyed. Kizmel smiled again.

"The people of the forest have their own ways of deception."

She pushed our backs, guiding us to the three-foot-deep depression in the wall and up against the surface, then pressing herself against us to hide us from view. Her ample bosom, tight stomach, and smooth thighs were pressed directly against me, and I was afraid that the game's harassment code would go off, but apparently that did not apply when it was an NPC initiating the contact. Kizmel, of course, had no idea what was running through my mind.

"Extinguish the torches," she commanded. I did as she said and dropped my light into a puddle on the floor. Once we were shrouded in darkness, Kizmel stretched out her cape to cover all three of us.

Oddly enough, while the cape seemed to be woven solid from the outside, it was sheer and see-through from the inside. All I could see was blackness, of course, but there was just enough green glow from the moss across the way to tell that the cape wouldn't block my sight.

That wasn't the only surprise to me. Despite not using the Hiding skill, its familiar hide rate percentage readout appeared on the left side of my view. Even more shocking, the number was at 95 percent. Kizmel's cape had a magic—er, charm—effect that activated the Hiding skill. Between this and the antidote ring, I was getting very jealous.

"You were saying earlier, Kirito?" Asuna asked at the lowest possible volume, interrupting my fit of envy. It took me a moment to remember what we'd been talking about.

"Oh, right. The people coming up from behind us are on that quest. It's the guild creation quest, the one the other frontier players were desperate to get started."

"…!"

Her eyes went wide in the darkness—she remembered. I was going to continue, but Kizmel gave us a warning first.

"Quiet. They'll pass by soon."

Asuna and I shut our mouths and swallowed hard.

Ten seconds later, we heard the rattling of armor on the move. I counted at least two heavily armored fighters, if not three. There were more footsteps, however; the party had to be five or six in total.

Finally, there came a rough shout, shockingly loud and careless in the midst of a dungeon.

"What the hell?! All the chests have been ransacked already!"

It was a very familiar voice, one that felt like I'd heard it just minutes ago. I had last seen him a whole fifteen hours ago, but something about the circumstances—the fact that I hadn't even been to the town yet or that his booming voice was so memorable—made me think, *Not you again!* Asuna's pale face grimaced in the darkness.

We held our breath for several seconds. The first player passed by us, so close we could reach out to touch him.

He wore thick scale armor with a chain coif that covered his entire head. It was too dark to make out the color of his tunic and pants, but they would be moss green, without a doubt. In his hands were a round shield and a rare one-handed ax. It was a crude weapon for the front line, but he nimbly spun it around in his fingers.

The next man to pass by also had a shield with his sword, and the third was unhelmeted. Instead, his hair was fashioned into large spikes that made his head look like a pointed mace. His eyes were sharp and his mouth was twisted in displeasure. He wore a steel breastplate and held a sword in one hand.

This man's name was Kibaou, and I'd been running afoul of him since the boss fight of the first floor. As an avowed opponent of the former beta testers, he had plenty of reason to hate me, and if he saw me here in the dungeon, he'd no doubt have a foul word—or two, or three, or four—to say to me.

The instant he passed by, Kibaou's beady eyes glanced at the hollow we were hiding in, and the hiding percentage dropped to 90. Fortunately, it did not drop enough to reveal us. Three more players followed him past, their raucous clanking growing fainter and fainter until it finally died out.

A few seconds later, Kizmel straightened up and returned her cape to its normal position. We heaved sighs of relief as we got to our feet. My partner looked worried.

"I felt more nervous than when we face monsters."

"Yeah. It probably wouldn't have turned into a battle if they'd seen us, though," I answered. Asuna's head waved, not quite a nod or a shake.

"Well, they might have demanded that we share what we found in the chests."

"I dunno. I don't think even he would go that far...I hope..."

Kizmel turned away from the direction the party had gone and asked, "Did you know some of those people?"

"Um, kind of...We're not exactly on friendly terms, you might say..."

"Oh? I'd heard that the humans in this castle had maintained a healthy peace for years."

"W-we wouldn't come to blows, of course. And we help each other out when fighting big monsters...but we're not friends."

There was no way to explain the difference between former beta testers and retail players to Kizmel, so my explanation had to be simple, but she seemed to buy the story. She grinned weakly and said, "I see. Then it must be like the relationship between my Pagoda Knights Brigade and the royal Sandalwood Knights."

What does she mean, Pagoda? I wondered. Asuna chattered in delight.

"Oh, that's lovely! Your knight brigades are named after trees? Are there any others?"

"There's the Trifoliate Knights Brigade, the heavy units. We are not on good terms with them, either."

"Ahh...In that case, if I get to join any of them, I'll go with the Pagoda Knights."

Kizmel grimaced awkwardly. "I'm afraid that there is no historical precedent for humans being awarded the knight's sword from the queen of Lyusula. But based on your accomplishments, you might be able to win an audience with her..."

"Really? Let's keep it up, then!" Asuna beamed, nothing but optimism on her mind. I, however, had extra knowledge that caused me to avoid her gaze. In the beta, I'd followed this quest all the way up to the dark elf castle town on the ninth floor, but that was as far as I got. When the quest concluded, the gate to the castle remained steadfastly closed...

"Well, let's get going!" Asuna bubbled, already an apprentice knight in her own mind, and slapped my back. I gave her a sullen affirmative and picked the two torches up off the ground, handing one to her. Dropping torches in water didn't affect their ability to light again, as long as they had durability points left. We scraped them against the stone walls to get the flame started again, peered out of the hollow, and trained our ears on the direction the party of six had gone.

If Kibaou's team was attempting the quest to establish their guild, they were heading for the second level of the cave. We'd already cleaned out all the spiders on the first level, so they could be at the stairs by now. The mobs down below would be tougher, but not enough to threaten a party of six.

I brought up my window and checked the map. We'd charted four-fifths of the first level, with only two spots left. One was probably the room with the stairs down, and the other was the room with the item we sought. We needed to head for the room away from the direction Kibaou was moving.

"Let's go this way..." I started to say, then caught Kizmel staring at me. I wondered why. Was she confused by the menu screen? Or simply pretending not to see it?

"...It has been a long time since I saw that human charm."

"Huh? Ch-charm?"

"Indeed. It is the art of Mystic Scribing, one of the few charms left to humankind after its magic was lost, is it not? The one that allows you to record knowledge, even physical items, within your mystic tome..."

Now that she mentioned it, a glowing purple screen that floated in midair at the wave of a hand was pretty much magic, no two ways around it. I nodded in agreement.

"Y-yes, that's it. According to the map in my Mystic...Scribbly book, we haven't checked this area yet..."

Behind Kizmel, Asuna tried to hold back a belly laugh at my pathetic answer.

We easily cleared out the spiders in one of the two remaining rooms, discovering a faint light blinking on the back wall. I sheathed my sword and approached to find a silver decoration carved in the shape of a leaf. At the base was a gleaming white gem like an opal.

I looked up and checked the fastener of Kizmel's cape on her left shoulder. The design and coloring were exactly the same.

"...It is the insignia of the Pagoda Knights. It must have

belonged to a scout who was investigating the cave. The owner cannot be alive anymore," Kizmel remarked gloomily. I offered her the brooch, but she waved her head.

"You must take that to the commander, Kirito. We ought to return for our report."

"...All right. I'll hold on to it, then."

I put the emblem in my pouch, and a message scrolled by on the left side of my view, announcing quest progress.

When I found this scout's memento during the beta after a long, hard slog, the entire party cheered triumphantly. But I was in no mood for that this time. It occurred to me that from the moment we rescued Kizmel in the forest half a day before, my mental concepts of quests and NPCs were subtly and steadily shifting.

Mobs respawned at a much higher rate in dungeons, so the spiders around the entrance were probably back by now. I trained my ears for the sound of many legs, torch in one hand and sword in the other.

But in a few seconds, what I heard was not the skittering of monsters, but the shouts of men.

"Crap...It's coming up the stairs!"

"Run, run! Back to the entrance!"

There was the crashing of metal armor and panicked footsteps. Then the screech of a very large monster, like dead wood creaking and cracking.

"No one said anythin' about such a freakin' huge spider! What the hell's goin' on?!" Kibaou bellowed. The irritation in his voice from earlier had been amplified into panic.

I turned to my two companions to confer.

"What should—"

"What should we do, Kirito?!"

"I will leave this decision in your hands!"

"—we...do..."

I never volunteered to be the party leader! I wailed internally, but it was too late for that. Now it was up to me to decide how to respond to this unexpected turn of events.

Ideally, we would hide, Kibaou's group would succeed at escaping, and the giant spider would return to the second level of the cave once it lost its target. But the likelihood of all these things happening was low. The nimble fishing spiders would have repopped at the entrance by now, so Kibaou's party wasn't likely to get out into the forest safely. In a worst-case scenario, they might wind up trapped on both sides. The "freakin' huge spider" had to be the queen spider, boss of the dungeon, so that would be a terrible situation.

The next best choice was for Kibaou's group to stop running and face the queen. From what I recalled, it wouldn't be too hard for a party of six around level 10 to defeat the spider without casualties. But that was assuming that all of them were calm and dealt with her special attacks properly. Kibaou's Aincrad Liberation Squad were steadfast in their denial of all beta testers, so none of them would have any advance knowledge of this unfamiliar monster.

That thought process took me two seconds. I spent another half second looking over at Kizmel's tense face.

Whether we got along with Kibaou or not, his party was an invaluable force in reaching our shared goal. We couldn't ignore their plight, but I was also hesitant to butt in directly. There was no way to know how they—particularly Kibaou—would react when the battle was over and they noticed Kizmel.

They might not attack directly, but I felt a strong aversion to letting them see her. Lately, I'd been trying hard not to let terms like *NPC* or *game* be spoken in her presence.

"We'll let them pass by and stop the spider as it chases. If we can get it into that big room over there, we should have enough space to fight," I said quickly. Asuna and Kizmel both stared at me. There were different thoughts behind the hazel-brown and onyx-black pairs of eyes, but both women nodded in agreement before I needed to spend valuable seconds trying to figure out what they were.

"All right. You can lead the way."

"If you have decided to fight, I will follow."

Kizmel was one thing, but Asuna's agreement took me a bit by surprise. There was no time to waste asking why, however; I had to consult my mental map of the dungeon and estimate Kibaou's route.

"This way!"

I waved my torch and started running after the sound of footsteps.

Within just ten steps, the corridor intersected with a wide cross path. Kibaou's group should come down that path from left to right, the queen spider on their heels. Once the players had passed, we'd grab her attention and pull her back to the room where the scout's memento had been. The party would continue running all the way to the entrance, perhaps running across some minor spiders near the entrance, but otherwise convinced they'd outrun the queen.

We leaned back into another hollow in the wall, Asuna's torch still lit but mine extinguished. I waited in the thicker darkness, timing when to charge. The ideal method of fishing mobs was through a taunt skill or throwing knives, but I didn't have either at my disposal yet—my only option was to swing my sword into the intersection and catch the queen as she passed by. And because I'd need to back away immediately, I couldn't use a sword skill with a movement delay after it.

I gripped my Anneal Blade and heard the shouts of the group again.

"It's an intersection! Which way's the exit?!"

"We just went through here! Straight, straight, straight!"

Six pairs of clanking footsteps approached. I flattened my back against the wall, watching the intersection with laser focus from five yards away.

Two seconds later, a gang of men raced across my field of vision. The man in the lead was still casually twirling his ax, but the others looked desperate. When running from a dangerous foe, the lightly armored types would always break away from the slower, heavier kind, but Kibaou's leadership kept his team tightly packed.

Once the party had rushed past, I heard a roar like scraping sticks again. I couldn't hear the sound of those thin legs, but the unique vibration of many spider legs hitting the ground traveled through my boots. Three seconds left, two…

Now!

I leaped forward silently, Anneal Blade raised for a compact swing. I wasn't looking for huge damage, but I needed to generate enough hate to make the spider change targets. The moment I started my swing, a giant form crossed the left side of my vision. First there were round, glowing red eyes, then legs the size of tree trunks, and lastly a bulging body.

"…!!"

With a silent scream, I struck the giant spider's flank. It was nothing more than a slightly charged normal swing, but it was enough for the point to pierce the dull purple exoskeleton and send green liquid shooting out.

"Kishashaa!!"

The spider bellowed in rage and stopped still as I pulled the sword out. I leaped back and raced for Asuna and Kizmel, not bothering to check if the spider was following.

When I looked over my shoulder, the queen spider had just finished a ninety-degree turn. My gaze met her many glowing eyes, and I noticed that the first of her two HP bars was slightly decreased. The name listed was NEPHILA REGINA. I knew that *regina* was Latin for "queen," which made her Queen Nephila. In that light, the silver patterns on her gleaming purple body did lend her a regal air.

"Looks like you got her attention," Asuna whispered, peeling away from the wall. The eight-legged queen crouched down, eyes flashing dangerously, as though displeased with the light of Asuna's torch. Then—

"Kshaa!"

It screeched and raced forward—but we weren't just standing

and watching. As soon as the first leg twitched forward, all three of us were off and running. These narrow corridors were no place to fight a foe with movement-disabling attacks.

After ten seconds of running, the opening to a large empty room appeared on the right. We darted inside and the two women spread out around me in the center. I scraped the torch in my left hand on the floor to light it again, just as the queen spider barreled into the room. It charged directly for me without hesitation.

I stood and watched the two front legs as they rose high in the air. As long as nothing had changed from the beta, the queen spider used the following attacks: jabs from the front legs, bites from poison fangs, a sticky spray from the rear, and a vertical jump that landed with a shock wave. The webbing attack would stick a player in place if stuck to the feet, and if it touched your head, there was no way to swing a weapon. The shock wave was similar in nature to the one used by the minotaur bosses on the second floor—if you lost your footing, you'd either stumble or fall over.

Without the time to tell Asuna and Kizmel about these attacks beforehand, I'd just have to instruct them in real time. Watching the spider's legs closely, I shouted, "When she jabs with her legs, the one that twitches will go first! If you don't get outside her range, both will hit you!"

Just as the words were out of my mouth, the right front leg twitched, and I jumped to the left. A giant claw slammed into the spot where I'd just been standing, and the left leg swung forward a moment later but couldn't follow me because the first leg was in the way. The instant it, too, stuck into the ground, I shouted a command.

"One sword skill!"

Uncowed by the unfamiliar boss monster before them, both women immediately brandished their weapons, blades glowing. I noted the glow out of the corners of my eyes and struck at the spider's legs with a Horizontal. The beast was hit by light and sound in triplicate, screeching hideously as a third of its top HP bar fell away. It had to be Kizmel's power that made that kind of damage possible.

At this pace, as long as we played it safe and limited ourselves to single skills, we could finish Nephila off in another six or seven rounds. I didn't take any chances, watching the spider closely after its delay wore off and it started moving again. She was only queen over a simple two-level dungeon, but she was a boss monster in her own right. I wasn't going to relax and assume that she hadn't been altered since the beta, the same way the floor bosses were.

The queen took a few skittering steps and crunched down with all eight legs.

"She's gonna jump! We have to leap out of the way just before she lands. I'll tell you when!"

The huge spider leaped upward, shaking the very air of the chamber. Once it reached the ceiling and began to fall, I cried out, "Two, one, jump!"

We leaped high as the queen spider fell, the shock wave effect passing harmlessly beneath our feet. Just before I landed, I prepared another sword skill.

In the midst of all the precise judgment and careful observation, I'd completely forgotten that the powerful and trusty elven knight was not a human being, but a programmed NPC.

It shouldn't be possible. An NPC didn't respond to abbreviated commands from a player like this over their preprogrammed algorithms. But nothing about her actions struck me as out of the ordinary.

Gauging the length of battle was extremely hard in a VRMMO, where all the senses were intensely occupied. It was typical to finish up a fight and say, "That was only a minute long?" or "It took us an entire hour?"

So when Nephila Regina, the giant spider queen, exploded with a splashy visual effect and we received our rewards, the first thing I did was bring up my menu to check the time.

Four twenty AM, which meant we'd only spent three minutes on the battle—but more than enough time for Kibaou's group to grow curious about the absence of the boss and come wandering back. If they did, we could hide with Kizmel's camouflage cape again, but it would be difficult to stay concealed after the monstrous sound of the spider's explosion.

I closed my window and turned to my high-fiving partners to put a finger to my lips. Fortunately, the dark elves were familiar with the sign to be quiet, and so Kizmel and Asuna lowered their hands. Next I gestured to wait and tiptoed over to the room's entrance. With my back pressed to the wall, I trained my ears on the hallway but didn't hear any approaching voices or footsteps for now.

If it was after four in the morning, when the hell did they leave town? Perhaps they'd been up all night working on the guild quest.

I spent three seconds half-annoyed and half-impressed by the Liberation Squad, but they didn't seem to be coming. They'd probably drawn the notice of some regular spiders near the cave entrance and got stuck in battle. I heaved a sigh of relief and returned to Asuna and Kizmel.

"Doesn't look like Kibaou's group noticed us. They'll probably head back in for the second level to finish their guild quest, so we can slip out once they're past us," I suggested. Asuna agreed but looked puzzled.

"How many minutes does it take for that boss spider to come back?"

"Umm…"

I started to search through my memory banks for that information from the beta, but Kizmel answered first.

"At that size, it will take three hours at the minimum for the cave to generate enough spiritual power to give life to a new ruler."

So Kizmel had her own interpretation for the phenomenon of mobs respawning. I was tempted to ask how this spiritual energy was different from the magic that had been lost from Aincrad, but this time it was Asuna's turn to head me off.

"With that much leeway, Kibaou's team will have plenty of time to search the second level safely. So we ended up helping them, without them realizing it. That kind of irks me."

"Ha-ha-ha. As they say, 'The forest sees all good deeds, and the insects all the bad.' The Holy Tree will ensure that you are blessed."

"Ah…I see. In the human lands, we say, 'One good turn deserves another.'"

"I shall remember it."

While they chatted, my brain busied itself with practical matters—it would be a pain to have to leave and deliver the emblem to the commander, only to be told to return to fight the boss spider again. But I soon noticed that something dark was gleaming on the ground nearby. It was a gigantic fang that had come from Queen Nephila's mouth. I tapped it just to be sure, and a label appeared, reading QUEEN SPIDER'S POISON FANG.

If everything went properly, we could give the commander the lost scout's insignia, receive the quest to kill the queen, then show him the fang to complete it immediately. I eagerly stashed the fang in my inventory and checked the clock to find that it was past four thirty. Kibaou's team would be back in the second level of the cave by now.

"Well, let's head back to the base camp," I suggested. Kizmel and Asuna both turned and nodded to me at the same time.

They looked totally unalike, especially with Kizmel's dark skin and pointed ears—but despite one being a human and the other an NPC, I couldn't shake the sensation that they were like sisters.

My hopes were rewarded when we made it back to the surface without running into Kibaou. We rushed through the forest to the camp south of us, avoiding battle wherever possible.

By the time the many rippling flags appeared through the thick fog, there was a faint purple glow to the light coming from the exterior edge of Aincrad that spoke of the eventual morning. The predawn chill of mid-December in the real world required a sweater and down jacket, but after the heat of our fierce battles, it felt good on the skin. Of course, any heat or cold coming through the NerveGear was just mental signals.

We passed through the thick magical mist created by the Forest-Sinking charm and into the narrow rock passage to the camp. Only then could we heave sighs of relief and undo some of the heavy equipment.

Kizmel, who had no in-game item storage, remarked with envy on our Mystic Scribing charms, as she called them, and looked to the rear of the camp.

"Kirito, Asuna, will you deliver the memento you discovered in the cave?"

"Y-yeah. That's fine..."

"Thank you. The scout who died was of the commander's blood...I do not wish to intrude upon your report. Forgive my selfishness."

I didn't need to ask if she was being reminded about the death of her sister Tilnel. Asuna reached out and brushed the dark elf's arm to soothe her.

"We understand. Don't worry, we'll give the report. What are you going to do next, Kizmel?"

"I will rest in the tent. Call upon me if you should need my services."

And with a weak smile, Kizmel stepped away. With a forlorn chime, one of the HP bars in the upper left disappeared. A small system message accompanied the change, alerting us to the departure of a member from the party.

With a clanking salute, Kizmel left and proceeded back to the right corner of the camp. I glanced over at my partner and, as I expected, saw a mixture of loneliness and unease in Asuna's face.

"Don't worry. She'll join us again, anytime we ask...I think," I reassured her.

But rather than turning on me in anger, Asuna simply said, "...Yeah."

She pulled the hanging hood up over her head, as though shifting gears, and remarked, "C'mon, let's go report on our quest."

The commander of the dark elven advance forces took the leaf-design emblem without a sign of emotion. It seemed that of all the NPCs here, only Kizmel's was anywhere near as advanced as she was, but after spending so much time with her, I couldn't help but imagine there was deep sadness behind the commander's stoic face.

A new quest log scrolled by once I had delivered the item, informing me of a new task: to defeat the spider commanding the nest. I hesitantly produced the queen spider's fang and set it down on the table. Fortunately, that fulfilled the requirements, so we were able to complete the second chapter of the campaign quest without leaving on another journey. Still, with ten chapters just on the third floor alone, there was plenty left to do.

We gratefully received our col, experience, and item—both Asuna and I chose the magic belt pouch that had a far greater capacity than its appearance suggested—initiated the third chapter of the quest, and left the commander's tent.

The night had fully broken by now, and there were more dark elves milling about the camp, but Kizmel was not one of them. I stopped just outside the entrance to the large commander's tent and turned to my remaining party member.

"...What next? We can call upon Kizmel to join us at any time..."

"Hmm..." Asuna looked down in thought, then shook her head. "Let's do that a bit later. I know this sounds weird, but...I think we should give her some time to herself."

"I see. And no, that's not weird. I mean, yes, she's an NPC...but more than that, she's our partner."

"I don't recall ever turning into your partner."

"...Yes, ma'am."

A tantalizing smell came wafting over from the dining tent.

I started to wander off in that direction, but Asuna pulled my sleeve back.

"We have something to do before eating."

"Huh? What's that?"

"Come on, you haven't forgotten overnight. We were supposed to have the blacksmith forge me a new sword once we collected the right materials!"

The equipment in *Sword Art Online* could be gained in one of three different ways.

First was the kind looted from monsters, whether simple mobs or bosses, also known as "monster drops." When combined with chest drops found in dungeons, this category was "dropped loot."

Next were "quest rewards" earned from completing a quest.

The last category was "shop made," crafted by a player or NPC blacksmith or leatherworker from special ingredients or material items.

In the five weeks since the game began, none of the three categories had proven themselves to be inherently better or worse than the others. My Anneal Blade +6 was a quest reward from the first floor, and Asuna's Wind Fleuret +5 was originally a monster drop. It was likely that as the player population's level rose, the value of quest rewards and NPC-crafted weapons would fall, meaning the best weapons would either be rare drops or player crafted. But that eventuality could be months and months away…or years, though I prayed it didn't come to that.

I trudged along, lost in thought, behind Asuna, her hooded cape flapping in the breeze.

Despite the seven hours of sleep I'd gotten the last night, after the heavy questing in the dark, the advent of the morning sun brought a fresh wave of fatigue down on me. By contrast, the fencer's stride was crisp and spry, so either she was that rarest of types among MMO gamers—a morning person—or she was trying to keep her unease away with the heel of her boot.

"Don't worry, it'll go fine," I mumbled as I rubbed my eyes, barely aware that I'd said it. A few feet ahead, the boots clicked to a halt. I barely stopped myself in time before colliding with her back. A voice made of 70 percent anger and 30 percent something else hit my ears.

"...I'm not worried about anything at all."

Even in my low-functioning brain state, I was aware that I shouldn't cross her right then, so I answered with a simple "Okay."

"Anyway, you'd better have saved up enough materials in battle. I don't want to have to go farm for more because we're a bit short," she said, turning back to me. When she spoke next, her voice was softer than before. "It can't always...be like this..."

"Huh? Like what?"

"I mean...I can't keep asking you for what kind of materials to make a weapon or how to beat a certain kind of monster. I have to learn how to figure that stuff out for myself."

"Ahh...B-but when I met you in the second-floor city, you knew exactly which monsters dropped which upgrade materials," I replied. Our reunion one week ago seemed like ancient history now. Asuna grinned wryly beneath her deep hood.

"Only because I memorized the details that were important to me from Argo's strategy guide. I don't know anything that isn't written down in a textbook. It's the same as I was before I came here."

"......"

This caught me by surprise. I searched for the right answer but could only shake my head.

"It's the same for me, too. I still have my beta knowledge to go on, but once that runs out, I'm just as lost..."

"You're wrong. The knowledge gained from a book and the knowledge gained from experience are totally different things. The reason I'm so nervous about creating a single weapon is because I've never experienced it before."

I noticed that my sleepiness had worn off by then. Choosing not to point out that she'd admitted she was worried, I kept my face straight.

"Then you can experience things starting now. The most important thing is to survive and keep moving forward...that's all. Use anything you can, as long as it's for that purpose—whether it comes from Argo's books or my brain. Each and every day will bring you more experience...and not the kind that comes in points."

I felt a bit self-conscious after that serious but uncharacteristic speech and looked away above the big tent. The first rays of the sun, pouring in directly from the outer aperture, caught the bottom of the floor above, dyeing it red.

"...Good point. It's the start of another day..." she murmured. Some of the strain had left her voice, to my relief.

I glanced back at her and added, "Also, there's one other thing I forgot to say..."

"Huh?"

"Unlike with weapon upgrading, there's basically no fail state for crafting. So there's really no reason to worry about—"

She cut me off with a punch to my gut just soft enough not to cause damage and growled threateningly, "You could have mentioned that earlier!"

Asuna stomped off angrily enough to break through the hard ground, and I followed at a careful distance until we came to the crafting section of the dark elf camp.

There were four tents laid out along the path, each waving its own identifying flag: item shop, seamstress, leatherworker, and blacksmith. The tents displayed their rarest wares up front, and my heart soared at some of the items unavailable in human territory, but the pricing was rough on the wallet, especially since I'd only just reached the third floor. I walked past the shops with considerable restraint and stopped in front of the blacksmith.

NPC blacksmiths were bearded macho guys as a general rule, but in keeping with the elven theme, this one was a tall and slender man with long hair tied back behind his head. The only visual identifiers that marked him as a blacksmith were the thick black leather apron and elbow-length gloves. But as the excellent smith's hammer in his hand suggested, this fellow's crafting skill was much higher than those found in the main town of the third floor. Now that Nezha of the Legend Braves had converted to a chakram warrior, this elf was the best crafter anyone could hope to visit at this point in the game.

If there was one problem here...

Asuna and I stopped before the tent. The dark elf blacksmith turned his sharp, tanned face upon us, snorted, and returned to his work. I felt a sudden surge of negative energy from beside me, so I pulled the cape sleeve away. This entire camp was outside of the safe haven zone, so if we did anything criminal, the guards would swarm onto us, beat us to a pulp, and toss us out of the camp—if the tough-looking blacksmith didn't take care of us first.

Fortunately, Asuna chose not to comment on the proprietor's lack of hospitality, throwing a glare at me instead.

"Are you sure this is going to work?" she muttered. I nodded vigorously. There were no guarantees when it came to upgrading, but as I'd said just a minute earlier, absolute failure was impossible when forging a brand-new weapon. Assuming that the crafter had the requisite skill proficiency necessary to create the item, of course.

I let go of the cape, and Asuna took a step forward. She politely asked the elven blacksmith, "Excuse me, can I ask you to forge me a new weapon?"

He replied with another snort, but the special shop menu appeared for Asuna. When dealing with players, the negotiation was usually face-to-face, but sometimes NPCs might not understand the meaning of the players' language, so a menu was provided to facilitate the transaction.

I wondered if the elf blacksmith also considered this window a type of magic charm. Asuna hit the visibility button in the corner of the window so I could see. She was about to push the CREATE WEAPON button with a slender finger, but stopped.

"...Oh yeah. There's something I need to do first," she murmured. A moment later, I realized what she meant.

"It's not a necessary step, though. You can do as you see fit, Asuna."

"I know...But I've made up my mind," she announced and turned away from the shopwindow to remove the Wind Fleuret +5, in its familiar green sheath, from her waist.

From the battle against the first boss to the trials of the second floor and now here to the third floor, the simple but beautifully designed weapon had served Asuna well. She whispered something to the sword that I couldn't hear, then offered it to the elf blacksmith. She chose to bypass the menu system and make the request herself.

"Please convert this sword into ingots."

I expected the elven blacksmith to respond with a third resounding snort, but instead, he simply held out his hand.

He couldn't possibly understand Asuna's attachment to the weapon, but he did silently take the Wind Fleuret and remove it from its scabbard. The brilliant, mirrorlike polish when it was new had faded, but the blade had taken on a deep luster since. The blacksmith inspected the rapier, nodded, and tenderly placed it in the forge behind him.

This was an honest, square brick forge, not the portable kind that Nezha carried around. It didn't have a bellows to power up the fire, but the flames rising from the surface were a mysterious blue green, likely the work of more elvish magic. The fire soon turned the silver blade bright red, and it began to glow from tip to hilt. Asuna clutched her hands over her chest as she watched.

Eventually, the sword flashed even brighter, then dulled, turning into a rectangular block about eight inches long.

When the light had fully subsided, the elf reached over with a gloved hand and picked the block out of the fire, handing it to Asuna. It was a single ingot, gleaming silver in the light of the morning sun. There were countless types of metal ingots in

Aincrad, from real materials like iron and copper to fantastical ones like mithril, and even I couldn't identify all of them by sight alone. However, it was clear that Asuna's beloved weapon had turned into a particularly rare and valuable material.

"Thank you very much," she said to the elf, taking the silver hunk in both hands. Asuna held it there for a few moments, as though assessing its weight, then opened her menu and placed it in her inventory. She closed the window, then slid the still-open shop menu over to resume her order.

She hit the CREATE WEAPON button, then hit ONE-HANDED WEAPON, then RAPIER, then SELECT MATERIAL. A smaller window popped up showing all of the eligible materials she pos-. sessed, split into categories.

When upgrading weapons, the only requirements were base materials and optional additives, but crafting a new one required a core material: the ingot. We could forge an ingot from the ores we'd collected in the spider cave, but those would be the basic materials in this case. Asuna didn't need my help with this one; she selected a number of materials, leaving for last the core from her Wind Fleuret—which was officially called an Argentium Ingot. Once all the required items were fulfilled, a final YES/NO dialog box appeared, along with the cost of creation.

Asuna gave the blacksmith another glance, thanked him for the work he was about to do, and hit the YES button.

With a swooshing sound, two leather sacks and the brand-new ingot appeared on the work platform next to the blacksmith. He silently picked up the two sacks, which were filled with the base, and added materials and tossed them into the forge. The sacks burned away, leaving only the materials within, gleaming red.

"I-I don't know about this...He was awfully blunt about doing that," I muttered to Asuna, who sighed in annoyance.

"You're the one who said you couldn't fail at forging a weapon. We just have to trust in the process now."

She's learned a lot about mental toughness since the time we asked Nezha to power up that Wind Fleuret on the second floor, I thought. The truth was, I hadn't told Asuna about one thing.

It was impossible to fail entirely at weapon creation—meaning that all of the materials disappeared and no sword appeared in return. But that didn't mean that the results were always fixed. The player chose a type of weapon, but what it looked like and what it was called were a mystery until the process was finished. Essentially, there was a wide range of potential stats for the completed weapon.

But it was impossible for the finished sword to be weaker than the Wind Fleuret it was based on—I hoped. The elven blacksmith might be unfriendly, but his skill was good, we gave him the maximum of basic and added materials, and all of Asuna's sentiment was poured into that ingot. Superstition or not, I believed that even in this world of digital data, that stuff made a difference.

As I pondered over these momentary thoughts, the materials in the fire melted together, turning the flames to a bright white color. The blacksmith tossed the ingot in, and the cold metal block began to sparkle.

"Buff, please," came Asuna's voice. I felt the index, middle, and ring fingers of my right hand gripped by a soft palm up to the second knuckle.

Of course, we had no active buff effects, and even if we did, the benefits wouldn't transfer through hand-to-hand contact. But instead of mentioning these things aloud, I simply brushed my thumb against the back of her hand, praying for a good sword to emerge.

The elf paid no mind to our rapt attention. When the ingot was sufficiently heated, he picked it up with his gloved left hand and moved it to the anvil. Smith's hammer spinning in his hand, the elf struck the metal rhythmically, once every two seconds. The clear ringing echoed through the morning air of the camp.

The number of strikes to finish the weapon was directly related to the strength of the finished product. A starter weapon like a

Plain Rapier or a Small Sword would only take five swings, less than an upgrade attempt. The Wind Fleuret and others of its level required around twenty blows. Therefore, counting up the number of hits as the process continued was both exhilarating and nerve-racking.

Ten, fifteen. The strikes continued.

Once the number passed twenty, I slowly let out the breath I'd been holding in. This essentially ensured that the sword would be better than the Wind Fleuret.

But once the hammer counted twenty-five, I felt the tension return. I stared closely at the spark-laden ingot, unaware that I was clenching Asuna's hand back.

My Anneal Blade was a quest reward, but a weapon of a similar quality was worth about thirty strikes. The blacksmith's hammer breezed past that number, then thirty-five, only stopping after the fortieth hit.

The shining white ingot slowly morphed into a new form: thin, long, sharp, beautiful. With one last flash, there was a gleaming silver rapier lying atop the anvil.

As we watched in silence, the blacksmith grabbed it by the ornately decorated hilt and lifted it up. He ran a finger along the slender blade and, to our surprise, commented on his work.

"...Good sword."

He reached back to a rack stuffed with countless sheaths and pulled out a bright gray one, slid the rapier into it, and handed it to Asuna.

At this point, I realized I was still gripping her hand tight. I hastily let go and shoved my hands into my pockets. She looked at me with a very strange look on her face, then accepted the rapier from the elf and bowed.

"Thank you very much."

This time, he did snort back.

Asuna grinned and started to hook her new sword to the fastener at her belt, but I grabbed her arm. She looked at me suspiciously, but followed as I pulled her away to an open area within the crafting quarter.

Once I stopped, she tugged her arm out of my grasp and frowned.

"What's the big idea? I got the new sword, safe and sound."

"I-I don't mean to complain about it. Can I just...see it really quick?" I asked, holding out my hand. She pouted but handed over her brand-new weapon.

The instant its dense weight hit my palm, I understood this was no ordinary weapon. I tapped the sword to bring up its properties, and we examined the results together.

At the top was the sword's name: CHIVALRIC RAPIER. That meant...it was a knight's rapier, I supposed. Its current upgrade level was, of course, +0. Next to it was the number of upgrade attempts remaining—fifteen.

"Nu-wha..."

An inexplicable grunt escaped my lips, the only outward sign of emotion, but on the inside, I was screaming, *How?!* My shock was so great that I felt like I could shoot upward and slam my head against the bottom of the next floor up, then fall back to the ground.

I didn't even need to look at the fine details of attack and speed numbers listed below. Fifteen upgrade attempts was about twice that of my Anneal Blade, which had eight. In the most simple terms, this Chivalric Rapier was twice as strong as my weapon. This was the equivalent of a fifth- or sixth-floor weapon.

It was cause for celebration, without a doubt. A weapon's stats had a direct correlation on the chances of victory—and in fact, "rate of victory" meant nothing here. In a world where *any* defeat spelled certain doom, every battle must be won. There was no such thing as too much power.

Unfortunately, it wasn't that simple. We weren't locked in a stand-alone RPG, but a VRMMORPG.

Looking at her beautiful weapon, with hilt, pommel, and even knuckle guard gleaming silver, I had the premonition—if not dread—that this rapier would change the fate of my partner.

"...What's wrong?"

I snapped back to my senses. Asuna was staring at me, so I hastily shook my head.

"N-nothing...I-I mean, it's not nothing. This sword...is ultra-good."

"Hmm. Ultra?"

"Ultra."

Suddenly, Asuna let out a little giggle. I didn't like being laughed at, but at least it got my mind back on the normal track. I coughed and returned her rapier.

Once she had fixed the gray sheath to her belt, I said, "Um... congrats on getting a new main weapon. If you ask me, your Wind Fleuret is still alive inside of it...but I guess everyone has their own way of seeing it..."

Her grin turned annoyed at the awkward, hesitant finish, but she thankfully did not cut me down with one of her usual barbs.

"Thanks. I agree...I feel like I'll still be able to get by with this new one."

"Ah, c-cool."

"As you probably remember..."

She stopped short, then had a wry expression of pain on her lips when she continued.

"...When I left the Town of Beginnings and headed for the labyrinth, I thought weapons were just disposable tools. I bought tons of those cheap Iron Rapiers, didn't bother with upgrading or upkeep, and just threw them onto the dungeon floor when they lost their edge. But...that was *me*, in a nutshell. I figured I'd just charge ahead, as far and fast as I could go...until I couldn't go any farther and died..."

She traced the knuckle guard of her new weapon with a fingertip. When she spoke next, it was in drips and drops, as though putting the texture of the silver into words.

"...To be honest, I still don't think I can have much hope. A hundred floors is so long...too long. But...once you reached out to me, and I got my Wind Fleuret and learned to power it up, I feel like I started changing, bit by bit. Not in the sense of beating the game and getting back to reality, but...taking each day as it comes. Having the hope of surviving each day. And to do that, I need to take care of my sword and armor, and study hard, and so on...I've learned how to do the necessary maintenance on *myself.*"

"...Your own maintenance..."

Asuna was a beginner, not just to *SAO*, but any MMORPG at all, and at the present moment, I understood much more about the game than she did. But I felt that she had just taught me something extremely important. I looked down at my hand.

There was probably a part of me that was avoiding thinking about the difficulty of beating the game, despairing that it would never happen. That's why I took on the mantle of beater, distancing myself from the mainstream group of clearers. Kibaou's Aincrad Liberation Squad and Lind's Dragon Knights had far more courage and ambition to look up at the hundredth floor than I did. There was only one reason I continued to fight: to make myself stronger.

Thirty-nine days before, right after Akihiko Kayaba himself descended upon the center square of the Town of Beginnings to herald the arrival of the game of death, I took off running for the next town. But not to get a head start on beating the game. I wanted to get a head start on surviving.

But even I ended up meeting a few others, getting involved, forming relationships.

Argo the Rat, information dealer. Agil the ax warrior. Nezha, the former blacksmith. Even Diavel, who perished against the first-floor boss, and Kizmel the NPC. And most importantly of all, the fencer before my eyes, Asuna...

I did have a responsibility. A responsibility to continue to fight, for the sake of those I'd met. I couldn't give up and abandon the battle because I was tired of it. The fact that they'd survived along with me was a source of strength and relief.

"...That's right," I said, still staring at my hand. Asuna responded, her voice free of the usual thorns, perhaps even...kindly.

"You have to learn to take care of yourself. When things are hard or sad, it's important to tell someone, rather than holding it all in."

"Uh...y-yeah..."

I looked up and saw a gentle smile on her face.

"And...what will happen if I tell you?"

Without hesitating, she replied, "I'll always be ready to treat you to a piping hot Taran steamed bun."

"Ah...you don't say."

I almost let my shoulders slump at that answer, then reminded myself not to hope for anything better. Plus, those steamed buns were pretty good—as long as you let them cool down first.

"Well, if I ever fail in my upgrade attempt, I'll call on you for a chat session. So anyway, back to the matter at hand," I said, hoping to change the topic. Asuna's ultrarare smile melted away like a flower of ice in the hot sun.

"Huh? Wasn't the matter at hand how my Wind Fleuret still lives on?!"

"That's right," I noted, pointing to Asuna's new partner. "Not to repeat myself, but that Chivalric Rapier is unbelievably powerful for the third floor. With a bit of upgrading, a single hit from it will easily eclipse the strength of my Anneal Blade plus six. That's a great thing, no doubt, but the question will be, how did you get such a powerful weapon?"

"Umm..."

She paused to think, then turned back to look at the blacksmith's tent, a number of yards away on the other side of the hasty fence that surrounded this cramped space. I followed her gaze—the blacksmith himself was invisible from here, but his lazy clanging reached my ears.

"If you overlook his rudeness, that blacksmith was good at his job, wasn't he? Wouldn't every weapon he crafts be about this good? If you overlook his rudeness."

"W-well...I doubt that's the case. We've had several fights now on the third floor, and the mobs aren't really any different from what I fought in the beta. If all of a sudden you're getting a weapon that's twice as powerful as it should be, the game balance is totally broken."

"So you're saying that maybe the blacksmiths in the main town are the same, but just this dark elf was updated to make better weapons? If you overlook his rudeness."

"Hmmm..."

I took my eyes off the tent and scanned the entire camp.

The night had completely worn off now; the deep valley was full of morning light. Beyond the last tendrils of morning mist, the guards, knights, and officers traded easy greetings, and the scent of baking bread wafted from the dining tent. It was exactly as I remembered it from the beta.

"...Anyone can reach this camp as long as they take on the 'Jade Key' quest. In that sense, I don't think there's much difference between this place and the main town."

"Well, you're not painting a very convincing picture. And besides, who cares if the game balance is destroyed because I got a way more powerful weapon than I should have? Better that than the reverse case."

"Um, yeah, that's true..."

Her opinion was absolutely correct. We weren't here to be gentlemen, to play nicely with the game's rules. We'd use any bugs or cheats possible to get out.

But therein was the problem.

If this Chivalric Rapier was indeed an irregularity in the system, an item that should not exist, there was always the danger that the management—if there were even any GMs other than Kayaba—would take action to deal with it, such as replacing it with a proper weapon or deleting it entirely.

But perhaps that wasn't the only issue. When we eventually

met up with the other frontline players to tackle the third-floor labyrinth and boss, the others would undoubtedly be stunned by Asuna's new weapon. And there was no guarantee it would all be in admiration...

"Let's do a test, then."

"Eh?"

I looked perplexed, not following her line of thinking.

"Let's ask him to create another sword and see if he repeats the phenomenon."

"Ahh, I see...wait." I nodded a few times, then pointed to myself. "When you say 'create another sword'...you mean me?"

"Why would I need to forge two swords? I can't fight with one in each hand."

"W-well, sure...but..."

Without thinking, I reached my hand over my shoulder to grab the hilt of my sword, then realized I'd put it back in my inventory. I put the hand on my head instead and rubbed my hair.

She was proposing that we test the dark elf blacksmith, if we overlooked his rudeness, to see if he would create a similarly overpowered sword, but that would require recreating the same conditions as with Asuna's purchase. Not only would I need to provide high-quality base and additional materials, but I'd also need a core ingot made from a powered-up, well-used weapon of my own. Meaning, the Anneal Blade +6 I'd been fighting with for over a month.

In truth, it was nearing the end of its usefulness as my main weapon. If I managed to use both remaining upgrade attempts successfully and get it to +8, it might last me until the fourth floor. But even here on the third floor, there were weapons better than this at +0, some of which were sold right from NPC vendors—they just didn't come cheap.

Ultimately, the Anneal Blade was a quest reward weapon that anyone could earn for themselves. It wasn't on the level of a rare weapon with only a few copies in existence.

And yet, there was a part of me that loved that sword and

wanted to keep using it until the very end of its life. It wasn't the specs, appearance, or handling of the weapon. It was the feeling of accomplishment that came with it, when I went straight from the Town of Beginnings to start the quest for this blade, using nothing more than my starter Small Sword. It was the feeling I got when I felt the weight of that new blade, which was nothing like my first sword. Part of the reason I stuck with the One-Handed Sword skill from the beta was knowing that I could get myself an Anneal Blade first thing.

But on the other hand, everything surrounding us had changed since the beta. We had to complete each floor as quickly as possible under the pressure of knowing that we only had one life to lose. The biggest priorities were efficiency and common sense. Personal attachment to items that needed to be replaced was a total waste of time. I even said this very thing to Asuna in the second-floor inn: If we wanted to survive, we had to constantly get new gear. That's what MMORPGs are like...

Looks like this is where we go our separate ways, partner, I told the sword in my item storage.

It was true that we ought to test the dark elf blacksmith's skill level, and it was true that my Anneal Blade would soon be useless. The timing was telling. I gritted my teeth and prepared to acquiesce.

But before I could say anything, Asuna sighed and admitted, "Of course, if you're not up for it, we should call the idea off."

"Uh...huh?"

"Doesn't it seem like that would bleed over into the result? Like, if you didn't want to make a weapon, the finished product might be bad."

"Wha...hey?"

"I mean, I wasn't sure at first, either, but when it came time to make the deal, I was ready. But it's clear from the look on your face that you want to go as far as you can with what you've got now."

"Hoh..."

"Let's think of a better way to test this. Plus, I guess just doing one more experiment isn't really proof of anything. If you're going to take the process seriously, you'd need all the best materials, enough to make a hundred swords, then watch for the best rate to make an extremely powerful sword…I'm sure the results would be all over the place, though."

Asuna stopped for a moment, lost in thought, then turned to look back at the blacksmith's tent.

"Then again…maybe we shouldn't do that to the blacksmith… to the camp as a whole. I mean, he's doing his best at his duty for the sake of the other soldiers. If we barged in and forced him to make a hundred swords we're not even going to use, it would probably just be an insult to his profession. I don't know, maybe I'm just being weird…"

She lowered her head, embarrassed, and looked up at me with her hazel-brown eyes. I grasped for the right words and eventually came up with "Okay, I won't do it" like a dumb younger brother following his smart older sister's lead.

I didn't want that to be the entirety of my response, so I kicked my brain into high speed and added, "But we still have business with the blacksmith. We'll want to get your new rapier up to plus five, and I need to power mine up a bit if I'm going to keep using it."

But as usual, big sister had a smarter answer.

"I'm fine with upgrading it, but won't we be short on materials? Ignoring my rapier for a second, your Anneal Blade is plus six already, and has eight max attempts, right? We'll want to use the maximum number of materials to get our chances of success to the top value…Why are you making that weird face?"

"Erm…Just thinking, you've really grown as a player. Perhaps it's not true that you only have book smarts without experience…"

I thought I was just putting my honest feelings into words, but she gave me an equally weird look in return, then let out a snort the elven blacksmith would be proud of.

"Oh, forget about me for a moment. What's the plan? Going out for more materials?"

"Actually, that won't be necessary."

I grinned and opened my window, scrolling through the item list until I found what I wanted. What materialized was a perfectly ordinary black leather bag with a single brand on the side. Asuna grimaced when she saw it.

"Isn't that the mark of the cow-men from the second floor? It better not be filled with something weird."

"Sadly, it is not."

I closed my window and grabbed something out of the sack. It was a gleaming black metal plate, about one by four inches. The same cattle mark was stamped onto the surface.

"Oh, it's just a metal plank. I don't recognize the color, though... It's not iron or steel," Asuna said, and she was correct. Metal planks were materials smelted from ores collected mostly in natural dungeons. They could be used for upgrading and crafting or combined into a larger, full-sized ingot. But while this was a plank, it wasn't just any plank. I grinned devilishly and explained the cattle sign.

"This was the Last Attack reward from Colonel Nato in the second-floor boss battle. This one plank will boost the upgrade success rate of any weapon below plus ten to the max, plus it allows you to choose whichever stat you want to boost..."

I could see Asuna's response coming from a mile away.

"You should have said that even *earlier*!"

The talented (if you overlooked his rudeness) blacksmith greeted us with his usual snort when we returned. We made seven attempts at the maximum of 95 percent success, and all seven were good.

Asuna's Chivalric Rapier was now +5, and my Anneal Blade went from +6 to +8.

There were still ten more of the cow-branded planks in the leather sack, but I decided to save them for a rainy day. With the bag back in my inventory, I drew my freshly upgraded weapon, now with four points to sharpness and durability each. There was a fresh, deep shine to the thick blade that gave it a prickly intensity. At this point, it might last to the end stages of the fourth floor, not just the third.

Satisfied, I snapped the sword back into its scabbard, then heard the same sound from next to me. We glanced at each other and grinned confidently. No true swordsman could resist the excitement of a good upgrade.

Her rapier back at her left hip, Asuna cleared her throat and said, "I'm going to pay you back for the five planks, just so you know."

"Well, I only beat Colonel Nato because of your help, so you don't need to bother. Either of us could have gotten the LA."

"Really...? Then I'll give you the next rare drop I get." She lowered the volume of her voice to whisper for my ears only. "But we still don't know what to think of the blacksmith's skill. If only there were a way to determine if it's a bug in the system or not..."

"Yeah, I know...Hmm."

I replaced my sword on my back and crossed my arms. The plan to attempt a mass order was shot down, and we certainly couldn't ask him ourselves...

No.

"Hey...that's it," I said, snapping my fingers. "We can just ask someone who knows plenty about this camp."

The valley that housed the dark elf base was mostly round, with the amenities such as dining and business on the eastern side, and the barracks and storage on the western side, with a main path through the center. It had the size and detail of a small village on its own; it seemed strange that it would be instanced for every individual party on the quest, given its scope.

Asuna and I left the business area, crossing the main street for the barracks section and stopping in front of a tent at the southern end. I lifted the familiar black pelt door and called inside.

"Hello, it's Kirito. May we come in?"

A voice immediately responded, "Certainly. I was just about to finish preparing breakfast."

We entered the tent, excusing ourselves first. My heart was initially set at ease by a gentle, milky scent, then went into spasms when I saw the elf knight rising from the cushions.

The five seconds that I witnessed Kizmel's black bodysuit the last night were stunning enough, and this morning, she was wearing nothing over her brown skin but a sheer gown that was significantly open at the front.

SAO's age rating was only twelve and up, right? Or maybe after it turned into a game of death, the usual standards stopped applying.

I felt a kind of pressure emanating from my right and took my eyes off the elf's skin as naturally as I could.

"I hate to bother you during your meal, but we wanted to talk about something..."

"If you have a new mission, I will gladly accompany you."

"That's great, but we're not leaving yet. I just want some information first."

"Ahh. In that case, we can talk as we eat. Have a seat and I will fix your portions."

She gestured to the soft, fluffy furs on the ground and turned back to the stove at the center of the tent. I felt like if I was polite and told her not to mind us, she would take it literally, so I thanked her instead. Asuna pulled her hood back and said, "We'll happily eat," showing just as much as interest as I in the smell coming from the pot.

We sat down on the furs, and I watched Kizmel take the lid off the pot and stir its contents. Asuna hissed into my ear.

"Stare too long, and you'll trip the harassment code."

"Huh? I thought that was only for physical contact," I replied, then cursed when I realized I should have denied looking at her at all.

The harassment code was a part of the game system that activated when certain "improper" activity was continued against an

NPC or player for a set amount of time, similar to the anticrime code. The first offense was accompanied by a warning and physical pressure away from the target, but repeat offenders would eventually wind up teleported into the prison beneath Blackiron Palace down in the Town of Beginnings.

For a time, some of the frontline players tried to see if it could be used reliably as an escape mechanism in the midst of danger. After all, the only way to instantly teleport while in the fields or dungeons was an extremely rare and valuable crystal—and those weren't even available on the lower floors.

But the research ended in absolute failure, nya-ha-ha, Argo the Rat had noted when she sold the information to me.

Not only did the automatic teleportation to the prison involve an unpleasant force like an electric shock knocking the player back—which I'd never felt myself—but it had to be initiated several times, and the other player had to be of the opposite sex. It was easier to simply run away from battle than spend a bunch of time fondling each other, and of course, *SAO*'s ratio of men to women was frightfully skewed. The phenomenon would work against an NPC, too, but few item-selling ladies bothered to hang out deep in dangerous caves.

On top of that, it wasn't easy to get out of the prison once teleported there, and some said that you'd drop items during the teleportation. Thus, the dream of conveniently using the antiharassment code to escape danger was crushed. It was simple curiosity that led me to buy this intel from Argo, not any intention of turning into a talented harassment artist—but at any rate, a simple stare would not set off the code.

Yet the whispering from Asuna did not stop.

"Uh-oh, here it goes. Five seconds, four, three…"

"H-huh? What…?"

I panicked, looking back and forth between Kizmel's legs as they peeked out of the hem of her gown and the steam rising from the stew pot. The countdown continued.

"Two, one, activated."

Thud.

Asuna carved into my right side with a solid punch. I rolled over in pain, wondering why *that* didn't set off the actual code. Kizmel turned back to us and smiled.

"You two get along so well."

The dark elf knight treated us to a dish of some starchy crop between rice and wheat, boiled in milk, and seasoned with nuts and dried fruit. It was firmly Western in style—or at least Aincradian—and yet something about its delightful taste was oddly familiar. The only problem was that the portion was too small. We treasured the small plates of the stuff with the wooden spoons she offered.

"This is really good," Asuna said wistfully. "I never thought I'd get to eat oatmeal in this game."

"W-wait...*this* is what oatmeal is?" I asked. I'd only ever heard the name before.

Asuna nodded. "Yes. The texture's a bit different, but the flavor is spot-on."

"Ohh," I said, impressed. Kizmel chimed in.

"Ah, so you eat milk porridge in your human towns as well? I did not know that. Perhaps someday..." She trailed off. Both of us looked at her, but the expression was hard to read.

Kizmel shoveled down the last of her porridge, or oatmeal, or whatever it was, and returned our gaze. "Kirito, Asuna, you said that you wanted to ask me about something?"

"Oh...uh, that's right. Umm, well..."

I wasn't sure how to broach the topic, so I decided to simply be straight and ask her opinion of the blacksmith's skill.

Kizmel's reaction was something between praise and unease. Simply put, he was talented but fickle, sometimes creating masterworks, but often outright refusing pushy or misguided orders.

At that description, Asuna and I looked at each other in understanding.

The Chivalric Rapier at her waist now had to be one of those masterworks. It was not the product of a bug or error, but a proper result that only occurred at a very rare frequency.

That part was good news, but the bit about "misguided" orders worried me. After all, what could be more misguided than asking him to craft hundreds of weapons based on the bare minimum of cheap materials? If he only produced crappy weapons in response to such an order, there was no way to test the odds.

He'd already made Asuna an overpowered weapon and succeeded in perfecting my sword. We didn't need, and couldn't ask for, a better set of results—but it just wasn't that simple. As a member of the frontier force of *SAO*, I had an obligation to spread the info I learned to other front-runners. They needed to know that the elf camp could produce weapons worthy of the sixth floor—as well as the possibility that you could keep the elf knights alive in the "Jade Key" quest...

I suddenly realized that I was so lost in thought, my spoon was scraping empty air on my plate, then cursed myself for not savoring the taste more.

"Thanks for the meal, Kizmel," I said. "The porridge was good, and you told us what we needed to know."

Asuna bowed her head as well. "I thought it was delicious. Thank you for the food."

"I'm glad to hear you enjoyed it. I will make much more tomorrow morning," Kizmel replied with a smile, taking our plates. "Now, what is next? We can spend more time in camp preparing, or we can head out for the next mission."

"...Actually," I said, shaking my head, "Asuna and I need to return to the human town for now."

4

KIZMEL OFFERED TO TELEPORT US WITH HER ELVEN magic—charm, rather—to a location near the main town, but Asuna and I gratefully declined. We headed through the narrow canyon, still choked with mist after the sunrise, and into the deep forest that made up most of the third floor.

I turned back to look at the camp we'd spent the last fifteen hours around and glanced at its rippling flags. A few more yards into the forest, and they would already be invisible. Asuna had the same concerns on her mind.

"...We'll be able to get back here, won't we?"

"We can make it back...I think. It should be marked on our maps."

"You think? It should?"

She looked even more skeptical now. I opened my menu and flipped to the map tab. Most of the Forest of Wavering Mists that made up the southern half of the floor was grayed out, with only the routes we'd traveled visible. But the locations we'd visited— the exit of the staircase from below, the queen spider's cave, and the dark elf base—were all marked by dots, so we'd be able to reach them again without getting lost...I hoped.

First we set off for the staircase pavilion through which we'd come to this floor. That required trudging through the forest without a path, of course, but it wasn't the main reason for the feeling of concern in our hearts. We were without our talented NPC guide—the elite mob Dark Elven Royal Guard Kizmel—and that left us feeling alone and vulnerable.

Perhaps we should have waited a few days to return to town and stayed here doing quests with Kizmel instead, I wondered. Asuna spoke up, her voice as weak as my own thoughts.

"Hey...About Kizmel..."

But her words faded out before she could form them into a clear question. I glanced over at the fencer, whose hood was pulled back. The fleeting smile on her lips seemed to contain a number of different emotions.

"...We can't keep relying on her the way we have. We're going to have to say good-bye to her someday..."

"Good point," I agreed, then spread my hands. "Besides, my beater knowledge doesn't help us out regarding Kizmel. Ever since you beat that forest elf guy in the original battle, we've been on a quest path that I've never been part of."

"Don't try to act like I did all of that on my own."

"Look, I'm just saying, like eighty percent of the damage was from your—"

An irregular sound came from the forest ahead, and I stopped in place, holding out my arm. Asuna took a fighting stance and focused.

Little rustling sounds grew louder and louder, a few seconds later, a silhouette appeared out of the drifting mist, low and long. It was not human, but insectoid...no, a mammal. There were five types of animal-based creatures in this forest, but only one of them looked like that.

I reached back for my Anneal Blade +8 and gave a brief explanation.

"That's a wolf. It doesn't have any annoying special attacks, but it'll howl to draw more of its kind when it loses half its HP. Once the gauge goes yellow, use sword skills to finish it off quick."

"Got it," she responded. I drew my blade. The shape beyond the mist suddenly charged, as though drawn by that metal rasp. The brilliant yellow mane from head to back and long, slender snout marked it as the foe I remembered struggling against in the beta: a Roaring Wolf.

I was the wolf's target, so Asuna backed out of range. The beast tensed up and pounced in midcharge. This leap attack came down nearly vertical, and if the player tried to simply guard against the wolf's six-foot-long body, they'd almost certainly get knocked back, if not into a Tumble status followed by the beast's fangs closing in. The better choices were to dodge out of the way or fight back with a sword skill, but antiair skills that moved from low to high were an acute weakness of the One-Handed Sword category. The best angle I had currently was the second blow of Vertical Arc, but it was extremely hard to place accurately, given that the first swing would miss.

I lowered my blade and crouched slightly. Watching the wolf's descent closely, I waited for the right moment, then leaped with all of my strength. My right leg took on a glowing effect, and my body rocketed off with an unseen force. The vertical kick as part of a backflip—the martial arts skill Crescent Moon—caught the Roaring Wolf right in the throat, and it flew back upward with a yelp.

The martial arts skill I'd learned with great pain—in more ways than one—from the bearded master on the second floor was an incredibly useful tool to have. Unfortunately, it did not add its own power to the player's limbs, so its damage couldn't match that of my sword. Despite the well-placed blow being classified as a counter, the wolf still had about 80 percent of its health left.

I wasn't sure if I had time to follow up with a sword strike before the wolf regained its balance, but I wanted to get in more damage before I handed the fight over. But before either the wolf or I had landed, I heard a voice shout, "Switch!"

The fencer flew into the fray from the right, cape streaming behind her. She held her Chivalric Rapier to her right side as she ran, starting the motion for the two-hit combo Parallel Sting.

I was a bit worried that she might not be used to the different weight of the new weapon, but soon I saw that silver shooting-star light again, and a thrust faster than my eye could follow caught the falling wolf.

With a heavy, satisfying slam, the Roaring Wolf shot away, spinning helplessly in midair, and smashed into a distant tree. The wolf's HP bar dropped precipitously, from 70 to 60—and down into the yellow zone.

"...Oops," I muttered. Rapier still held out in front of her, Asuna said, "Uh-oh."

We immediately raced forward, but the wolf was already getting to its feet and let out a long howl from its lengthy throat. Soon, more howls responded from elsewhere in the forest.

Asuna stopped and glanced at me, then shrugged and pleaded, "Well, I didn't know two hits were going to do so much damage."

It took nearly ten minutes to take care of the pack of wolves that gathered. It was always dangerous to get in a drawn-out battle with monsters who could summon allies, but we were close enough to the camp that we could retreat if necessary. At least then, the worst we'd suffer was Kizmel's disappointment.

We sighed with relief and returned our swords to their sheaths once the fifth and final wolf was dead before it could call yet more allies.

The Anneal Blade +8 performed even better than I expected, but the true stunner was the Chivalric Rapier +5. Fencers lived and died by the number of strikes they could inflict, and each of Asuna's thrusts was as heavy as a two-handed spear. And there were still ten potential upgrades left. I shuddered to think at what it could do if fully upgraded.

The fencer herself strode through the dapple shade of the trees, oblivious to my astonishment. She was probably more concerned with the rapier's feel and balance than its numerical stats. She wanted that feeling of trust, the reassurance that she could keep fighting to her heart's content with that sword.

No doubt, feeling was crucial. In the days of games on a monitor before the NerveGear came along, the way a gamer's mouse and keyboard felt and responded was of the utmost importance. I knew more than a few players who stockpiled multiple units of their favorite devices, just in case the manufacturer stopped selling them.

But I couldn't help but feel that prioritizing gut feeling over numerical logic in this VRMMO was living dangerously. Ironically, the only "proof" I had to back my suspicion was another gut feeling, but it was undeniable.

"Wait," Asuna suddenly muttered, and I nearly walked directly into her. I paused in my awkward, unnatural pose, scanning the surroundings. I'd been deep in thought, but not carelessly so. I didn't sense any monsters around, either visually or audibly.

No, wait...

There was a high-pitched metal *clang* somewhere far off. It happened again, then again. The sound was not in a rhythm, but it kept happening.

"Sword combat?" Asuna wondered, turning to me. I nodded. This was *Sword Art Online*—the sounds of battle were not uncommon.

The problem was that the Forest of Wavering Mists did not feature weapon-swinging enemies like the kobold and tauruses of the floors below. The only possibilities were dark and forest elves fighting, elves against players...or worst of all, PvP—players versus players.

I wanted to believe it was not the last option. It was hard to imagine people setting up a proper duel out in this dangerous area, and if it wasn't a duel, it had to be...

I forced myself not to think about that.

"Let's go check it out, just in case."

Asuna looked unsure for a moment, then said, "All right."

The audible range of a battle depended on terrain, weather, and the status of those listening, but in any case, it was not particularly wide. We stayed low, following the source of the sounds for several minutes, then noticed flashes of light amid a grove of trees ahead—the sign of sword skills in action.

A few yards ahead, we put our backs against the trunk of a particularly old and large tree, then peered around either side.

The first thing I noticed was a semicircle of five players with their backs toward us. They wore matching blue doublets with silver highlights, the unmistakable sign of Lind's Dragon Knights. The blue-haired man in the center with his long hair pulled into a ponytail had to be Lind himself. He raised his curved Pale Edge high, timing his orders. But the sounds of battle were coming from beyond the waiting group of five.

I leaned out farther, curious as to who or what was fighting, so that I could see beyond the group.

The first thing I noticed was a whirling green cape, platinum blond hair, and long ears. That was not a player, but a forest elf knight—exactly identical to the Forest Elven Hallowed Knight that Asuna and I fought the night before. The snow-white elf had his back to Lind's group as he struggled in violent battle with someone else. His back was completely exposed, but none of the five made any move to strike. Which meant…

"Are they in the middle of the 'Jade Key' quest?" Asuna wondered, her back to mine.

"I think so…And they probably took the forest elf's side. Which would mean the elf is fighting…"

Suddenly I felt a tremble jolt through my back from Asuna. She must have come to my conclusion. On the other side of the Dragon Knights and the elite forest elf would be another dark-skinned, purple-haired Dark Elven Royal Guard…In other words, a second Kizmel.

It was possible. In fact, it was inevitable. Anyone could take on this campaign quest, which meant that the battle between forest and dark elf had to be occurring at every moment somewhere. It was extremely strange to think of many Kizmels existing at once, but we had no right to demand that every other player in the game avoid the quest. All we could do was watch as the two elves fought to their mutual deaths...

But that wasn't true. I knew from experience that it was possible to avoid a double KO, to ensure that the champion selected would survive.

And I learned that fact because I was working with Asuna yesterday. If it had been just me alone, I would have been trapped by my beta knowledge, focused solely on defending myself rather than defeating the forest elf. But Asuna took everything dead seriously, using all of her power to challenge an elite foe far stronger than herself, and won. Of course, Kizmel did most of the damage, and I fought very hard myself, but that outcome would not have transpired without Asuna's presence.

With that in mind, it was clear that Lind's blue team knew what they were doing with this quest. Either Argo had already released the first volume of her third-floor strategy guide just a day in, or they learned about the quest through other means. At any rate, the fact that they were sitting back rather than taking part in the fight meant that they knew what would happen, and were waiting for the enemy elf to unleash a major attack, prompting the friendly elf to perform the self-sacrifice to win the fight.

What should we do? I bit my lip in frustration.

Should I leap into the fray, advising Lind that if they did their best to defeat the enemy elf, the survivor would be a powerful companion in the campaign? But Lind was nearly as suspicious of me as Kibaou—would he really listen?

The other factor was that if we did that, Asuna and I would be assisting in the murder of a second Kizmel.

It would be shameless sentimentality, of course. We sided with Kizmel on nothing more than a whim and callously slaughtered the forest elf. There was no right or wrong between the elven races. If we'd chosen, for whatever reason, to help the forest elf, we'd have killed Kizmel, spent the night at the forest elf base, and forged a pact of friendship with him instead. And just moments before, I'd been scolding myself about the dangers of prioritizing sentiment over logic.

...But.

I bit my lip even harder. A hoarse voice sounded in my ear.

"Sorry...this is your call, Kirito."

Deep internal conflict was evident in Asuna's words, as few as they were. She was grappling with the contradiction, just as I was.

Damn these quests, I muttered to myself.

I'd just discussed the inherent contradictions and dilemmas of MMORPG quests with Asuna the last night. There could never be just one hero in a world with thousands of players logged in at once. Everyone had the right to experience the story as the protagonist. Even now, with the stakes turned deadly—*especially now.*

But sometimes, different players following different stories would intersect. We should not have come so close to contact with Kibaou in the cave this morning, or Lind in the forest right now. If that happened, the story lost its consistency. It was no longer unique.

The ideal way to handle this was to spirit away every player or party into its own instance the moment a quest began, isolated from contact with anyone else. But it was also impossible to generate dozens, if not hundreds, of maps and dungeons at the same time. It was surprising enough to me that the elf base was an instance. Plus, too many instances removed the entire point of an MMO. How could you share a world where no one was connected?

As I gritted my teeth, the battle between the elven knights rose in intensity. Based on the state of their HP gauges, if I wanted to convince Lind, there was no time left to make up my mind.

But in fact, this was not the time for hesitation in the first place. Preserving the integrity of the story was not what mattered here—it was escaping *SAO*. I ought to do everything I could to increase that possibility.

"Let's go," I murmured, and I felt Asuna agree.

Suddenly, the positions of the fiercely clashing elven knights switched ninety degrees, and I saw the dark elf who had been blocked by a green cape until this moment.

The black-and-purple armor, long saber and small kite shield, dark skin and pale purple hair were exactly the same as Kizmel's. But that was all.

"Huh?!" Asuna exclaimed. My eyes were wide with shock.

The dark elf knight, hair slicked back, was just as tall as the opposing forest elf. The arms were bulging and muscular, and the face was beautiful and proud—and masculine.

As I watched in astonishment, the dark elf knight leaped forward powerfully, evading the forest elf's longsword and swiping upward to catch him with a solid blow. The blond knight was knocked back several feet, grunted, and collapsed.

Rather than chase down his opponent, the dark elf glared menacingly at Lind's group. His saber took on a purple glow. Lind lowered his scimitar and raised his shield.

"All members, defend!"

His four companions raised their shields or large weapons in defensive stances. We'd lost our chance to intercept the encounter. If we darted out of the trees, Lind's group would panic, and possibly lose their defensive positions.

The dark elf let off a sword skill directly at the tightly clustered defenders. He slid forward to close the gap and slashed faster than the eye could follow with his saber, left to right. With each collision of purple light and shield, a roar and sparks burst forth—but none of them fell.

I thought they'd successfully held strong, but the elf wasn't done. Spinning like a top, he unleashed another sideswipe, then again. These three attacks together were a high-level saber sword skill called Treble Scythe.

The second blow knocked down the team's defensive wall, and the third sent them all sprawling. They landed with an enormous clatter about six or seven yards away from where Asuna and I watched, behind the grove. All five of their HP bars plunged into the yellow.

I knew what would happen next, and presumably, so did the team. But my pulse raced out of my control, virtual sweat forming on my palms. I could feel a tension just short of outright panic from the five players looking up at the approaching dark elf.

Asuna took a step forward, and I hastily reached out to grab her hood.

The dark elf spoke in a voice as sharp as steel. "If you'd followed my warning and left, this would not have happened. Foolish humans...accept the punishment for your actions."

It was the exact same line I'd heard in the "Jade Key" quest during the beta. The dark elf held his saber with both hands overhead, pointing straight for Lind. Lind raised his shield out of impulse, but it would not stop the coming blow.

The elf's weapon began to glow, accompanied by a keening vibration.

"I am your foe, Knight of Lyusula!" bellowed the forest elf, who was back on his feet and charging. He struck with astonishing speed, longsword glowing green. The dark elf was unable to evade in time. He caught the strike with his saber, and the resulting shock wave sent Lind's group sprawling to the ground again. Even the tree trunk we hid behind trembled with the force of the collision.

The two elves were locked in a stalemate, their blades grinding. But the forest elf, whose HP bar was in the red, slowly began to give. When the saber was pushed right in front of his eyes, the forest elf cried out.

"Holy Tree of Kales'Oh! Grant me the final sacrament!"

A brilliant, yellow-green shine erupted from the forest elf's chest. When it had spread to cover his entire body, it shot out rapidly to engulf the surrounding area. It did not look like an attack, but the dark elf's HP bar quickly drained to nothing, and the forest elf's emptied with it. Still locked in combat, their swords joined in a standstill, the two fighters slowly collapsed.

Every detail was as I remembered it. I had witnessed this scene three times in the beta—once for my own quest, twice while helping a party member. Whether on the dark or forest elf side, the event and dialogue were all the same.

At the time, I hadn't given it much thought, other than that it was a common development, but this time, it felt as though I'd been stabbed through the chest. I could only take short, gasping breaths, and I clutched the end of Asuna's cape.

Before he perished into motes of light with the dark elf, the forest elf imparted his final message to the Dragon Knights. Only a small leather pouch was left behind on the grass, which Lind reached out to pick up.

A greatsword-wielding man named Hafner, who was something like the second-in-command of the group, plopped down onto the grass and exclaimed, "Whew! Man, that was scary!"

I could vividly recall him swearing at Nezha for using the money from his sword to buy himself a feast when the blacksmith had admitted his crimes after the second-floor boss battle. It seemed like he'd been repaid with a weapon of similar level. Shivata, another of the scam victims, was present in the group as well. I didn't know the names of the other two, but I recognized one of them.

The man on the right, holding a blunt flail on a chain, smacked Hafner's shoulder bracingly.

"You're just fine, Haf. That was an auto-defeat event."

"Whatever. You looked pretty scared to me, too, Naga."

"Can you blame me? That elf's cursor went past red into black. I've never seen one that high."

"Yeah. That was insane."

Based on their conversation, neither seemed to be beta testers. Nor were Lind and Shivata, who were speaking a short ways off. I snuck a peek at the fifth member.

He was a thin man wielding an Anneal Blade like mine. He wore a chain coif that hung low on his head, so I couldn't see

higher than his mouth, but I didn't think he was present for the second boss battle. I was pretty sure I'd never seen him before, but there was something eerily familiar about his manner.

I wanted to check with Asuna, but they were standing just thirty feet from the tree we were hiding behind, and I didn't want them to detect our whispers. I could probably stroll out with a friendly greeting and not get a bunch of swords in my face, but they weren't going to be happy to see me, either. It was a good place to use my Hiding skill, but if they saw through it, that would only make the situation worse.

Fortunately, they had no idea we were there, and at a gesture from Lind, the five huddled for a meeting. I could only pick up isolated phrases at that hushed tone, but I began to get a sense of the topic.

"...is supposed to be to the north of the forest...we get there, then start on quests...next destination is shared with the guild quest, so we'll follow that...evening is the first overall meeting at the town, so if we get the guild established by..."

...*Aha*, I thought.

Based on the way he was talking, it seemed their quest info came from a different beta tester, not Argo. I guessed that it was probably the unidentified fellow with the Anneal Blade. I made a mental note to buy info on him from Argo, then concentrated on the conversation again.

But now they were talking about how to deal with the monsters of the forest, and I didn't catch anything of note. They raised their fists in salute at the end of their talk, then headed off to the north.

Once the clanking of their heavy footsteps disappeared, I heard a frosty voice command me to let go. I turned and realized that I was still gripping Asuna's hood tight.

"S-sorr—"

I hastily let go, and she snorted and put her hood back on. Asuna's expression shifted from angry mode to questioning mode.

"What do you suppose that was about...?"

I wasn't sure which part of the conversation she was referring to, so I shrugged my shoulders.

"I don't know. I was certain that we'd see a second version of Kizmel...but it was a totally different person."

"Even though the forest elf was clearly the same guy..."

"That's the weird part. If they were both different, it would mean the system rolls different NPCs every time the fight event is generated. That would at least make sense," I noted, arms crossed.

Asuna sent a glance my way from beneath her hood.

"Was it always the same people during the beta?"

"Yeah. I only participated in this particular battle three times, but the forest elf was always a long-haired blond guy, and the dark elf was always a short-haired lady...basically, Kizmel. At least, in appearance."

"Hmm..."

Asuna thought over my answer for a few moments, then shook her head. "I suppose we can't say anything for sure until we at least witness this scene one more time. But we should get moving now. The mist is thickening."

Just as she said, the western end of the little grove was already turning white. If we got lost in the unique mists of this forest, we'd only have a visibility of fifteen to twenty feet, and the monster encounter rate would rise. Fortunately, the staircase we were heading for was to the northeast, so we didn't have to charge into the mist.

"Gotcha. They said the strategy meeting was tonight, so we've got some time. Let's try to avoid combat where we can."

I headed away from the tree, and only after several steps did I realize that Asuna wasn't following.

The fencer was frozen next to the tree, staring at the empty space where the battle event had just taken place. Eventually, she snapped out of it and trotted over to catch up. I was going to ask her what she was looking at but reconsidered. The march over the dark forest floor resumed.

* * *

We managed to stay ahead of the tide of mist and ran into only two monsters along the way, so it did not take long at all to reach the staircase.

The shadowy mouth of the passage down to the second floor opened in the middle of the mossy ground. It had been less than a day since we'd come up those stairs, but it felt like several. Asuna stared at the opening, apparently lost in the same thought.

"You don't think that time flows differently in that elf camp... do you?"

"I don't think even the NerveGear can affect the passage of time," I said, laughing it off. She glared at me.

"That's not what I'm saying. It can send this realistic data to our sensory centers, so maybe it can adjust the way we perceive time. That's all I'm wondering."

"The way we perceive it...So even if only one day has actually passed, it feels like three?"

"Yes...Wait, forget I said that. There's no use for that function."

"Huh?"

I stared at her in confusion. She blinked a few times, searching for the right words, then murmured, "I just don't want to rely on false hopes."

In a flash, I understood what she meant. She'd been hoping that these thirty-nine days in the world of *SAO* were a shorter period of time in real life—say, ten days. Or just one. Maybe even a single second. How much easier her life would be if that were true.

But sadly, it was clearly impossible for one's mind and senses to be accelerated to hundreds of times the normal speed during a full dive. I didn't know the fundamental properties of how the NerveGear worked, but even I could guarantee that.

Instead of agreeing that it would be escapist fantasy, I put words to a thought that rose unbidden from deep in my chest.

"...You said it was all about surviving today—I always thought that was a perfect statement. It never occurred to me to think about stacking each and every day as I go along."

The fencer looked like she was choosing her words carefully again. She grinned faintly.

"Are you the type of person who has trouble sitting down to study every day?"

"Definitely. I was the type to spend one desperate all-nighter studying before a test, then forget it all once the test was over."

"I figured. But I suppose you deserve my thanks—you dedicated so much of your personal memory capacity to the *SAO* beta test, you've helped me out in countless ways."

"...Should I take that as a compliment?"

"Of course. Now let's get moving for that main town. It's not far, right?"

"Yep. Just take the east fork at the branch ahead, and it'll be in sight in no time. It's called, um...S...Su...It's s-something." I groaned at my lost memory.

Asuna sighed. "I take back my compliment."

We left the staircase behind and walked along the forest path for five minutes until a wall of thick logs appeared, blocking our way. This reminded me that the difference between the camps and the town was that the town was built with lumber from cutting down the forest trees.

The path was swallowed up by a large cast-iron gate. The familiar bustling sound of all the human towns was coming from beyond the gate. In the beta, I felt relieved to go from the elven base to the comfort of town. For some reason, I didn't get that feeling this time.

When I noticed Asuna hiding farther beneath her long hood than usual, I considered breaking out my favorite bandanna disguise, then thought better of it when I realized that few players were likely to be around at this time of day. At we reached the gate, I hailed the halberd-bearing guards—round eared, of course.

"Um, what's the name of this town?"

The craggy-faced NPC stared down at me, then growled, "It is the town of Zumfut."

"Thanks," I replied and started down the tunnellike passage through the gate.

Asuna noted wryly, "It didn't even start with an *S*."

"Y-you can always ask to find out the name. The important part is where to find stuff within the towns…"

"In that case, can you guide me to your recommended place to sleep?"

"Sure thing. Any particular requests?"

Asuna thought that one over very seriously.

"I'd like to say that I want a bath…but we'll just be back at the base camp by tonight. As long as the beds are nice, the area is quiet, and it has a nice view, anything will do."

"…I doubt there's anything else you could even add to narrow it down further," I grumbled quietly.

As it happened, though, finding quiet places with a good view was quite easy in Zumfut. The town itself was not made of ordinary buildings but three gigantic trees that stood together like monstrous baobabs. Their trunks were a hundred feet wide and well over two hundred feet tall. The insides of the trunks were hollowed out into many-floored structures, so the farther up you went, the better the view, and the more distant from the noise of the surface.

When we exited the tunnel, Asuna's eyes went wide as she saw the massive, broad trees looming overhead.

"Whoa…They're like skyscrapers…"

"On the inside, too. I think it goes up to twenty floors? The view from the top is stunning, but there's just one problem."

"…Which is?"

"No elevator."

Asuna said she didn't mind that, so I pointed her toward the tree to the right—they were arranged in a triangle.

The space between the three trees was Zumfut's teleporter

square. It was already a day since the gate had been activated, but there were still people walking through the blue portal a few times every minute. Those with starter equipment or no gear at all had to be tourists up from the Town of Beginnings. I hoped they wouldn't venture outside of town, but the fact that those who had chosen to stay safe felt secure enough to come visit was a reassuring sign.

The northern end of the plaza was a semicircular meeting place, like that in Tolbana down on the first floor. Most likely, this was where the strategy meeting Lind mentioned would take place. We approached the southeast baobab with the square to our left.

A wide staircase went up to meet the elevated entrance to the tree. Next to it was a bulletin board of the classic kind: parchment fixed to a flat wooden board. Right smack in the center was a large announcement.

"The strategy meeting starts at five o'clock. That's going to leave us with plenty of time," Asuna murmured. I suggested we rent a room before coming up with ideas of how to pass the time.

At the top of the stairs and through the natural knothole in the trunk, the great hall of the first floor filled my view. Players and NPCs chattered happily as they strode over the wooden floor, which had been polished to such a shine that the rings of the tree's age stood out bright and clear. The outer walls of the hall were lined with shops selling food, and in the center was a large, spiraling staircase that led up to the ceiling.

"Wow," Asuna exclaimed as she approached the stairs, marveling at how the steps and handrails extended directly out of the grain. "So everything in here is just one giant piece of wood. It must have been incredibly hard to carve it all out."

I was tactful enough not to point out that everything here was generated digitally and not actually physical in nature. Instead, I nodded in agreement and rapped on the handrail with my knuckles.

"If we go to the baobab in the back—technically, I think they call it the Yew Tree—you can meet the mayor near the top, and he'll talk your ear off about how hard it was to carve these out. It's actually where you start the first mission of the guild quest."

"Ahh...I wonder if the guilds and wood-carvers have any connection."

"Now that's a truly long story, but the short version is that long ago, you had three different groups carving out the three trees and getting into all these fights. So some warrior-slash-blacksmith-slash-carpenter guy united the entire town, and in recognition of his feat, some king from another floor gave him the sigil of a guild leader..."

"Ahh."

"Anyway, that hero's descendants have been the mayors of Zumfut ever since. The mayor now says that the precious guild sigil has been stolen, and the guild quest is all about getting it back for him."

"Ahh."

"...I'm guessing you have no interest in guild-related stuff, Asuna?"

"Not at the moment," she said flatly. Her attractive lips twisted into a bit of a sneer. "I mean, according to Argo's book, don't guilds set it up so that a certain percentage of the money you make gets automatically deducted?"

"Y-yeah, that's right. In fact, that's one of the best things about the leader's sigil..."

"I'm not saying that I'm desperate to keep all of my money. I'm just saying, I don't like that kind of heavy-handed system, forcing you to participate in that way."

"I see," I replied, but I sensed something dangerous in her response.

At the exit of the stairs from the first to the second floor of Aincrad, what seemed like ages before, I'd told Asuna that if someone she trusted invited her to a guild, she should accept. That there was an absolute limit to what she could accomplish alone.

I knew full well that Asuna was not the type of person to swear loyalty and service to someone else. But at the same time, I knew she harbored a special quality that I didn't possess. She had the talent to inspire others, to lead. It was hard to imagine her leading her own guild, but if she was perhaps a high-ranking officer in a large guild, she might shine brighter than anyone else...

"Asuna was still frowning. "What about you? Did you join a guild in the beta?"

"No...I didn't..." I muttered, trying to avoid the uncomfortable sense of being seen right through. "But it wasn't because I hated the tax system, or didn't want to work under someone's command, or anything like that. It was just..."

"A matter of efficiency?"

Once again, she had me pinned. I raised my hands in surrender.

"I guess. *SAO* is rare for an MMO in that it's more efficient gaining experience alone or with a partner than in a large party...at least, in the early stages. In the beta, all I cared about was how far I could get in a month."

I considered mentioning the theoretical limit of playing solo I'd been thinking about just moments before, but it didn't seem to be necessary at that point in time.

"I see," Asuna said, though I wasn't sure how she'd interpreted my answer. At least the frown was gone. She was about to say something, then reconsidered and turned to the staircase, clicking her boots to change the topic.

"Well, let's get climbing these stairs. Did you say the tree had twenty floors? Do the lodgings cost different amounts depending on the floor?"

"No, the only factor is the size of the room and whether it has windows or not. You get better views higher up, the only difference is how long it takes to get there."

"I see. And...just so you know, I'm not racing you up to the top."

"I-I didn't say it was a race!" I protested, but Asuna had already leaped over the handrail onto the stairs and was flying upward. I hurried after her and caught up, but as she had seized the advantageous inner position, I needed to run a longer distance just to keep up. As movement speed in *SAO* was dictated by equipment weight and agility points, speed-oriented Asuna had a distinct leg up on me, a more balanced player. I ended up chasing her all the way to the top floor, wheezing heavily with my hands on my knees, despite there being no point.

Asuna watched my anguish with cool disinterest. "I win. As the winner, that gives me the right to choose a room."

"Th...that's not...fair. You said...it wasn't a...race..."

"It certainly wasn't. Anyway, where's the clerk...? Ah, over there."

I stared at her grudgingly as she strode across the spacious hall. "...Hmm?"

Something about that last line stuck out to me, but she was already speaking to the NPC with the inn menu open. Normally, check-in happened on the first floor (or what was otherwise the lobby) of any inn, but larger facilities like this one had a special NPC on each—wait, why was I thinking about this now?

For some reason, I snuck up stealthily to where Asuna was earnestly perusing the list of empty rooms. She poked the window when she found one she liked, entered the length of stay, and paid the fee, then closed the window and turned to me with a very rare smile on her face.

"I got a nice-looking room on the south side. It was a bit expensive, but since we're each paying half, it's not so bad. This way!"

She pushed me from behind, jolting me into motion. The center of the circular floor was the staircase hall, and there were two concentric circles of rooms along the sides. Therefore, any room on the inner circle did not have windows to the outside.

Naturally, Asuna had chosen a room on the outer circle. She squeezed the knob on the door reading 2038, and it identified her as the owner and opened accordingly. Two seconds after watching the cape wave through the open door, I made up my mind to follow.

This was easily the best view I'd ever had in any room. Not only was it spacious, but the entire south wall was one glass window, which gave us a two-hundred-foot-high view of the forest and the outer perimeter of the castle beyond that. Asuna pulled back her hood and pressed herself against the window as she looked out through it, then she spun around with a burst of excitement.

"This is amazing, Kirito! We can see the entire Forest of Wavering...Mists..."

Her chatter slowed considerably as the sentence continued, until she finally realized what had happened.

Asuna's frozen smile wore off, her mouth grew tense, and a red blush started creeping up from the base of her neck. She opened and closed her mouth two or three times, looked left and right as though seeking something, then picked up a strange-looking fruit that had been left on the table for decor.

With perfect overhand form, she pitched the fruit directly at my forehead and screamed at a painful volume.

"What are you doing in here?!"

Now, I might be a careless, thoughtless person in many ways. But in this one instance, I felt my reaction was justified.

This isn't fair!

The pink-and-purple striped fruit was—fortunately or unfortunately—extremely hard, and rather than exploding into chunks against my forehead split into two clean halves. Because we were in town, I felt the impact but suffered no damage.

I caught both halves in my outstretched hands and took a bite of one. The milky-white flesh was crispy and pleasant, with a flavor somewhere between an apple, a pear, and a lychee.

Asuna breathed heavily with smoldering rage as she watched me chow down on the fruit. Eventually, she realized that most of the responsibility for the current situation was on her shoulders, and she kicked the ground timidly.

"...I'm sorry. Clearly, this wasn't your fault."

"Well, I could have said something when I noticed what was happening," I answered, planning to stop there so that I still had some ammo to use against Asuna at a later time, but she still looked so uncomfortable that I had to offer a better olive branch. "I just followed you in the door, the same way I walked

into Kizmel's tent when we were staying there...But you paid for this room, so I should have checked with you first."

"No, I'm the one who dragged you into this...I'm sorry for throwing the fruit at you."

Asuna's facial effects finally wore off, and she regained her normal expression. "You said that any party member can go freely in and out of an inn room, right?"

"Yep."

"How does the cost work, then? Does it subtract the money equally from everyone?"

"That depends on the setting you enter when renting the room. Remember how there was an occupancy number on the window? If it's set to one, you pay the whole cost, and if it's multiple people, then the cost is split."

"..."

The odd expression on her silent face told me that she was remembering it had been set to a room for two. In that case, my wallet had already suffered the loss of half the cost of a deluxe room, but that wasn't anything I couldn't make up.

"Don't worry, if we split the party up, I'll still be able to rent my own room...but only if I get back the cost of what I've already spent here."

"..."

She didn't respond to my half-joking suggestion, either. Eventually, she came to a conclusion of some kind.

"...We're not spending the night here, just using it to rest until this evening's meeting, right?"

"W-well, that was the plan. I want to be back at the dark elf camp by tonight..."

"...Okay, let's leave it at that, then."

"L-leave it at what?"

"Well, I only paid the price on the assumption that we'd be splitting it. It would be crazy to spend that amount on my own without even staying the night," Asuna announced, then scanned the room for the beds on either side and pointed at the one on the east wall. "This one will be mine. And just so we're absolutely clear, there's a border right here that must be respected."

She indicated a line straight down the middle of the room with her toe, then walked over to her sovereign territory and removed her Chivalric Rapier +5, breastplate, hooded cape, gloves, and boots. Loose and comfortable, she sat down on the bed and looked up at me.

"I'm going to take a little nap. You ought to get some rest yourself."

"Uh, okay," I said.

We needed to conserve money where we could, we needed to rest when we could, and we'd be spending the night in the same room—well, tent—anyway. This wasn't the time to be succumbing to the Confusion status effect. Wait...*SAO* didn't have a confusion effect.

At any rate, I moved to my territory and removed my Anneal Blade +8, coat, and other armor. When I sat down on the bed, I was facing directly at Asuna, which felt awkward, so I rolled back into a lying position. Appropriately for the price we paid, the pillows and mattress were soft and comfortable, and I felt sleep approaching quickly. I'd been up since two in the morning. After all we'd been through, I had earned a bit of a nap...

"About our earlier conversation," Asuna said from across the room. My eyelids opened up about three-quarters of the way.

"Which was?" I prompted, looking up. Asuna was still sitting on the side of the bed, boots off and feet dangling. Her response took me by surprise.

"About the experience gain being better with one or two people than a whole party."

"...What about it?"

I raised my head, then recalled that Asuna had been about to say something back at the staircase when I'd first mentioned it. But perhaps that was just my imagination.

"Just wondering, alone or with a partner, which is better?"

"Which...? Oh, meaning which gives you better experience points?"

The fencer nodded. I lowered my head back against the pillow again, blinked a few times to clear the sleep away, then thought my answer over.

"Hmm...It's not as simple as one or the other. The reason you don't gain as much with a full party is because it's really hard not to have some strength go to waste. You can't surround a small monster with six people and swing away wildly. If you break into two halves of three, it's hard to time when to switch out. It'll be different once we find a map with a whole bunch of extra-large mobs to fight all at once, though...And of course, the more people you have, the safer it is," I prefaced, then actually answered her question.

"Soloing or playing with a partner are basically the same thing. With a two-man team, if you can hunt twice as fast as solo, your rate will be better. But that's difficult to do. You need to be able to switch from one player's sword skill directly into the other's..."

At this point, I finally realized what Asuna was wondering about. I looked back at her and our eyes met directly, so I quickly glanced back at the ceiling and coughed to hide my embarrassment.

"W-well, that's the ideal outcome, but it takes a lot of time to work together that smoothly. But at this point, safety is more important than efficiency, so in that sense, you'd want to have a partner rather than fight solo..."

"Kirito, if I'm ever more of a hindrance than a help, you'd better tell me," she announced, clear and firm. I held my breath.

The fencer stared me down with a calm expression nothing like her fluster just minutes ago. She put her fists on her knees and continued, "Like I told you back in Tolbana, I left the Town of Beginnings so I could continue to be myself. But...maybe I've forgotten that feeling, bit by bit over time. We've been fighting side by side since meeting up in Urbus...but if that's making things harder for you, or causing your leveling pace to drop, that's not what I want to do."

"…"

So she could be herself.

I didn't know enough about how other people thought to truly understand those words. I didn't even know how *I* was processing this insane game of death we'd been trapped inside. It frightened me, of course, and I wanted to be free of it. I didn't want to die, and I felt hatred for Akihiko Kayaba for orchestrating it all.

As a result of this, I'd focused on nothing but making myself stronger since the day the game began. I prioritized efficiency, gathered information, tested out my ideal build, and gave up on everything else.

So the fact that I was now working with Asuna the fencer was the result of a decision—that doing so would improve my chances of survival. There was no other reason. There…shouldn't have been.

"…You're very strong," I finally put into words. "You're not holding me back in the slightest. In fact, with your new Chivalric Rapier, your damage per second is higher than mine. But it's not just about DPS numbers. Your poise in battle, the execution of your sword skills—I'm in no position to claim you're not good enough. On the contrary…if you decide to keep working with me, I'd be grateful."

It felt silly to say these things while I was rudely lying on the bed, but Asuna only straightened her back, still and silent. I thought I detected her slender body trembling slightly.

Wait, what does that reaction mean?

But before I had more time to wonder, she said simply, "Oh. In that case, I guess I'll stick around for a bit."

"Um…cool. Glad to hear it."

It felt like we ought to shake on it. I lifted my head off the pillow, but Asuna was already lying on the bed firmly in her own territory and rolling back toward the wall. With her back turned to me, she whispered, "Well, I'm going to take a nap until noon. Good night."

"Um...okay. Sweet dreams."

I lowered my head back down, wondering what her deal was. It felt like I ought to take this time to think things over, but the sandman was attacking again, and I only had enough willpower to set an alarm before closing my eyes and succumbing.

Across the surface of my mind, little thoughts rose like bubbles, then popped.

So much stuff happened in the span of this one day.

At this rate, we're gonna be really busy with conquering the third floor.

I guess it's not that bad knowing there's someone there to watch your back...

At that point in time, I had no idea that just seven hours later, external factors beyond my control would threaten the dissolution of our team.

5

"WE ARE WELL AWARE THAT OUR REQUEST IS UNREA-
sonable," intoned the scimitar-wielding man, his long blue hair
tied into a ponytail—Lind, now the first leader of the official
DKB (Dragon Knights Brigade) guild.

"But I need you to understand this. Now that the top players
in the game have been split into two camps, it is imperative that
our two guilds eternally remain on good terms, working together
in the pursuit of defeating the game."

Compared to the late knight Diavel, who laid the foundation of
the DKB, Lind's expression and speech were stiff and awkward,
but there was a certain stateliness to him, as befitting a man who
had led his large group for ten whole days.

The spiky-headed Kibaou, leader of the ALS (Aincrad Liberation Squad), the other official guild, was also on the stage. But
unlike Lind, he was silent, sitting cross-armed and cross-legged
in a chair. Even after Lind's speech, he sat, mouth twisted but
shut tight.

Lind's words were not meant for Kibaou. The scimitar warrior's
sharp gaze was not pointed at the DKB or ALS, but the true
outcast of outcasts left over, the only beater who had publicly
admitted to his participation in the beta test.

Me.

* * *

About five and a half hours earlier, our energy and motivation refilled after the nap in our lofty (in more ways than one) inn room, Asuna and I descended the long stairs—without racing this time—refilled on food and potions, and started all the single quests available in Zumfut before leaving town. Not to return to the dark elf camp, but to get down to the dirty business of earning experience.

Gaining experience in an RPG was practically a job, and each player had his or own way around it. Most could be categorized as quest first or hunt first. The former raced across the map, completing and turning in quests for bonus experience. The latter found camping spots with the best monster spawn rates, killing them over and over for points.

If anything, I was one of the hunt-first types, but I started changing my way of thinking after the second-floor boss battle. In the beta, the battle ended with Colonel Nato and General Baran, but the advent of King Asterios and his terrible lightning breath nearly brought our raid party to ruin. If Argo the Rat hadn't cleared out all the local quests and noticed the possibility that a new boss had been added, then most likely Lind, Kibaou, Asuna, and I would all have died. Money, items, and experience weren't the only things to be gained from a quest.

But of course, farming monsters over and over also gave you something other than just col and experience. It provided the player with actual skill—the experience of practice in battle. In this VRMMO, where combat was fought by moving the avatar like one's real body, this kind of experience was just as important as the numerical kind, if not more so. Even if the attack speed number was the same in their menus, the initiation speed of an expert in a sword skill and one still new to it was, in fact, subtly different. Also crucial was the player's ability to gauge distance and sense danger.

So it was that Asuna and I greedily planned to head out into the forest, stopping to battle at particularly effective spots as we worked on fulfilling the various hunting and gathering quests from town. In the five hours until sunset, we slew countless mobs, crushing them into polygonal dust. After turning in seven complete quests each, I had risen one level to 15, and Asuna had earned two to reach 14.

Tired and satisfied, we indulged in a toast at a tavern. At ten minutes until five o'clock, we headed off to the first strategy meeting of the third floor.

There was already a crowd of players crammed into the bowl-like assembly grounds between the three giant baobab trees. I saw the familiar, friendly face of Agil the ax warrior, so I greeted him and got an earful of jibes about how Asuna and I were still a party. I had just promised to give him the Vendor's Carpet from Nezha, which was still at the inn down on the second floor, when the bells rang five o'clock. The support and tongue of Zumfut's bells were carved directly out of the baobab trunks, and they had a soft, pleasantly woody sound to them. I sat down in the corner as the wistful melody of the approaching night played out, then applauded along with the group when Kibaou and Lind appeared on the speaking platform together.

Including the two on the platform, I counted forty-two participants at this meeting. There had been forty-seven (actually, forty-eight) at the second-floor boss battle the previous day, so we were down a full party. The six who hadn't shown up were the Legend Braves.

The reason they'd made such a splash in the battle despite not meeting the average level of the raid group was the effect of their incredibly powerful gear. But they confessed that they'd raised the money for that gear through a scam and donated their equipment to the rest of the group. It would take them some time to regain the strength to join the frontline players, but with enough willpower, they would be back.

Meanwhile, Lind and Kibaou finished their brief introduction, and the real meeting began.

The first order of business was an official announcement that the blue and green teams, the largest groupings of players among the raid, were now real guilds. I was as impressed as everyone else. It took quite a number of errands, hunts, collections, and battle events to get the sigil necessary for the guild—though it was still far less work than it took to complete the elven war campaign quest. I seemed to recall that in the beta, it took twenty hours of play on average to complete the guild quest series. It had only been a day since we opened this floor, so Kibaou and Lind must have foregone food and sleep to finish it. Even Lind must have been surprised that the Liberation Squad had kept pace with the Dragon Knights, given their aversion to beta knowledge.

Next were the unveiling of the official names and acronyms of the guilds, their current member lineups, and a casting call for new faces. However, the only people in the group of forty-two who weren't already affiliated with one of the two groups were Agil, his three friends, and Asuna and I.

I had no intention of joining either guild, of course, and Asuna said she wasn't interested either, and I suspected the same went for Agil. When none of the six of us raised a hand, I expected that phase one of the meeting would be over.

But instead, Lind, leader of the DKB, made a most unexpected announcement.

"I would like the doors to my guild to be as wide open as they can be. Our only requirement at this time is that the player be at least level ten."

Kibaou abruptly stood up next to him and shouted, "Level nine for us!"

A blue vein briefly pulsed on Lind's forehead, but he regained his cool and continued the speech.

"Everyone participating in this meeting who hasn't joined either guild should meet the requirements. So if you simply raise a hand, you will be gladly welcomed. However, there is one condition which applies only to certain people. This was decided after discussion between me and Kibaou."

This time it was Kibaou's turn to look cross but resigned. At this point, I was still looking around, curious as to who would need special conditions. So when Lind stared straight down at me, I nearly stumbled down the stairs of the assembly grounds.

"Kirito," he said, voice hard. Finally, I understood what was going on. He wanted to make it clear that I couldn't join because I was a beater. This didn't come as a surprise, and I wasn't planning to join anyway.

"Yeah, I get it," I started to say. But Lind's gaze shifted to the left, and he called another name.

"...and Asuna."

Asuna's shoulders twitched, her face hidden beneath her hood. Even I couldn't see her expression from my seat next to her.

Lind watched the two of us sit in silence, then cleared his throat before continuing, "Before you are approved to enter our guild, there is one more condition on top of the level requirement. One of you must enter the DKB, and one must enter the ALS."

"...One each?" I repeated, not understanding his point. Asuna gave no reaction.

Lind cleared his throat again and explained quickly.

"As was made clear during yesterday's boss battle, Kirito and Asuna are head and shoulders above anyone else in our general group. The two of you made off with the Last Attack bonuses of all three bosses in that fight, after all. I do not bring this up to criticize you, of course. But it does not benefit any of us to have the both of you join either guild. Our combined strengths are roughly equal for now, and you would cause a severe imbalance by joining either side."

Kibaou's forehead took on the bulging vein this time, probably because he took offense at the idea that their teams were equal *for now*. I listened to the explanation of the first guild leader in *SAO* without paying it much mind.

"We are well aware that our request is unreasonable. But I need you to understand this..."

* * *

My first thought was *How serious are they being?*

Lind and Kibaou's demands boiled down to one thing: They wanted me and Asuna to join separate guilds, if we chose to at all. But the "if" conditional was a total nonstarter. I had zero intention of joining either group. Lind must have known that to begin with, and for Kibaou to welcome me into his guild would defy their cause of antagonism to all former beta testers.

They didn't need to make this grand public display. A simple question of "Do you want to join a guild, yes or no?" would have settled the matter. Instead, the members of both the DKB and ALS whispered among themselves nervously, and Agil had his hands spread, head shaking with the folly of it all. Nothing about this reflected well on Lind. How could this decision possibly benefit them?

My mind was full of nothing but question marks, but Lind seemed to be waiting for an answer, so I felt obliged to stand and speak.

"Umm…I hate to say this after you said we were head and shoulders above the rest, but I have no plans for the future to join either guild. In fact, I figured that both of you would have expected this answer."

Kibaou snorted theatrically, and Lind seemed to falter self-consciously, but his familiar hard expression was back in a moment.

"I understand. By the way, may I ask your reasoning for explicitly choosing not to enter a guild, under the circumstances?"

"Huh? Um…"

I wasn't sure what he meant or how to answer.

By "under the circumstances," was he referring to *SAO*'s current state? Lind seemed to be assuming that creating a guild was the ideal solution to the current, contradictory aims of "beating the game" and "surviving." Based on that premise, his point of view did not match mine, but I did not have the time or obligation to explain my entire philosophy to him.

"It's not based on some grand, explicit choice. It's just not my style...that's all."

"Ahh. So you are stating that you have no intention of joining or leading a guild for the moment."

Now it was my turn to grimace. "Sure, you could put it that way. If I'm not going to be a guild member, I certainly don't want the responsibility of being a leader..."

...Aha, so that's what this is about.

Something in what I said hinted at Lind's true intentions. He was trying to get me to make that very statement to a public audience. He wanted to crush the creation of a third guild forming before it could begin.

But what a convoluted, silly way to go about that. Who was going to step up and join a guild called the Black Beaters? He could have just asked, "Are you going to make a guild, yes or no?" Hell, if he'd simply ordered me not to start a guild, I would have happily agreed.

On the other hand, I could understand that he was worried about the possibility that if I was excluded from the start, I might create my own guild out of spite. This cautious, roundabout way of doing things reminded me strongly of someone else: the original leader of the blue precursors to the DKB, Diavel.

Three times before we fought the boss of the first floor, I received an offer to buy my Anneal Blade through Argo the Rat. The offers were coming from Kibaou, who'd been a lone wolf at the time, but it was Diavel who was giving him the orders. Diavel wanted the Last Attack bonus on Illfang the Kobold Lord, in order to better grip the reins of leadership. So he sought to remove his biggest obstacle—me—by buying my weapon away from me. Again, it was a very convoluted way to go about it. If he'd just asked me to let him have the LA, I probably would have agreed—for a price, of course.

I didn't think that Lind was aware of Diavel's machinations, either at the time or now. It was half coincidence and half imitation of Diavel's ways that led Lind to pursue this strategy.

Suddenly I realized that he was still staring sternly at me from the podium.

Even though it had been ten days since we first met, I felt like this was the first moment I'd truly looked him in the face. Lind always seemed blander, less distinct when put next to Kibaou, but his sharply slanted eyes had a powerful strength behind them now.

As far as I knew, he had never truly let his ugliest, most basic emotions explode outward in public since that one occasion: when he demanded to know why I let Diavel die, right after the battle with Illfang.

The next time I saw him, Lind had dyed his hair blue and donned silver armor, just like the late knight, and assumed control of the blue group. Perhaps he chose that path out of respect for Diavel, or a feeling of rivalry, of desire to surpass his mentor. Perhaps he actually wanted to *be* Diavel.

That third option's gonna be pretty tough, Lind, I thought.

Diavel was a man of contradictions, someone who sought to lead the best players in the game while hiding the fact that he himself was a beta tester. He was playing a role that could easily see him hoisted by his own petard, but that also made him strong and a fascinating individual.

It occurred to me that if *SAO* had not turned into the deadly trap it was now, he might have been a great PVPer. The name Diavel came from the Italian word for "devil," Argo told me, but if that was the reason behind his name choice, what drove him to call himself a knight? I didn't know, of course, and pretending that I did was a disgrace to his memory.

At any rate, Diavel left Aincrad entirely without revealing a number of truths to his friends, and no one could fill his absence.

As though sensing my line of thought, Lind's stare grew even sharper. He continued, "So you have no intention of being involved in any guild. Do I have that correct, Kirito?"

"Sure, that works. I'll still take part in the boss fights, of course...assuming you let me."

The guild leader nodded a few times at my answer. "Understood. We will discuss the matter of the boss at the next meeting. That is all I wanted to know."

I sighed with relief once his gaze left me and sat back down on the stone steps.

Next, he turned to Agil's group to ask if they had any intention of joining either guild, but all four of them declined. It seemed to me like they were going to make their own guild, but Lind did not ask about that. In the end, the DKB and ALS both wound up with an even eighteen members. There might be ferocious competition for new members between them, but as long as it swelled the ranks of the frontline clearers, that was a welcome development.

I'm glad that's over, I thought to myself, then realized something.

I had answered for myself during that public interrogation, but I never checked with Asuna to see how she felt. She had her hood so low and was staying so quiet, it was as if she was testing out her Hiding skill, and I'd totally forgotten about her presence. Lind asked me and Agil; why didn't he check with Asuna as well?

I turned left to look at her. Her hands and legs were perfectly still and aligned, just as she'd sat during the first meeting down in Tolbana. The profile I saw peeking out from her hood was calm, and she didn't appear to be upset.

"Um..." I started, then swallowed what I was going to say. There was a pale fire smoldering in her narrowed eyes.

She was more than a little upset.

The one player who could deal the most damage per second out of all forty-two present was burning with a righteous fire that threatened to consume her entire being.

"Let's head into the next topic. I'd like to ask Kibaou to lead the ceremonies now."

Kibaou stood up, sensing that it was finally his turn, but I was not watching him. My eyes were frozen at a random spot in space, neither on the stage nor on Asuna's face.

We'd been party members and travel companions for the last several days. Even I could sense that she was incredibly angry.

But I could not immediately discern why. There must be three potential reasons: (1) me, (2) Lind, (3) Kibaou. But I had no idea which one of the three it was.

Reason (3) was probably out. Asuna did not think much of Kibaou—when we nearly crossed his path in the cave this morning, she made a face of disgust—but all he'd done so far at this meeting was introduce himself, then sit in a chair the entire time.

I wanted to believe that (1) wasn't true. It was wrong of me to declare no intention of joining a guild without seeing how she felt first, but she would probably have interrupted and made her anger clear if she really felt that way. Plus, the smoldering flames in her eyes were trained at a point directly over the stage several dozen feet away.

Based on the process of elimination, the target of her glare had to be (2) Lind. Most likely, it was something in the DKB leader's speech that had made her furious.

Even as I considered these options, Kibaou was theatrically gesturing to the crowd.

"Listen up, we're lookin' ta finish this floor in the span of a week! That means gettin' to the labyrinth in four days and beatin' the boss in another two! Our best option to make that happen is numbers! We can't keep up this pace with only forty-whatsit folks every time! We gotta get out there and recruit folks what got a bone to pick with this damn game!"

The members of the crowd dressed in green roared with approval at this statement. Increasing the strength of the front-line group was a crucial task, to be sure, but taking on new members and increasing the speed of our conquest were contradictory goals. The harder these two guilds tried to push the frontier forward, the further they left those down in the Town of Beginnings in the dust. Orlando's Legend Braves had attempted that upgrading scam specifically to close the stark level gap between them and the best players.

But that aside, I had a more pressing duty at the moment. I needed to prevent Asuna from tearing Lind a new one. She was keeping herself under control for now, but the moment the meeting ended, she would leap up and confront him. The other DKB members would be furious, and it would also close the book on her eligibility to join the guilds, which would gladly welcome her if she just asked.

I tuned out Kibaou's lengthy speech, turned to my left, and steeled myself to speak. But before I could get the words out, her voice emerged from the hood, strained and gravelly.

"You can't stop me. I've been able to resist what he says before, but this time he's crossed the line, and I'm going to speak my mind."

"...By 'this time,' you mean how we'd have to join separate guilds?" I asked, just to be sure, but Asuna did not respond with a yes or no—probably because she thought it went without saying—and pressed on, her voice even harder.

"Whether I join a guild or not and who I hang around with or not are my choice. I might be able to put up with his pushy attitude and speeches, but I can tell that deep down, he believes it's his job to guide others and tell them what to do. He believes that giving people hard orders will ultimately be to their benefit. He even believes that what he's doing is some kind of self-sacrifice."

"..."

I felt a cold sweat break out on my back, even though I knew she wasn't talking about me. If I ever caught wind that someone said these things about me, the withering criticism would made me sulk in an inn room for a week.

But if Asuna's remarks were accurate, then Lind's convoluted scheme to prevent me from making my own guild wasn't meant to firm up his own leadership of the playerbase, but as an attempt to guide me into my proper place as a player. He thought that wearing a blue uniform and taking part in the frontline community would reform me. I would be reborn from shunned beater to respected member.

That would indeed be overstepping the boundaries of his responsibility, but on the other hand, I felt like Asuna might be overthinking things. She continued on as if hearing my thoughts aloud.

"I know how it goes. I've been hearing those words on the other side ever since I was a kid."

"…!"

I held my breath. Asuna almost never talked about her life back in the real world—in fact, this might be the first time.

She'd described her motive for picking up her sword and leaving the Town of Beginnings: "For me to be myself." I probably didn't fully understand what that phrase meant yet, but her resistance to Lind's orders meant that they would prevent Asuna from being herself. And that had to be more important to Asuna than hanging around in an ambitious guild.

However.

However…

Even as I was lost in thought, Kibaou's impassioned speech was reaching its climax onstage. He challenged us to set the next town as our goal for tomorrow and read the most important pieces of information from the latest edition of Argo's strategy guide. Even anti-tester Kibaou was just barely able to accept the guides as "trusted secondary sources." It felt awfully convenient to me, but if that helped justify Argo's position in being independent from the frontline crowd, that was a good thing.

Still, it was important to prevent any situation in which Asuna might draw the ire of the others. Kibaou's speech was about to end, and she was preparing to go after Lind as soon as it finished.

Asuna had qualities that I didn't possess. She had the qualities of a leader meant to guide a great number of players. I didn't want to let her dash that possibility on the rocks by antagonizing the majority here at the very start of the game. Then again, I'd done that very thing right after the first boss fight…

Suddenly I realized one very important truth and held my breath again.

It wasn't a coincidence. This clash with Lind, the self-professed leader of the top players in the game, was inevitable. As long as

Asuna worked with me, it was bound to happen at some point. I was a beater, and I used my store of knowledge from the beta to help myself, and Asuna as my partner, gain a lead over the other frontier players. What was the Chivalric Rapier at her waist if not proof of that fact?

I felt disappointment and anger that I had just now realized this obvious truth, as well as a powerful doubt and hesitation. I bit my lip.

Up onstage, Kibaou theatrically gazed in a full circle around the meeting grounds and prepared to finish up.

"...And that's why, from now on, whichever guild spots the boss chamber first gets ta call the shots in the battle. If there ain't no further questions...which I assume there ain't, then that brings our first strategy meetin' of the third floor to a close. Let's finish it out with a cheer!"

Seeing that Kibaou had raised a defiant fist in the air, Lind reluctantly got to his feet. At the same time, Asuna leaned forward. Her skinny legs tensed, preparing to leap forward.

"...We're gonna crush this boss within a week!!"

"Yeah!!" the crowd roared in response. I held out my left hand and clutched her wrist.

Her hood turned to me and she growled, "Don't try to stop me."

"Sorry, I have to."

"I don't care if he...I don't care if all of those guild people hate me. I have no intention of joining them. I'd rather go back down to the Town of Beginnings than sit here and take that nonsense," she claimed boldly. A breeze ruffled her hood and the red light of the sunset caught her hazel eyes, shining like two shooting stars.

I stared right back into those burning pits of fire and shook my head.

"Don't do it, Asuna. You can't antagonize them."

I sucked in a deep breath, preparing to tell her that we ought to split apart.

I knew full well that this was the kind of thing Asuna hated most: a pushy, heavy-handed act supposedly done for the sake of the other person. But at this point, I had no other words to use. I couldn't let Asuna make herself the enemy of the main player force in the game, even if it meant that she hated, shunned, and insulted me, never to adventure at my side again.

It was the absolute limit of a solo player.

The fact that no one could save you.

SAO was programmed with a depressing number of negative status effects. Stunning, paralysis, poison, bleeding, blindness, dizziness, et cetera...These things could be overcome with the help of friends in a group, but they all threatened the life of any solo adventurer. In a normal game, where a player could be revived at any time, it might be worth the risk to play solo. But in this extremely deadly game, where a single mistake could be the end of everything, the only reason I was able to play alone in the first two floors was my stock of knowledge from the beta test.

That lifeline would last me to only the tenth floor. Eventually, I'd be forced to survive in unfamiliar maps against unfamiliar monsters. Already, the things I knew about the boss monsters had been proven insufficient. As the dangers increased exponentially, working with a full party or a guild would be crucial. But the longer she spent with me, the more Asuna risked falling into my position—or one even more perilous.

I had to tell her. It was time to break apart the temporary partnership that had sprung into existence with a Windwasp hunting competition. She had to swallow her anger at Lind and Kibaou and, if not soon, eventually join a guild, whether the DKB, ALS, or someone else.

But it was as though my throat resisted the order to turn the air in my lungs into words.

Asuna met my gaze in silence. Just seconds ago, her eyes had been burning red with rage, but now they were filled with something else that defied my understanding.

The other players in the square roared with enthusiasm, then broke off into smaller groups and chattered excitedly. Agil's group was seated in a wall in front of us, so no one noticed or interrupted our silent tension, but it also couldn't last forever.

I gritted my teeth and finally managed to make my stiff throat produce something...but what emerged was not what I expected in the least.

"If...if I died today...what would you do?"

Even though she couldn't have expected that question, her expression didn't change an ounce, as though she knew it was coming.

"Nothing would change. I'd still run as far as I could go." She paused, then asked, "And you? What would you do if I died?"

Despite asking her that very question just seconds ago, I had no immediate answer.

What would I do after Asuna died and all traces of her existence disappeared from Aincrad? I'd certainly return to being a solo player, but I couldn't imagine what I would feel and think after it happened.

Again, very suddenly, I realized one simple truth.

I was pulling Asuna away from the main group and into a high-risk environment. Of that there was no doubt. But there was only one reason I was doing that: I didn't want her to die.

The first time I met her in the labyrinth on the bottom floor, I broke my personal rules and spoke to her because that very feeling was my first instinct. I wished to see more of that shining, shooting-star Linear and where it would go from here. That same sentiment was at the core of my current attempt to keep her from snapping at Lind.

Perhaps, rather than arguing about breaking up the team or joining guilds, I should just say that simple statement. But once again, my throat had sealed itself shut.

My bad habit of seizing up when it mattered most was nothing new. Ever since I left behind my very first friend, Klein, in the back alleys of the Town of Beginnings, thirty-nine days before... In fact, ever since I started living in my home in the city of Kawagoe, Saitama Prefecture, I'd missed my chance to say what truly mattered, over and over.

But now, now that I'd realized this...

I prayed and fought, but my throat refused to turn the air it accepted into words. Everything physical in this world was digital data, so it wasn't my real throat that had seized shut. It was my brain itself, my mind, connected directly to the NerveGear. Over years of experience, I'd shut down my own mental pathways.

Just when the words I needed to say were about to evaporate in a sigh of resignation, I felt a faint voice speak into my ear.

Kirito.
If there's something you want to say, now is the time for you to do it, while you can. Your ability to do so makes you very fortunate.

The quiet but beautiful whisper seemed to belong to the dark elf we'd left far behind in the depths of the forest. Perhaps I was remembering something she'd said at that tiny graveyard at the rear of the camp, late that night. Perhaps my mind was putting its thoughts into Kizmel's voice all on its own.

But that phantom voice did prod me onward. The words I'd given up for lost made their way out of my mouth, bit by bit, into the virtual air.

"I don't...want you...to die."

For just an instant, Asuna's eyes grew wider.

"So...please, just hold it in. It's quite possible that Lind and his guild might save your life and mine someday. Please don't think you'd rather die than be saved by him."

At the very end, my voice shook pathetically, like a pouting child on the verge of tears. I looked down and finally let go of Asuna's arm. Awkwardly pointing forward, I saw that most of the players had descended upon the stage, showing off their weapons and trading collected materials. Agil's group of four were huddled tightly, conducting a meeting of their own.

Completely spent by the mere four sentences I'd just spoken, I waited for my erstwhile partner's response.

After about five seconds, she said simply, "I'll hold it in, then."

At that, I let out the air that had built in my chest with a long, slow exhale. It couldn't have been easy for Asuna to hold in the anger at having her strongest beliefs insulted. I wanted to respond to that, but there were no more words. I simply nodded.

After a bit, I heard the whisper in my ear again.

You did well, Kirito.

I had to grin at that. I really had to be losing it, if I was imagining Kizmel's voice in order to encourage myself...

"..."

No.

Wait. Hang on. Unless.

A number of other phrases circled through my brain. I slowly reached up with my right hand, feeling the (supposedly) empty space near my ear.

My fingertips met a soft and squishy surface.

We said brief good-byes to Agil's team, headed out the rear of the meeting area, and quickly strode down the main street and out of the town gate. Another hundred yards down the road, out of the hearing range of Zumfut's bustle, I stepped just a bit off the path and into the darkening forest.

Asuna followed me without comment, though the skeptical look on her face demanded an explanation for the sudden move. Rather than elaborate, I turned to an otherwise empty spot and asked, "Are you there, Kizmel?"

Asuna's eyes went wide with surprise, and she looked all around.

For a while, there was no response but the chirping of birds and rustling of leaves, but it was broken by the sound of rippling cloth. A laugh emerged from the opposite direction of where I was looking.

"So you noticed."

I spun around just in time to catch sight of the dark elf whipping her long cape back. Even with her Hiding status removed, the knight's tall form seemed to be melting into the dim shadows of the trees. Her onyx eyes glittered with mischief.

"How could I not notice?" I asked, choosing not to note that she was the one who spoke to *me*. Until I heard that whisper in my ear, I never would have imagined that Kizmel had not stayed back in the dark elf camp but used her cape's hiding charm to make herself invisible so she could follow us the entire time.

I just stared at the grinning Kizmel; I didn't even know what to ask first. Asuna filled the gap.

"Uh...Kizmel...? How long have you been there...?"

That was indeed a big issue. If Kizmel had trailed us ever since we left the base camp, she would have witnessed the scene where Lind's team started on the "Jade Key" quest—and sided with the forest elf knight against the male dark elf.

Contrary to my fears, the slain dark elf wasn't an identical replica of Kizmel, but it still must have been a difficult sight for her to process. If she had been present while we watched, how did she interpret that sight?

But Asuna did not share my apprehension. Like Kizmel, she tossed her hood back and pressed the elf further, her face reddening.

"...Were you also...in the room with us?"

That was another major issue. Even setting aside the simple fact that we did nap in the same room together, there was also the question of if we said anything embarrassing that we wouldn't want overheard. I tried to remember what had happened eight hours before, but fortunately, Kizmel shook her head.

"No, I spotted you in the meeting place at the center of the town. It wasn't until the late afternoon that I used the teleporting charm to come within range..."

That was right—she had mentioned such a power. I was partly relieved, but my suspicions had not been entirely undone.

Was this development even supposed to be possible? Were NPCs not registered with a party allowed to leave their designated areas of activity and chase down human players?

And when Kizmel whispered in my ear at the center of Zumfut, it was within the safe haven of town. Even if it were possible that a player being chased by monsters could run into town and actually have them follow him in, the frighteningly powerful guards at the gate would dispatch the creature at once.

Plus, Kizmel was a yellow-cursored NPC to us, as we were actively taking part in the dark elf side of the campaign, but she would be a red-cursored monster to any other player. It must be true to the guards of Zumfut as well, so if her Hiding effect had worn off for any reason, the results would have been disastrous. Of course, Kizmel was tremendously strong by herself, so she might have been able to hold off the guards long enough to flee into the forest.

I tried as best I could to corral all of these questions into one simple enough to ask.

"So, um, why did you come all the way to the human town…?"

Perhaps it was my mind playing tricks on me, but I thought I saw her face blush a bit out of shyness, but her expression was serious as she answered, "It was my duty."

"D-duty?"

"Yes. The commander has given me a mission: to serve and protect you. You did not return for many hours after leaving this morning, so I simply left to see how you were doing."

"Simply, huh? Is it really safe to go all the way into the middle of town like that? What if your hiding—er, deception charm wore off?"

Now her face seemed to take on a note of pride. She stroked the oddly gleaming cape.

"This Mistmoon Cloak is most effective at the evening and morning hours when sunlight and moonlight switch places. Its charm will not break, even with a little physical contact."

"Aha…I see," I replied, looking at my fingertips and recalling the squishy sensation, while Asuna's brow furrowed in slight consternation,

"…He touched you?"

"Yes. You might be surprised; Kirito is quite—"

"*Quite* the cloak, I must say!" I interjected hastily, trying to steer the conversation away from the brewing storm clouds. I broke out in a nervous sweat just thinking about what part of Kizmel I might have touched and how close I'd come to being automatically thrown into the game's prison for harassment. But for now, the questions were over. I looked upward.

The sky—technically, the bottom of the floor above—peeking through the branches was almost entirely purple, with just a few traces of red remaining. I'd been planning to eat dinner in Zumfut after the meeting, but I didn't want to wander back into town with Kizmel tagging along out of sight, and I also couldn't force her to just wait out here in the forest, abandoned.

"Asuna, I'm thinking we should just go back to the camp. Is that okay with you?" I asked. She shot me a glance that said I'd still have to answer on the previous topic, but kept her face neutral as she replied.

"All right. Especially since Kizmel came all this way to see us."

She shut her mouth but appeared to want to say more. I peered at her patiently, prompting her to continue. But Asuna looked down at the ground and prodded a bluish-purple mushroom with the toe of her boot.

"Um…I was thinking, maybe we should just stay around the elf camp all the way up to the boss battle."

"Huh? W-well…I guess we can get all the info we need on the state of progress from Agil and Argo, and there are plenty of supplies at the camp…but I thought you really liked that hotel room in Zumfut."

"I got to see the view once, and that was enough. Besides, I don't want to be anywhere near those guild people right now."

"…I see."

Once you caught a case of Stay-Away Syndrome in an MMORPG, it could be extremely hard to break (as I knew from experience), but I understood how she felt, and I didn't have any room to argue otherwise, so I took her comment in stride and turned to the elf.

"Kizmel, do you mind if we stay in the tent with you, starting tonight…and lasting for a week or so?"

"I do not mind," she said simply. Her smile was more beautiful than any NPC's expression—more beautiful than any player's, in fact. "I would be delighted for you to call it home. Let us live together until our goals are met."

"…Great, thanks."

The phrase *live together* seemed to take on a new, fresh meaning coming from her. Asuna nodded in agreement but turned away just as quickly. In the dying rays of the sun, the contours of her rapier, breastplate, and fine cheek lines were a blazing red.

Sadly, the teleportation charm from the dark elf camp to the forest near the main town was a one-way ticket, so we had to retrace our steps from the morning, only now through the gloomy evening mists.

There was no avoiding the monsters, of course, but Asuna and I had recently earned significant upgrades, and we had the powerful elf knight as our travel companion. Both Kizmel and I were level 15, but as an elite unit within the game, her power was not dictated by level alone. We traveled with Asuna and Kizmel in the front and me in the rear. Any mobs who approached from the right were dispatched with a single attack and sword skill from Asuna's Chivalric Rapier +5, and those from the left were met with the same by Kizmel's long saber. I barely had to lift a finger. I still got the shared experience and col from being in the party, but it felt a bit disappointing to not take part, and my mind began to wander due to inactivity.

On the one hand, I thought about the DKB and ALS, who had effectively split the frontline player population between themselves, and our duo's role in all of it.

I told Asuna I didn't want her to die, as a means to prevent her from throwing herself at Lind. That wasn't just an excuse I made up on the spot—it was how I really felt. But as a result, I'd extended the terms of our temporary partnership. The logical part of my brain deduced that her odds of survival rose if she was part of a big guild, but I just couldn't tell her we needed to break up the team. I still didn't know why the words caught in my throat.

At any rate, I had to take responsibility for my statement. I had to make her more powerful, to dedicate myself even harder to that task. I had to teach her more, not just about her movement in battle, but her stats, the types of gear, and other knowledge of the game.

That day marked a week since we teamed up on the second floor, and during that time, I'd held to a simple stance: If she asked, I answered. Over and over, she demanded to know why I hadn't said something or other earlier. Perhaps it was my resignation to the role of beater. But now was the time to snap myself out of that passive attitude…

But on the other hand, the subconscious parts of my mind grappled with something else entirely: the mysterious actions of Kizmel, the NPC knight.

What was she, anyway?

It was beyond obvious that she was not an ordinary NPC. Her natural conversation style and ample emotional range were on a clearly higher level than the shopkeepers, guards, and hotel clerks in Zumfut, and even the other dark elves in the camp with her. It was as though Kizmel thought, felt, and expressed herself, unbound by the normal constraints of NPC algorithms. Otherwise, she would never have boldly followed Asuna and me into the human town far from her home base.

If she wasn't a normal NPC, there were two possibilities.

One: For some unknown reason, Kizmel was granted a high-functioning AI, rather than the simple chat bots that only responded to a set of keywords.

Two: Also for some unknown reason, Kizmel was actually a

player. Or to be more precise, a human role-player who was acting out the character of a dark elf.

Both were hard to believe. I wanted to think that the latter could not be the case. If that were true, the person behind Kizmel wasn't a fellow prisoner of *SAO* but someone aligned with those who had plotted to turn it into its current trap...one of the administrators.

There was no way Kizmel could be Akihiko Kayaba, but even if it was an accomplice of his, I couldn't see them earnestly helping us advance in the game. Perhaps I ought to consider the possibility that she was plotting to lead us into some kind of trap ahead...

"...!"

I shook my head vigorously to dispel that dark notion. I didn't want to be suspicious of Kizmel. The last thing I wanted to do was imagine that the earnest sadness as she mourned at the grave of her sister Tilnel was nothing but a cynical act.

I looked up and fixed my gaze on the back of the fencer ahead and to my right. I had to protect Asuna, to make her stronger. Strong enough that if I died, she would be able to survive this perilous world on her own. That was my responsibility now that I'd chosen not to break us apart.

But what if Kizmel really was leading us into a trap? If there was even a slight chance of that being true...

"Kirito," came a voice from my left. I looked up in surprise and locked eyes with the dark elf. The consternation and concern in her face were so natural that I felt shame for my suspicion, and my desire to learn the truth about her grew even more.

"You have been silent for quite some time. Is something the matter?"

"Er, it's nothing. Just thinking..."

"Ahh. Sometimes it is best to speak your worries aloud and free yourself from their weight."

Asuna turned back and added, "That's right. I've noticed recently that you're the type of person who gets depressed on his own because you overthink everything. Just speak up before you get any stupid ideas."

"Well, that's…true, I suppose…"

I glanced around under their withering stares, but there was no escape. Yet I couldn't say the things I'd just been thinking. Instead, I put on an awkward smile and thought up a lame excuse.

"J-just thinking, you're both so strong and handy to have around…"

"What in the world would make you think so hard about that?"

"Uh, just, erm, thinking, uh…which one of you I'd want to have as a wife…"

Wait. Scratch that. Reload from save point.

My eyes darted around, looking for the LOAD button. Asuna gaped at me in total disbelief, then sucked in a deep breath and bellowed, "Are you really that stupid?!"

Meanwhile, Kizmel grunted in understanding without batting an eye.

"I'm sorry, Kirito. That will require Her Majesty's permission," she said, utterly straight-faced.

"N-no, that's perfectly all right," I reassured her, shaking my head and hands. My mind immediately went down an escapist tunnel—instead of MMOs, maybe I should have played those games with all the romantic choices to make instead. A teenager who loved dating sims wouldn't have gotten himself trapped in this situation. Maybe there really was a market for full-dive romance games with deadly stakes. But what would you have to do to die in such a game…?

Asuna snapped me out of that ugly spiral with a chilly "We're here."

I nearly asked her where that was, until I remembered that our little journey had a destination after all.

Ahead, the thick forest opened up, and triangular flags could be seen rippling in the trailing mist. It was the familiar sight of the dark elf base.

Biting back a rueful sigh at my own relief, I decided to forget the shameful display I'd put on just a minute ago and picked up my pace to catch up to the women.

In the end, I left both the fighting and the navigation to the other two. It was hard not to feel like my stock had fallen during the trip from Zumfut to the camp, but if there was one thing I learned, it was that nothing good came from moping on my own.

Whether Kizmel was AI or human, it didn't change the fact that we helped her and she helped us. I wanted to be around Kizmel for as long as possible—and I was sure Asuna agreed on that point. That was all I needed for now.

If progress continued in accordance with Kibaou's challenge to the crowd, the boss battle against the third-floor boss would take place in six days: December 21. Until then, we'd accomplish as much as we could using this camp as our home. We'd continue with the campaign quest, acquire new armor and upgrade it, increase our skill proficiency, and gain information. There was a mountain of tasks to see to.

When we passed through the narrow canyon of magical mists and into the camp, I breathed in a lungful of the strangely scented air and told myself it was time to get cracking.

6

IN THE LONG-DISTANT PAST...

The world was split into the forest elven kingdom of Kales'Oh, the dark elven kingdom of Lyusula, the human Alliance of the Nine, the underground realm of the dwarves, and various other groupings along racial lines, and while there were skirmishes at times, the land was at peace.

But one day, something happened, and a hundred varied regions from around the world were cut in circles from the earth and summoned up to the sky. The circles were under two miles across at the smallest and over six at the largest. They were stacked in a conical formation to form a gigantic floating fortress a hundred floors tall.

This castle held its countless towns and villages, mountains, forests and lakes, and never again returned to earth. The magic powers that caused the old civilizations to flourish were lost, and with them, the nine kingdoms of man. Most towns reverted to maintaining themselves, and the floors lost contact with one another. A great length of time passed. Legends and tales of the Great Separation still existed among the two elf races, the only people to keep their kingdoms intact from that fateful time...

"...and that's how the story goes," I said, summarizing the backstory of Aincrad's genesis as best I'd learned it that day while

I leaned back against the tent. A watery voice answered from behind my back.

"Hmm...So it feels like we learned some stuff, but none of it is very useful."

"Pretty much," I replied, looking up with my hands folded behind my head. Beyond the steam issuing from the exhaust pipe built into the roof of the bathing tent, the bottom of the fourth floor gleamed dark and foreboding.

According to elf legend, someone had yanked the ground straight out of the earth and connected it all with a framework of steel and stone so that the pieces were stacked one atop the other. Of course, the true creators of *SAO* were Kayaba and the Argus staff, and the legends of the Great Separation were nothing but background info they'd added to the game, but it was hard not to be curious about it all. Who had created this floating castle and why? Was it the whim of a godlike figure, or the work of a human, or elf, or something else?

Asuna was pondering a similar topic within the bath. When she spoke, there was a bubbling filter applied to her voice.

"By the way, it doesn't seem like there's much in the way of gods to this story. When I read or watched fantasy stories as a little girl, there were always a bunch of different gods with fancy names."

"Hmm, you may have a point there. There are churches in the bigger towns, and NPC priests, but I don't even know what god they're worshipping...Then again, that might actually be fitting, based on most fantasy-themed games. All they have is a vague godlike figure."

"Because the player is supposed to fill in the blank for herself? Then I guess your god must be the god of Last Attack bonuses. You managed to win yourself the bonus against today's field boss, after all."

I tried to answer her half-joking response with another of my increasingly weak excuses.

"I-it's not like I'm going out of my way to win them. I just play a character build that excels in attack power, which happens to raise the chances that I'll get the last hit...Besides, if we're talking about gods, then yours must be the god of the bath or something. It ensures that everywhere you go, you find lodgings with baths attached...In fact, that reminds me of my place back in Tolbana—"

A ball of water smacked the other side of the tent wall behind my head. I remembered that I was supposed to have erased that memory and hastily changed the topic.

"A-anyway, aside from us, it looks like only Lind and the DKB are working on the campaign quest. Seems like a waste, especially since Argo put out Volume One of her Elf War strategy guide."

"And we added a lot of information on our own. But maybe everyone saw that guide and got a bit intimidated. I mean, it said right there that the campaign doesn't end until the ninth floor. Even Agil said, 'I don't think I've got the time to mess around with a long-ass quest like that.'"

I snorted at her surprisingly accurate impression of Agil.

"Well, I guess there's always the option, once we reach the ninth floor, of rushing back here to blaze through the entire questline. Plus, you'd be at a much higher level, so it probably gives you a better chance at saving the elf champion in that first duel," I noted, then realized something.

Challenging a campaign quest that spanned seven floors was predicated upon the player's assumption that we'd make it to the ninth floor anyway. I had gotten that far in the beta already, and I hadn't been thinking about anything but leveling since we started the quest, but at the present moment, the ninth floor seemed like a distant fantasy, a future too difficult to fathom at our current rate. Once you started looking up, you had to think about the fact that there were ninety-seven floors over our heads.

"...But you know what?" Asuna started from within the tent,

as though reading my mind. There was a heavy splash and the sound of wet feet slapping against the wood deck. I heard her sit down right on the other side of the heavy, hanging flap.

She continued, "It's not as scary as it used to be, to think about all the floors left. I'm still trying my hardest to survive each and every day, but now I'm looking forward to seeing the dark elf queen's palace, for example. If the dozens of floors ahead of us were all ripped from the surface centuries ago, then there must be all kinds of sights and sounds to experience. It's more of a feeling of anticipation."

"...I see," I responded simply, impressed once again with Asuna's strength of spirit. It seemed like an inadequate statement, so I searched for something else to add. "I bet there are all kinds of baths up there, too."

A sharp elbow (I think) slammed into the small of my back through the heavy tent wall.

Sunday, December 18.

Three days had passed since the first strategy meeting in Zumfut. We hadn't returned to the human town since then but stuck to the dark elf camp, completing quests, collecting upgrade materials, and buffing up our skills to earn mods.

With a fresh new level gained, I was at 16, and Asuna at 15. This was probably as far as we'd get here on the third floor. During the beta, the recommended level for fighting the boss was three times the floor number—which would probably change as we got further into the game—and we were already half a dozen over that number. Accordingly, the experience we were receiving dropped precipitously. Killing mobs in the forest and dungeons barely moved the EXP bar in the least.

More surprising to me was that Kizmel actually earned a level-up to 16 during our journeys together. I accidentally congratulated her on the level-up when I saw the customary flash, but she already interpreted the number as a kind of sword rank and did nothing more self-aware than thank me.

With the help of our even-stronger knight companion, the campaign quest proceeded smoothly, but as Asuna had noted earlier, we didn't really learn any more about the birth of Aincrad than before.

After the "Jade Key" and "Vanquishing the Spiders," the third act of the campaign was a collection quest titled "The Flower Offering," in which we gathered items to offer to the memory of the slain scout from the previous quest. The fourth act, "Emergency Orders," was another search for a missing scout, but unlike in the second quest, we successfully rescued the elf this time. But the fifth quest, "The Missing Soldier," revealed that the scout we'd brought back to the camp was none other than a forest elf using a disguise charm.

I knew how it all went already, of course, and I was considering whether or not to expose the imposter during the fourth quest, but not only did I not know how to undo his charm, there was also the possibility that the campaign might fall completely off the tracks right then and there. I kept an eye on him after we got back to the base, and raised an alarm after he tried to steal the Jade Key from the commander's tent, but I soon lost sight of him thanks to his elven hiding abilities. It was better than in the beta, when the key was stolen from under my nose, but the imposter still had to be chased. We formed a temporary party with the camp's Dark Elven Wolfhandlers, plus Kizmel, and followed the imposter scout's tracks directly to a large forest elf camp.

It was at this point that we had to pause the quest, for earlier that day was the battle against the field boss that guarded the cave leading to the labyrinth.

We defeated the boss on the first attempt, with no fatalities. Aside from the outcast beater jumping in and stealing the LA bonus again, it was a rousing success. But I couldn't help but feel that the sparks of anger that had been smoldering within the group were rapidly turning into a raging fire with the creation of the two big guilds.

"Hey, Asuna," I shouted at the bathing tent, rubbing the sore spot on my back. The only answer I got was the sound of the exit flap being lifted. I turned to see a slender silhouette leaving the tent, profiled against the dying light.

She was in the water just a minute before, but the leather-tunic-clad figure showed no signs of having just bathed. One of the convenient things about virtual bathing was the instant drying effect, but as the most vocal bathing admirer of the front-line team, you'd think Asuna would not like the deviation from realism.

Thanks to this mental diversion, the question that eventually left my lips was not what I'd meant to ask.

"...Don't you ever feel like changing outfits?"

Even in the dim light, the furious crevice between her eyebrows was as clear as day.

"Is there a problem with me not changing?" she snapped, voice freezing cold. I rapidly shook my head back and forth.

"N-no, no problem at all. I just wondered if you felt like wearing something that...fit the mood better once you were done bathing. You know, like a yukata, or a bathrobe, or a single T-shirt..."

Too late to stop the words, I decided to blame the last option on my subconscious bringing up what my little sister always wore after a bath, but Asuna held it in and did nothing worse than twitch her eyelids for a few moments. She looked down at herself and sighed.

"...As I'm sure you remember, I do have extra outfits. In fact, most of my storage space is packed with them."

I did remember. When I had forced her to use the MATERI-ALIZE ALL ITEMS command in Urbus so she could retrieve the sword that had been swindled from her, the room had exploded with small, frilly white articles of clothing.

Asuna pinned me with a sharp gaze to ensure I didn't go remembering too many of those details, leaned against the tent support, and stared up at the night sky.

"But those clothes aren't meant for my own enjoyment."

"Huh? Why did you buy so many of them, then?"

"I didn't."

I blinked in surprise, then understood. Many copies of the same crafted items often represented a means, not a purpose.

"Are you saying...you crafted those yourself to raise your Tailoring skill?" I asked softly. Asuna nodded. "B-but, when did you do all of that? It wasn't after we teamed up on the second floor, right?"

"No, it was before. You know how when you farm monsters on the second floor, you end up with tons of wool and cotton items? I just decided to use them on a whim..."

"Gotcha. I usually just sell them off to an NPC once I get a big stock of them. I'm surprised you were in the mood to work on a crafting skill. Isn't it boring?"

For some reason, she did not react. After watching her stand there silently, I noticed something. At present, it wasn't the length of time that was the issue with crafting skills. It was the number of slots.

At level 1, a player started with two skill slots. It expanded to three at level 6, four at level 12, and five at level 20. From that point on, every ten levels provided a new slot, as far as I knew.

At level 16, I had four slots, and they were all filled with battle skills: One-Handed Sword, Martial Arts, Search, and Hiding. Asuna had four slots as well, but I realized I'd never asked her what skills she was using, aside from Rapier. She wore a metal breastplate when out adventuring, so she had to have Light Metal Armor, but the other two were a mystery. If one of them was Tailoring, why would she choose that?

Asuna claimed she did it to get rid of the materials, but skill slots were crucially important factors in a character's build, not something to be chosen on a whim. As a frontline player, it made much more sense to ditch the crafting skills and maximize her battle potential and survivability with Hiding or Search like me, or perhaps Acrobatics or Weight Limit Expansion. Asuna didn't need me to explain these things to her. She understood the logic.

Asuna seemed to recognize the confusion in my gaze. She

glanced at me, looked down, and caught me by surprise once again.

"Just so you know, I removed Tailoring from my slot. And most of the clothes, I turned back into fabric."

"R-really? So it was all just a whim, nothing more?"

"That's what I said, isn't it? But…that's not all there was to it…"

"Meaning…?"

"It's a secret. I'll tell you someday, if I feel like it."

There seemed to be a hint of a smile behind that standoffish answer. Asuna pulled off of the tent pole. "So, what about you? If you want to take a bath, I'll stand guard out here."

"Uh, that won't be necessary. It'll only take three minutes. You go ahead to the dining hall."

"Okay. While we're eating, you better tell me what you got out of that giant spider today."

"Yeah, yeah," I replied, getting to my feet. Asuna waved and marched off to the nearby dining tent. I watched her go, then stepped through the hanging door flap of the tent.

For the last five days, we'd made a practice of beelining for this bathing tent when we returned to the camp, and I would stand guard at the entrance while Asuna bathed. At no point in any of this had a dark elf of either sex attempted to visit the tent while someone was inside. It felt like standing guard wasn't even necessary, but it was hard to get over that idea when the only thing separating you from anyone else was a simple flap of fabric.

On the other hand, a man had little use for bath-place security. I stepped onto the wooden deck installed within the tent and hit the REMOVE button three times on my equipment mannequin, sending all of my gear into storage. I shrank back at the immediate chill and headed straight for the large bathtub at the rear of the tent. If it weren't for the fear that the dark elves might be drawn by the sound, I would have leaped into the water. Instead, I slipped in as gracefully as I could manage.

The bathtub was at least seven or eight feet long—heating that much water seemed like it would be hard, but it was just another elven charm at work. The water was a pale green color, brimming with a pleasant scent like mint or cypress. Once I was up to my shoulders, I felt a delightful heat and pressure enveloping every inch of skin. It made sense that Asuna had such a fixation on bathing, but it was also distracting to notice the ways in which it didn't match up to the real thing. Something about it just didn't quite feel *liquidy* enough.

In a general sense, I did my best not to think of my body and everything else in Aincrad being a polygonal creation. I was afraid that if I imagined any of it being fake, that my subconscious might think that this didn't matter, that I could always retry any mistakes. The fighting, eating, and sleeping were certainly realistic enough, but there were times when the cracks in the edifice were noticeable. That must have been why I never took to bathing much...

But...no, that was an excuse. Even in the real world, I wasn't much of a bather as a little kid. Maybe the baths here were actually more suited to me, given that I didn't need to shampoo my hair, scrub my body, and dry off.

Small pots filled with what I assumed to be shampoo and soap were lined up at the edge of the deck, but I'd never used them. Perhaps Asuna was using them to gain some kind of statistical advantage. Was that the kind of question it was safe to ask?

Two minutes had passed. I stood up, ready to finish my brief bath.

Suddenly, someone lifted the entrance flap of the tent from the outside.

Did Asuna forget something in here? No, there's nothing on the wooden deck.

Is another player coming for a bath? No, this is an instance.

Is it a forest elf hit man, coming to kill me? No, that looks like the brown skin of a dark elf...

I stood there, frozen, clutching the rim of the bathtub. The visitor's onyx eyes blinked just once, and she spoke as though nothing was amiss.

"Oh, I didn't realize you were in here, Kirito."

I expected her to continue with *I'm sorry, I'll come back later,* but the armored dark elf walked straight through the entrance and reached out to the clasp on her shoulder piece.

"Do you mind if I join you in the bath?"

The key to survival in *SAO* was judgment: Observe and identify the situation quickly, analyze all possible actions, and react based on your best expectations. In the half second that Kizmel waited for my answer, my brain raced faster than ever before. Depending on my choice, I might wind up clapped into chains in the prison beneath Blackiron Palace.

I recalled a magazine interview published during the beta test, claiming that implementing the anti-harassment code was an extremely difficult decision for the development team.

Unlike physical attacks and theft, drawing the line around "inappropriate contact" that constituted a crime was a very tricky task. At first, they considered simply leaving the policing of manners and morals up to the playerbase. A hardcoded detection system might misdiagnose certain cases, and there was the fear that the code could be twisted in unintended ways by wicked players.

But the fact that NPCs were visually indistinguishable from players and the fact that this was an experiment in a totally new genre forced their hand, and they eventually added the code. The fact that players could find young female NPCs and grope them to their heart's content in the full-dive setting ran afoul of the game ratings agency's ethical standards. I couldn't help but wonder what made that different from being able to PK someone, but that had always been a case of different standards. The interview this information came from was with the Argus staff rather than Kayaba, but they probably had their own bone to pick with the real-life factors forcing their decision.

At any rate, the addition of the anti-harassment code to *SAO* was meant to curb inappropriate actions toward NPCs of the opposite sex, not players.

But in that case, how would the system react if an NPC chose to barge into the bath with the player? Would the code stay put as long as the player didn't touch the NPC, or would I run afoul of it just for looking at her with all gear removed? Or was this situation so far beyond the regular bounds of the system that it would ignore everything entirely?

My brain was at its maximum capacity—I could imagine white smoke issuing from the top of my head.

"G-go right ahead. I'm just getting out," I said. That was the proper social response, regardless of how the system worked. There was just one problem: I had all of my clothing removed and couldn't leave the bathtub. Some male players thought nothing of their virtual nakedness and changed outfits in the middle of town without hesitation, but I sadly did not share their courage.

I hung to the rim of the tub, waiting for the moment Kizmel looked away to emerge.

"I see. Thank you," the elf woman said, turning to the washing station on the right side of the tent and pressing the magic clasp.

With the same familiar jingle from the other day, the armor and cape vanished with a flash of light. She was wearing a single silk undersuit. The sight of her brown skin peeking through the fine, sheer black lace put me under a stun effect, but I'd seen that before. I tried to maintain focus and leaped from the tub when she turned away. I had my menu open before I even hit the ground, instantly popping the UNDERWEAR button. The security of fabric around my waist gave me the courage to continue to my shirt and pants—

Jingle.

The beautiful, dangerous sound rang out again. I automatically looked to the right and saw the bodysuit disappearing from Kizmel in a shower of light.

"Nbwha…"

A nonsense syllable escaped my lips, and I lost my balance in midair. Naturally, I stumbled upon landing and fell into a

Tumble status, landing with a pathetic splat on the wood deck. Kizmel started to turn around.

"What's wrong, Kiri—"

"N-n-n-nothing! It's nothing!"

"Oh? Be careful; the bathing area can be slippery," she said, like a mother scolding a clumsy child. She turned back to the wall just before the point of no return and sat down on a wooden bathing chair. Reaching into one of the small urns lined up on the counter, she removed a thick liquid and spread it on her skin. A sudden surge of white suds flowed forth, coating her bare back.

I wasn't just sitting there, staring; I crawled toward the exit on all fours rather than wait for the Tumble to subside. The problem was that my wild jumping had left the wooden deck slick and slippery, slowing my progress. I had gotten about six feet across the room when…

"Since you're here, would you do me the favor of washing my back?" came the knight's request from on high.

In the end, I was not sent to Blackiron Palace for inappropriate contact, but I didn't know if that had anything to do with Kizmel's unique nature within the game. The bathing tent had its own brush for scrubbing, which meant I didn't need to touch her skin directly.

The fact that I did not refuse to sit on the chair behind the knight and scrub her sudsy back with the brush was most certainly not out of the desire to test the limits of the anti-harassment code. It was Kizmel's confession that she hadn't had anyone to scrub her back since Tilnel's soul had been called back to the Holy Tree.

The death of Kizmel's sister and the very war between the forest and dark elves were nothing more than a background setting that had been applied to Kizmel. It was impossible to imagine . NPCs going about their routines and actually fighting and dying in combat where no player could see. It was the old quandary about the sound of the tree falling alone in the forest. The memo-

enemy is slain, but I perish as well. I fall to the ground, and you look down upon me with sadness in your eyes…Every time I have the dream, your clothes and your companions are different…but your face is always the same at the end…"

"Ahh," I murmured.

My eyes then went wide, and I silently gaped.

That dream.

Was it…

Memories of the SAO beta test?

I was so shocked, I nearly asked Kizmel this question, knowing she couldn't possibly understand it.

The only thing that prevented me from doing so was a steely voice that piped up from beyond the hanging entrance flap of the tent.

"Kirito, how long are you going to keep me waiting? It's been nearly ten minutes."

It was, of course, the fencer who had gone off to the dining tent before I bathed.

Didn't I tell her I was only going to take three minutes? I recalled, far too late to do anything about it. Beyond that, the overwhelming danger of the situation—Asuna standing outside, separated by only a flap of cloth, while I scrubbed the back of a totally naked Kizmel inside—left me unable to formulate a response.

I sat there frozen, brush clutched in my hands, and heard a more menacing statement this time.

"Well, say something. I'll give you three more seconds before I walk in there."

She was clearly angry about being stood up for dinner. The dining tent's menu was probably seasoned whitefish (Asuna's favorite) or the rooty brown stew. Oddly enough, though the elves in this world didn't cut down living trees, they also weren't vegetarians. I could have sworn I'd read a story once about an elven heroine who didn't eat meat.

But this wasn't the time for distractions. At the two-point-eight-second mark, I summoned my courage and sucked in a breath.

"S-sorry! I'll be out soon, just give me one more minute!"

The flap was already lifted several inches at that point, but it dropped back to its hanging position.

"…I'll give you two minutes out of pity. I'll order your food, too, so stop by if you want to eat."

Her footsteps trod away. I let out my breath in relief. When Kizmel spoke, there was a jovial, teasing note in her voice.

"Do you human warriors not normally bathe together?"

"N-no, especially not men and women together. What about elves?"

"The knight's manor at the palace has separated bathing quarters, but this is a battleground. We cannot expect luxuries."

"I see. Um…can you tell me more about that dream some other time?"

Perhaps Kizmel did possess memories of the beta within her. I was fascinated and deadly curious, but I felt I needed to process this information before I knew what to ask her.

She leaned just a little bit toward me and muttered, "Yes. I, too, would like to know what that dream means…"

It felt like she was talking more to herself than me.

Eleven forty-five at night.

My eyes popped open at an alarm that only I could hear, and I waited for my senses to fully return before sitting up.

The lamp hanging off the center pole of the tent and the fires of the heater below were both extinguished, but there was enough moonlight coming through the exhaust vent in the roof to see by. In the center of the pelt-covered floor, Kizmel and Asuna lay close together, fast asleep.

NPCs acted like players in that they went to sleep at night, but in their case, they simply closed their eyes and went inactive according to the rules of their programming. At least, that's what I'd always assumed—and perhaps it was true, for NPCs other than Kizmel.

But six hours ago, she told me that she had a mysterious dream every night.

At that point, the possibility that someone in the real world could be role-playing as the dark elf knight disappeared entirely. Bringing up the topic of the beta test destroyed the illusion of a simple NPC, and my appearance now was completely different from the beta days. Someone on the development side would know that, and they wouldn't say something like "Your face is always the same at the end."

So assuming Kizmel was a true NPC, what did that dream mean to her? The function of dreams was still largely unexplained as far as humanity knew it. Did it mean that Kizmel's host program was still active and calculating while her process slept?

I challenged the "Jade Key" quest three times in the beta, and I remembered seeing her die in each case. Was that data accumulating in her system, and her program was simply trying to find some kind of logic to this memory that should not exist?

Did she remember the beta because she was an exceptional NPC?

Or had she gained her exceptional nature *because* those memories still existed within her?

A gentle night breeze through the gaps in the entrance flap ruffled my hair. I recalled the day this game of death began.

I left my first and only friend, Klein, back in the Town of Beginnings, raced through the open fields, and didn't stop until I reached the village of Horunka deep in the forest. I was heading straight for the quest that would reward me with an Anneal Blade—the weapon I still used today.

The quest was offered by the mother of a sickly child and required me to hunt plant monsters for a special herb. In the midst of that quest, I ran across another former beta tester for the first time. He invited me into a party, and when we'd collected enough herbs for one of us to turn in the quest, he tried to kill me with a monster trap.

Instead, I just barely survived and returned to the village to give the mother her herbs. When I did the same quest in the beta, I took my sword and raced off for the next place of interest, but for some reason, this time I watched her prepare the medicine and followed her into the child's room next door.

As I watched the sick little child NPC named Agatha slowly recover thanks to the potion, I recalled how I had cared for my sister when she was sickly. The emotions that had been building up inside of me since I learned that I was trapped in a game of death suddenly burst forth, and I wept into the blankets of the bed. Agatha reached over, looking concerned, and rubbed my head, over and over and over until I stopped...

"..."

I took another deep breath and pushed the memories out of my mind.

Kizmel and Asuna were lined up together, fast asleep like sisters. After bathing and eating, we went back out into the forest and, with Kizmel's help, completed all the quests we picked up in Zumfut. We'd have to turn them in later, but after a solid four hours fighting spiders, treants, and wolves, they must have been exhausted. Did NPCs even have a fatigue stat, though?

I could have stood to sleep some more myself, but there was another mission to be undertaken tonight. I crawled along the floor, slipping out of the entrance with a minimum of disturbance, and took another deep breath.

That lungful of crisp, cold air shook me fully awake, and I snuck away through the night camp. I passed the now-familiar night guards with a wave and headed through the canyon into the forest for the third time today.

The Forest of Wavering Mists was dangerous at night; when the heavy mists rolled in, there was nothing to see but a blue-gray haze. I had a solid grasp of the terrain by now, though. I proceeded through the forest, mindful of the presence of monsters, and in less than ten minutes, I reached the familiar staircase leading back down to the second floor.

Bathed in pale moonlight, the stone structure appeared to be empty, but as I drew nearer, a silhouette melted out of otherwise thin air from the shadow of one of the pillars. This player's Hiding skill was on par with Kizmel and her cloak of invisibility.

The person I was meeting grinned, three painted whiskers crinkling beneath her heavy hood.

"Seven seconds late, Kii-boy."

"Sorry. Blame it on the train driver."

Her hood shook ruefully at my earnest attempt at humor.

"I can sell you some better jokes, if you're looking to improve."

"No thanks, I'll manage with what I've got. I hate to rush you, but...did you learn anything about what I asked for?"

"Always the impatient one, you are. The hastiest rats are the ones that don't make it back to the hole."

My grinning guest hopped up onto a collapsed pillar nearby and crossed her legs. I took a position leaning against the pillar facing her.

Argo the Rat was the first, and best, information agent in Aincrad. I'd known her for a long time (if a month counted as "long") but barely knew anything about her personally. I was pretty sure she was a girl, pretty sure she was somewhere between her late teens or early twenties, and pretty sure she was also a beta tester. She collected information from her beta experience, as well as nuggets bought from me and other testers, and compiled them into her own series of strategy guides that she sold through NPC item shops throughout the game. Most important of all to remember was her motto: Any information with a price would be sold.

That meant that if I asked Argo to sell me personal information, like her height, weight, favorite foods, skill layout, and so on, she would do it...as long as I paid the price.

Fortunately, the cost of the information I wanted in this case was quite reasonable. I pulled a five-hundred-col coin out of my coat pocket and flipped it to her, which she caught nimbly between two fingers. The coin danced along her fingers before disappearing entirely.

"Thankee. I'll tell ya what I know so far." The grin on her whiskered face disappeared, and she continued in a low voice, "Seems like there's only one player who joined up with Lind's Dragon Knights Brigade since reaching the third floor. His name's Morte, he uses a one-handed sword, and he never takes off his metal coif, even in town…That's all I got for ya."

"Morte," I repeated, thinking that it sounded like a type of candy.

A man wearing a coif. That had to be the man I saw in Lind's team of five the other day. He was probably a beta tester like me and was feeding Lind information on the campaign quest…

Suddenly, I recognized a contradiction there.

"Wait…but at the last strategy meeting, which I assume you were watching, the DKB still had eighteen members, same as during the last boss fight. So if Morte joined, does that mean one person dropped out? And was it voluntary or forced?"

Argo waved my suspicions away.

"Nope, the eighteen at the meeting were the same from the boss battle."

"…Do you know all the names and faces of the DKB?"

"I wouldn't be much of an informant if I didn't. Same goes for the ALS."

"It was silly of me to ask," I said, raising my hands in surrender. "So…Morte just joined up on the third floor but wasn't present at the meeting. And the reason for that is…"

"A mystery to me, 'fraid to say."

"You'd have to ask him or Lind to know why, I guess."

I played back my recollection of the strategy meeting in Zumfut three days ago. But I couldn't remember the faces of the other seventeen dressed in blue. Part of it was that I sat at the very top row of the stadium-style seating, so I could only see the backs of the others present. And halfway through the meeting, most of my mind power was spent worrying about the imminent explosion of anger from Asuna.

Still, it had to be a problem that, forty days after this game started, we were still putting our lives in the hands of other players whose names or faces we couldn't even recall.

I wasn't going to get into the business of selling information anytime soon, but it wouldn't be a bad idea to put more effort into remembering people. It just wasn't a skill that came naturally to me.

I asked Argo, "So how did this Morte character get into the guild?"

"Looks like he requested to join. The day after the third floor opened up, Lind introduced him as a new recruit to the other main members of the DKB guild—well, technically it wasn't a guild yet at that point."

"Ahh...So it was Lind who took his request directly. I'm surprised that Lind would just rubber-stamp him like that. Maybe Morte is just that powerful...How does he seem to you?"

It was just an idle, curious question, but Argo grimaced atop the stone pillar and rocked back and forth.

"The thing is, I haven't seen this Morte fellow for myself yet...I staked out the pub the DKB is using as a base in Zumfut, but I haven't seen anyone who matches the description."

"Wow...If even you can't spot him, he must be trying to hide himself..."

"That's what I think. If it's on Lind's orders, then perhaps he's supposed to be a secret weapon to help them jump past the ALS. I'm sure he'll be involved in the boss battle, so at the very least, I'll check him out there."

"Please do. Well, I've certainly gotten my money's worth of info here."

"Glad to hear it," Argo grinned. She hopped off the five-foot-tall pillar without a sound and raised her hand to her face. The coin I'd paid to her just a minute ago was there in her fingertips, glinting in the moonlight.

"By the way, Kii-boy, any interest in selling some intel?"

"Oh? What kind?"

"Like where you've been staying with A-chan since we got here."

"Not selling that," I replied immediately. Argo grinned again.

"I see. You didn't immediately deny that you were lodging with her. But don't worry; I won't go selling that juicy nugget."

7

SOMEONE ONCE WARNED ME THAT A FIVE-MINUTE chat with the Rat would end up costing you a hundred col. I wondered how many times that would happen for me to learn my lesson.

I trudged back into the forest, shoulders slumped. Every once in a while, I stopped to open my window and ensure that I was moving in the right direction—in the last four days, I'd mapped almost 90 percent of the forest.

Getting back to the dark elf camp didn't require a map by now, but that wasn't my destination. I set down coordinates in the center of the Forest of Wavering Mists, which covered the southern half of the floor, and made my way carefully for them. I was not heading for the town of Zumfut or the queen spider's cave but the large forest elf camp to which the imposter soldier had fled. I couldn't bemoan my carelessness now; this was the real point of my solo night expedition.

I had experienced "Infiltration," the sixth quest of the campaign, during the beta. To complete it, I had to steal a scroll of orders from the forest elf camp. In it were top-secret commands from the leader of the forest elves, who was situated in their home base at the north end of the forest. Having done it before, I knew the contents of that "top secret" mission: to use a disguising charm and steal the Jade Key from the dark elf base. If that mission failed, the agent was to wait for reinforcements and lead an assault on the base...

In the beta, I was in a party of four with another four hired dark elves, and we led a midnight assault on the camp, killing all the enemy soldiers to steal those orders. If I tried to complete this quest with Asuna, Kizmel, and some of the soldiers from the base, we would probably have to use the same method.

But now, I felt a strong resistance to that idea. I didn't want to force Asuna and Kizmel to kill a number of forest elves in their sleep, even if they were our foes.

I knew that was an illogical, meaningless, emotional reaction. And it was easy to imagine that if I completed the quest on my own and informed Asuna of that fact, she would be furious.

I could have explained it all to her, attempted to convince her. But Asuna—and likely Kizmel as well—would have resisted my request that she stay back at the base. And the way I intended to beat the quest was only possible alone.

My idea was not to steal it by the sword. I was going to sneak into the camp by myself and take it through stealth.

Now that a single fatal mistake was permanent, and I couldn't just revive myself at Blackiron Palace, it was the height of stupidity to take such a risk on nothing more than an emotional reaction. Even worse, this quest had no bearing on clearing this floor and furthering the ultimate goal of freedom.

But even if I hadn't teamed up with Asuna on the second floor and had adventured alone on the third floor instead—which easily could have happened on a whim—I would still be tackling this campaign quest alone. I'd have to complete the quest to steal the orders as a solo player anyway.

I had plans. Based on the title of "Infiltration," one assumed that the quest had been designed for a player to beat it without drawing his sword. By the end of the beta, the orthodox strategy was for a player with a good Hiding skill to sneak in and do the job alone. At this point in time, my level and skill proficiency was far above what the quest required.

On the other hand, there was no guarantee I wouldn't cause an accident of some kind and be forced to fight the entire camp on my own.

But after the week and five days I'd spent with Asuna on the last two floors, I understood that my personal values were shifting. In the past, I cared for nothing but effective mob farming, quick quest completion, and maximum money and experience gain. That was what I needed to tackle the ultimate goal of winning my freedom—fixed parties and the background stories of quests were extraneous fluff that only got in my way.

But what if there was something here just as important as efficiency? I couldn't express what that thing might be in words yet. But here I was, hiking through the woods at night alone, for that mysterious sake. Something I treasured enough to open myself to incredible risk.

Despite being lost in thought, I managed to travel over a mile without drawing the attention of any nocturnal mobs and arrived at my destination just before one o'clock.

The forest elf advance camp was located atop a hill looking over a river that ran through the Forest of Wavering Mists from east to west. There was only one entrance to the semicircular fence that surrounded the camp. There were guards manning the entrance, of course, and my Hiding skill was woefully inadequate to sneak through without detection. I might be able to bump the Hide Rate number a bit with Kizmel's Mistmoon Cloak, but from what she told me, it did not work quite as well against other elves. I supposed that was why the forest elves had to use disguises to sneak into the dark elf base—a similar invisibility cloak would not have done the trick.

So infiltration via the entrance was off the table. The brittle fence, made of dead, whitened wood, would split with a deafening crack when pushed against, so climbing was not an option either. But as a proper beater, I knew the way in, of course. If I descended to the river a safe distance away from the camp and snuck along the waterside, I could position myself just below the tent with the item I needed. There was a sheer cliff over twenty feet tall from the foot of the canyon to the top of the hill, but there were roots conveniently placed just so an opportunistic climber could scale the wall, as long as he wasn't outfitted in heavy armor—theoretically.

If I managed to pull this off, I could sell that nugget of info to Argo for the second volume of her Elf War guide. Lind's guild were the only other people attempting the campaign for now, but the information would be very useful to those who wanted to catch up to the frontline team.

I circled the hill from the south to the west and found a relatively gentle slope that would take me down to the foot of the cliff. I stared out at the pleasantly gushing river, spotting the occasional shadow of a large fish beneath the surface. I was in the mood to fish one up and salt grill it, but I didn't have the Fishing or Cooking skills. That reminded me of Asuna's hobby Tailoring skill, but I had to scold myself for getting distracted during a mission. I steadily slipped along the rocky shore.

After about ten yards along the water, aided by nothing but a pale sliver of moonlight, I came to a dead stop. It felt like someone was watching me.

I scanned the surroundings, but there was no silhouette of man, beast, or insect, either in front, behind, or above. The idea that I could "feel" someone's gaze was even more impossible in Aincrad than in real life. Detecting other players and moving objects in the game required direct visual, auditory, or olfactory signals from the NerveGear. It was absolutely impossible for me to notice that someone was watching.

Even still, I couldn't move. I was held still by a dread chill, something I'd felt several times since being trapped in this game of death. I continued to look around, rooted to the spot.

In the end, what made the difference—possibly between life and death—was the Spotting Bonus mod I'd earned for reaching skill level 100 in Search. As the name suggested, this mod made it easier to find hiding targets.

As my gaze swept from right to left, I detected a vague, shifting outline in the shadows on the far bank. I stared hard at the spot, wide-eyed. If someone was hiding there, my constant gaze would be dropping their Hide Rate. But if I was focusing on the wrong spot, my would-be attacker could slip around my backside and catch me by surprise.

For ten seconds I concentrated on the far bank, resisting the urge to turn around.

Suddenly, color bloomed within the shadow. A figure appeared as though from the cliff itself. The mod was meant to help me against the forest elves, but the cursor that appeared over the figure was not the yellow of an NPC or the red of a monster, but the green of a player.

After the cursor, I saw the dark gray of scale mail. It did not appear to be metallic but close-fitting scales that clung to his torso and gleamed wetly. His gloves and boots were made of the same material. A longsword hung at his left hip. And dangling from his head to his shoulders, a fine, chain mail coif...

"...You," I growled.

It was him. The man I saw in Lind's party three days earlier. The newest member of the DKB, who I'd just learned was named Morte.

But why would he be here in the middle of the night, all alone?

No.

There was something more important than that. Morte was hiding—and he stayed hidden as I entered the canyon.

Hiding itself was not a crime. I did the exact same thing when Kibaou's party passed by in the queen spider's dungeon. But Morte did not happen to be here and then hastily hid when he noticed me coming. If that was the case, I'd have noticed him first, thanks to the Search Distance Bonus mod I earned at skill level 50—or at the very least, we'd have detected each other simultaneously.

No, Morte had been hiding here all along. He expected someone to come through this passage at the foot of the hill behind the camp. Someone who had to be pursuing the Elf War quest, on the side of the dark elves. Only two people on the third floor currently fit that description: me and Asuna.

He was waiting for us.

Pure, righteous fire must have poured out of my eyes in that moment of understanding. Just twenty feet away, his right hand twitched.

But in the next instant, a bright, cheery voice that was completely out of place broke the silence.

"Welp, looks like I got spotted!"

Just a bit louder, and his voice would have been audible in the camp above. He lifted his fish-scale gloves and made a show of pretend applause without actually making a clapping noise.

"Pretty good job. I've never been revealed like that at this distance, in this kind of darkness. And you totally spotted me on a sheer hunch, not with your eyes at first, right? You don't have some kind of Sixth Sense extra skill, do you?"

His voice contained both a playful, boyish innocence and a grating theatricality. He was about my height and size, but I couldn't see his face due to the coif that hung down to his nose.

Upon closer look, the border of that metal hood was torn and ragged, with fine tendrils of chain that hung down like locks of hair. It was probably just the design of the item, not a sign of wear and tear, but it looked creepy all the same.

"You're Morte from the DKB?"

He had been using reasonably polite speech, so I could have stood to return that level of courtesy, but I wasn't in the mood after learning that he'd been trying to spy on me. The man didn't seem to be bothered by my brusque response. He did the show of fake applause again.

"You get your info quick for not hanging around the town at all. Yep, the name's Morte. Guess you could say naming's not my *forte*, ha-ha-haaa."

I recoiled a bit at his slimy evasion of my curiosity. I'd never run across someone of his type in *SAO*. Klein had been a breezy, lighthearted kind of guy before the game turned deadly, but compared to him, this Morte fellow was totally inscrutable.

He bowed politely, dangling chains jingling. I took a step toward him.

"I don't suppose I need to introduce myself. Seems clear you were hiding with the expectation that I'd pass through the area."

"Ha-ha, why, you make it sound like I was waiting to ambush you, Kirito," he said casually, indicating that he knew my name. There was a wide grin on his face, but as usual, I couldn't see his eyes.

"Sound like? That's what you were doing," I accused, barely holding back the bile I felt rising to my throat for reasons unknown. Morte's smile never wavered, and he shuffled his shoulders in some strange mockery of a dance.

"Well, you got me, then."

"...Was it on Lind's orders?"

"Ha-ha-ha, y'know, he's got potential, I'll admit. But no, this was my decision. I mean, Lind's not a beater; he just wouldn't understand. How could he know that you'd pass by this river to sneak into the camp?"

"But you did know...which means you were a beta tester, too."

"Just call me a beater. It's a stupid nickname, but that's what I like about it. Did you know that 'beater' is the name of a kitchen implement in English? Like for beating eggs. Makes you want to whip everything in this game up into a froth, ha-ha-haaa!"

Even at low volume, his bubbly voice was crystal clear, and he remained steadfastly polite. So why did I find it all so annoying?

I took a step back, intending to demonstrate that I would not put up with his silly chatter without a point.

"If you were waiting for me, then get to the point. As I know you're aware, I've got a quest to complete."

"Gosh, this Elf War quest really takes me back. I hear that only like three people managed to complete the whole questline in the beta, including you. I ran out of time before I could finish."

Morte held up his hands in panic as I started to turn my heel. "Whoa, hang on, friend. I'll tell you what I want. What I'm asking for."

"...Asking for?"

"That's right. Look, here's the deal: I'm asking if you can forget about this quest and turn back."

I stared at him in stunned silence, then shrugged my shoulders just as theatrically as he had earlier. "You know I'm not going to turn back now. And what does it have to do with you? The DKB's working the forest elf side of the campaign, right?"

One of the basic rules of the Elf War quest was that each party proceeded individually. The main bases of either side were instanced maps, and it was impossible for Party A completing quests on the dark elf story line to somehow disadvantage Party B as they worked the forest elf story. Yes, the individual quests sometimes overlapped at non-instanced locations, such as the spider cave earlier and this camp now, so that multiple parties could be in the same place at the same time. But with a bit of waiting, everyone could complete their goals safely. Besides, Lind's team was on the forest elf side, so they wouldn't even get the quest to steal the commander's orders.

So whether I completed this quest or not, it would have no effect on Morte or the DKB.

But Morte simply grinned, jangling the metal threads of his hood, and wagged an index finger back and forth.

"Actually, it *is* my business. I'm afraid I can't actually explain how it is, though. I mean, if I could do that, I wouldn't have been hiding, would I? Ha-ha-haaa."

"...What?" I nearly overlooked the menace hidden within his statement. My eyes narrowed. "You're saying...that you weren't hiding in order to call out to me and negotiate...but to interfere and stop me by force?"

"Why, that would be silly of me. I mean, I'd get tagged as an orange player if that was the case. That'd be an awful easy way to get kicked out of the guild I just joined, ha-ha-haaa," he said, waving his hips back and forth. But the menace returned with his next statement.

"The thing is, I won't get flagged just for performing a song, see? I really like singing, you understand. If they had karaoke in one of these towns, I'd be hanging out there all the time."

…*What are you…?* I wondered, eyes narrowed. Then I understood.

Morte was threatening to cause a racket as I was trying to infiltrate the camp. The dozen or so elven warriors sleeping in their tents would immediately burst out, ready to fight. If I was spotted by that many foes at once, it would be difficult to escape. If I was unlucky, and they surrounded me…

"So you're trying to MPK me," I murmured, remembering what had happened forty days before. The face of the man who'd tried to kill me remotely through a monster trap steadily faded from my memory, replaced by Morte's.

But the mysterious beta tester didn't play up his devious plot. He grinned disarmingly.

"Oh, I'm not suggesting anything that awful. I mean, you'd be able to slip right out of their grasp, wouldn't you? All I'm asking is that you hold off on that quest for a day."

"A day…? What difference will a day make?"

"Well…"

He slowly held up his hands and made an X over his mouth with his index fingers.

"Sorry! That's a secret! But you'll understand, come tomorrow. All I'm asking is that you go back to wherever you're hanging out for tonight."

"And if I refuse?"

I was getting tired of his slimy, smarmy nature. I wanted this meeting over with.

Morte took the fingers off his mouth and pointed them directly at me instead.

"Why don't we settle it the way we did in the beta? You remember how guild members would settle disputes, don't you?"

"...With a coin toss?"

"Ha-haaa, but you wouldn't accept that result, would you? No, I'm talking about the other way. The cool, exciting way."

It took me two seconds to realize what Morte was suggesting. For another two seconds, I glared at the swordsman on the far bank. When I spoke, my voice was as low and gravelly as it could go.

"...Are you being serious?"

"Oh, my serious switch is always on, partner."

He lowered his left index finger and used it to trace the pommel of the Anneal Blade at his waist.

That settled it. Morte was proposing a duel.

The idea of a dueling system itself was not new to MMORPGs. Many games that otherwise removed the ability to PK implemented a dueling system where two players could agree to fight. In *SAO*, PK-ing was legal outside of towns, but anyone who committed a PK became a criminal, which turned their cursor from green to orange and prevented them from entering town.

Duels, on the other hand, were legal anywhere and invoked no crimes. They happened with wild frequency in the beta, as a test of strength or a means of settling scores.

But once the retail game came out, I had never challenged or been challenged to a duel. Even in a duel, when a player's HP reached zero, he was dead. Which meant that in today's Aincrad...

"...If we duel, one of us will die."

Morte practically squirmed in delight at my observation.

"Well, Kirito, if you insist...Kidding, kidding! I mean, a complete duel would be super-dangerous, right? Oh, but it's much safer in half-finish mode. That way, the duel ends as soon as one of us gets to the yellow zone. A lot milder, if you ask me, ha-ha-haaa."

Aside from the "full-finish mode," in which a duel continued until one player's HP reached zero, there were a "half-finish mode," where an HP bar down to 50 percent ended the duel, and a "first-strike mode," where the first clean hit won the match.

Unsurprisingly, the over-before-you-blinked first-strike mode and the unsatisfying half-finish mode were rarely ever used in the beta; I'd forgotten they even existed. But as Morte said, a half-finish duel would not result in death.

It was dangerous to allow yourself to lose 50 percent of your HP, the very numerical embodiment of life in Aincrad. But if I refused, Morte could make good on his promise to shout and disrupt my quest. Then again, even if I dueled him and won, he could still break his word and shout anyway...

"Is there any guarantee that if you lose, you won't interfere with me?" I demanded, staring into the darkness beneath the coif. He shook his head in a show of mock affront.

"Oh, I wouldn't pull a dirty trick like that. If I broke my word, I'd be too Morte-fied to show my face again. But let's say I lose. Then my HP would be at fifty percent, you know? It'll take a while for a healing potion to kick in, and I wouldn't be able to shout, because the long ears in camp might hear, and some other mobs might approach from behind, ha-ha-haaa."

"..."

It was a weak guarantee.

I had the choice of not exposing myself to needless danger and swallowing Morte's condition for today. There was no reason I had to complete this infiltration quest tonight. According to the road map Kibaou set up at the strategy meeting, this was the day (now that midnight had passed) that we started on the labyrinth, and in two days, we would be challenging the boss. There was plenty of time for questing.

But if I left the camp then, I would never know Morte's motive for staking out this location.

It was easy for a beta tester to assume that if I didn't show up in town, I was busy with the Elf War quest. But it was impossible to predict with such accuracy that I'd be visiting this camp on this night. It would be one thing if he bought that information from Argo, but I had just met her, and she would have offered to sell me the fact that Morte bought my info.

That made it highly likely that Morte was waiting in this spot for hours and hours on nothing more than an assumption that I'd come by. Why would he go to all that trouble just to prevent me from finishing one single chapter in a lengthy quest?

It wasn't curiosity that made me stay but a feeling of peril, a need to understand before I could leave. I nodded.

"...All right. Let's have a duel to see who leaves. But you need to throw in another chip on the wager."

"Oh? Awful pushy of you."

"Of course. If I lose, I have to call off the quest, but if you lose, you just go home. That doesn't add up."

"I see, I see. So what am I supposed to wager, then?"

"I want an explanation that makes sense. I want to know why you did this."

Morte rocked back and forth like some kind of toy, but he soon nodded in agreement.

"Allll righty. I can't guarantee that you'll understand it, though."

Now that we'd reached a deal, I had no obligation to listen to his prattling. But I couldn't just tear into him right away, either. If the sound of our sword fight reached the camp above, the elves would wake up and be on alert.

"Let's change spots, then. There's a place upstream with some open space."

"Roger that. Man, I'm getting so nervous thinking about a duel with *the* Kirito. Can we take a photo to commemorate after the fight? Oh, wait, we haven't gotten to the point where screenshot items show up yet. Aww, too bad."

I took my eyes off Morte and his babbling and started walking upstream, to the south. Morte sprang after me on the far bank of the river, dancing along.

After about thirty yards, there was a circular clearing next to the river. Usually such landmarks held something of interest— perhaps this was a good place for fishing—but this wasn't the time to be peering into the water.

I proceeded to the center of the clearing and turned to my

right. Morte turned to me at the same time. The grin was still slapped across his face, but I felt that his concentration was just a bit sharper than before.

"Okeydoke, so I'll send the request."

He swept his right hand to open the menu and smoothly tapped a series of commands. A smaller sub-window popped up before me. It read: MORTE HAS CHALLENGED YOU TO A ONE-ON-ONE DUEL. DO YOU ACCEPT? YES/NO.

At least the name Morte wasn't an alias. Sadly, my knowledge database was woefully inadequate to indicate if his chosen name was supposed to mean anything.

Above the YES/NO prompt was a series of check boxes for the duel mode. The center option, for a half-strength finish, was selected. I looked up.

Across fifteen feet of water, Morte still had his coif on. The more space covered by headgear, the better the defense, but the poorer the visibility and hearing. The chain veil hung down below his nose, so he must have been staring through it like netting. Combined with the darkness of night, his vision must have been severely affected.

My vision and hearing were at maximum efficiency because I wore no helmet, but a good blow to my head would cause tremendous damage. On the other hand, even if I did have a helmet, a clean hit to the head would still cause temporary dazing and stun effects. Such negative status effects were fatal to a solo player anyway, so my thought process was simple: avoid head damage at all cost, and bothersome headgear will only make it harder to avoid, so no headgear.

In that sense, Morte's coif was baffling. Compared to one of the bucket-like great helms, the coif offered little protection, but it robbed just as much eyesight. There had to be some reason that he wouldn't remove it, even in a duel.

It belatedly occurred to me that I should have dared him to add the reason for his coif to the bet, but now was the time to concentrate. I flipped my mental switch to battle mode.

Without taking my eyes off of him, I slammed the YES button. The sub-window shifted and began a sixty-second countdown.

During the beta, many complained that a full-minute timer before the duel began was overkill. But the development team made no moves to shorten the timer while the test was running.

Despite not having dueled in months, the timer still felt long to me. I drew my Anneal Blade +8, held it up in an orthodox mid-level stance, and spread my legs front and rear.

But Morte showed no signs of drawing his blade, despite the active countdown. He just stood there, watching. Just as I began to wonder what he was up to, it hit me.

I had accepted his challenge without a second thought.

The most important factors for survival in *SAO* were knowledge and experience.

I had been in countless duels in the beta. I had acute knowledge of which skills were best for a one-on-one fight against a player and how to use them.

But this was different—a duel in the official release of *SAO*, where the stakes were deadly. And I had never once tried a duel in these circumstances.

Morte probably *had* been active in dueling since the change. He might have done it dozens of times. He knew something I didn't know. And based on that knowledge, he was simply staring at me, learning what he could from my stance and location, waiting to draw his sword until the last moment.

Nobody did that in the beta. We groaned over the length of the timer, chatting with any onlookers or waiting with boredom, then unleashing our best sword skills as soon as the timer hit zero. That was the duel I knew.

But after the moment forty-three days before that changed everything, the old way went out the window.

Sixty seconds: a span of time allotted to observe the enemy and formulate a strategy.

I glanced back down at the window hovering in front of my chest. The countdown was around forty-five seconds remaining.

Back to Morte. He stood straight, swaying slightly. I gleaned nothing from his stance. In comparison, I had my Anneal Blade held out in front of me, crouched slightly, center of weight leaning forward. What did he see in my stance? How would he read and react to my first movement? I could change my stance, but would that just give him more information instead?

I checked the counter: thirty-five seconds. That endless timer from the beta seemed to be ticking twice for every actual second now. There was no time for thinking. Could I signal a pause and request a do-over? No, I wasn't that shameless, and once the timer started, the duel was inevitable. I realized that I was losing my cool and starting to panic, and the first bead of virtual sweat trickled down my forehead.

Twenty-five seconds left. Perhaps I should give up on striking first and see what he did instead. There was fifteen feet of water separating us. It was certainly shallow enough to cross, but I could easily fall into a tumble just from running through it, to say nothing of striking with my sword. Morte wouldn't just rush across the water…

But hang on. Fifteen feet could be crossed quickly with the Sonic Leap skill. And if used right as the counter ended, there wouldn't be enough time to escape the accuracy range of the sword skill. Fortunately, Sonic Leap started with a high stance, and I had the blade held neutral, so he wouldn't know I was going to use it.

Ten seconds left. The countdown started to beep audibly with each second.

Five seconds. Morte finally drew his sword. His Anneal Blade had a slick gleam to it, the sign that he'd put a lot of work into upgrading it.

Four seconds. Morte swung the sword up into a careless high stance. The blade started glowing light green, the sign that he was about to use a sword skill. The stance and color meant…Sonic Leap.

Three seconds. Was his plan the same as mine? But the counter wasn't over yet. Hitting the opponent during the countdown to a duel outside of the safe haven of town was considered a criminal act. His cursor would go orange.

Two seconds. If I was going to evade, I had to jump to either side now. But I stayed pointed right at Morte and raised my sword to a high position. He probably intended to hold the premotion of the sword skill until the countdown finished, but he'd started far too early. It was going to cancel out before the duel began.

One second.

But just as the counter read 01, Morte leaped off the ground. The high-speed slash screamed across the water, green trail reflecting off the surface.

Then I understood.

There was no need to wait until zero to let the skill fly. If the blade hit the opponent's avatar and caused damage even a mere 0.001 seconds after the bell, it would not set off the criminal code. Morte understood that well and timed his move perfectly.

Zero.

A purple DUEL!! sign appeared over the river, but I did not see it. Morte's body, like some dark, monstrous bird, blocked my view.

I was planning to use Sonic Leap when the duel began. But that naive plan of mine was ultimately what saved me from the ignoble result of a defeat simultaneous to the start of the match.

Because I had my Anneal Blade held up, not yet in the motion for the skill, I just managed to turn it flat and absorb Morte's attack in time. If he'd hit me right on the head, it would have stunned me, if not consumed half my health right in one go, and left me unable to stop a follow-up attack.

A tremendous shock ran through both hands—right gripping the handle, left pushed against the flat of the blade for support.

Player sword skills had a special weight to them that far outclassed monster attacks. He didn't just rely on the system assistance for speed and power but jumped and swung downward for extra momentum. Orange sparks and green light exploded just inches from my eyes, clouding my vision.

Longswords were among the hardier one-handed weapons, but

they had a weakness. If a powerful shock hit the flat side of the blade head-on, there was a chance for the weapon's durability to drop to zero at once, resulting in the destruction of the item.

My sword creaked unpleasantly as it blocked Morte's Sonic Leap. But the faithful partner who had held fast since the first day of the game did not give. The blow was so powerful that if I hadn't just upgraded the durability stat to +4, it might have broken.

"Grrh…"

I grunted and gritted my teeth, waiting for the enemy's sword skill to finish. If I could withstand the blow fully, Morte would be left in a brief, vulnerable pause. The lights exploding before my eyes grew steadily weaker, bit by bit…

But just before the skill was finished, my right foot, planted in the soft ground of the riverbank, finally gave in to the pressure and slipped. My body sank abruptly, and I had to leap backward to avoid falling. At the exact same moment, the glow left Morte's blade.

As soon as I landed, I leaped forward.

When his pause ended, Morte lifted his sword again.

"Raaah!"

"Shwaa!"

After the two shouts was a single clash. Twice, then three times, the night forest rang with the eerie, resonant *clang* of two copies of the same exact blade striking with force.

Even without the benefit of a sword skill, Morte's talent with the blade was considerable. He wasted no effort with his swings, aiming for my critical points with the shortest possible movements. I had to parry and sidestep desperately just to block these unique attacks, somewhere between slashes and thrusts.

He had the clear upper hand in the number of strikes, but that suited me fine. The more I concentrated on this battle, the quicker the remnants of that ugly panic faded. Once my mind was as honed as a steel trap, I would be ready to counterattack.

"*Shuaa!*"

Furious at the failure of his surprise attack, Morte emitted a bloodcurdling screech and thrust at my heart. Thrusts were difficult to parry due to the precise timing required, but they were much easier to sidestep. I stepped forward and to my right, tilting sideways, and swept my blade from left to right as I evaded his sword point.

My sword, upgraded to +4 sharpness, cut through the fish-scale armor and knocked down Morte's HP bar for the first time. It wouldn't have been enough damage to win even under the first-strike rules, but at least I finally had the advantage.

"*Shhhu!*"

Morte leaped backward, hissing in anger. Finally, that cocky leer was gone from his lips. If I let him take his distance, he might come back with another unexpected trick. I darted after him, keeping within sword range. Morte attempted more of his thrusting swings, but I calmly dodged or deflected each one.

As Morte retreated, still attacking, his boots hit water. I didn't have the time to look at the ground, but I knew I'd pushed him against the river. If I put more pressure on him, I could lure him into another major attack. And if I evaded that, I could actually use a sword skill to finish him off...

A large splash sounded nearby, but it was not Morte falling into the water. In fact, he was already quite deep into the river. His right leg had just kicked up a wave of water; a sheet of tiny drops danced before my eyes.

He was using this blinding water attack either to flank me or to launch a counterattack. I retreated quickly, staying away from the droplets and watching Morte closely. Beyond the spray of water, I caught a flash of purple. It was...

...not a sword skill. That was the purple of the menu.

I had no idea what he was doing, opening his menu in the midst of a duel, but that was not possible with his sword in his right hand. I didn't see it in his left hand, either. Perhaps he had returned it to its sheath—no, not that either. He must have dropped it into the river and had to open his window to get a new one. But I wasn't kind enough to let this opportunity pass.

"Raaah!"

I held my sword high overhead, screaming with animal aggression. The same instant, a faint swishing hit my ears.

That sound was familiar. But by the time I realized what it was, I couldn't stop the slash already in progress.

The flying sheet of droplets finally reached its peak and began to fall. On the other side, Morte's left hand held a round shield that hadn't been there a second before. It was of a simple, unassuming design, but the spun-metal luster spoke faithfully to its quality as an item.

My sword descended and struck Morte's shield dead center, generating a vivid clash effect. We both staggered backward, as though pushed by the sparks of the collision.

I desperately fought back against the virtual inertia, hoping to recover even a tenth of a second faster than my foe.

No matter how familiar Morte was with the menu, he couldn't possibly have opened his equipment screen, hit the left-hand icon, then picked out the shield from his inventory when it appeared, all in that brief amount of time. The swishing noise I'd heard was none other than the Quick Change mod that allowed him to flip to a preset equipment loadout with a single button.

Which meant the shield wasn't the only thing in his hands now. I couldn't see his right hand, as it was held behind his body, but it must have been clutching a new sword. The instant he recovered his footing, Morte would launch a counterattack.

I tried my hardest to tilt over to my right within my stagger animation, hoping to evade his attack and deliver my own counter. In *SAO*, the book on shield users was to flank them on the shield side. In the ultimate first-person combat game, the shield was both a trusty source of defense and a wall that blocked eyesight. Plus, nobody won a duel by doing nothing more than defending. This was basic information I'd learned way back in the beta, but the basics were useful in any situation.

Back from his delay just a step before me, Morte's twisted lips opened and emitted a fierce shriek.

"Shaoo!"

His gauntleted hand struck like a black viper. I expected one of his vertical thrusting slices, so I jumped off my left foot, sidestepping to the right. His round shield rose upward with his attacking motion, and I tried to swipe a counter below it.

Whoosh!

A dull, heavy roar cut the air.

Morte's right hand was not clutching a sword. And his swing trajectory was not vertical.

It was an ax, a dense blade on the end of a handle over two feet long. I recognized that individual type of ax: a Harsh Hatchet.

He spun like a top, ax whirling on a flat plane right for my left flank. I couldn't dodge or defend. The dark head of the ax struck me squarely in the side, in the exact same spot that I'd hit Morte just moments earlier.

The blow was heavy enough to lift me off the ground and took away close to 20 percent of my health, as well as knocking me into another stagger.

The overwhelmingly powerful two-handed ax was a favorite of many players, but its one-handed counterpart was something of a niche weapon. Its power was equal to that of a one-handed sword, but without the benefit of thrust attacks. Its greatest bonus was the severe delaying effect its heavy attacks inflicted, but it was very hard to land them—unless you used a different weapon to lure the opponent into thinking you would only use thrusts, that is.

"Hrgh," I grunted, coming again to a belated realization.

Morte's repeated spamming of sword thrusts was nothing but a feint to set up this ax blow.

If true, that meant this Harsh Hatchet was his true main weapon, not the Anneal Blade. This was not an idle experiment without the actual weapon skill behind it—he would come after me with a sword skill next.

Morte's entire body twisted back on itself like some kind of rubber toy. The ax, held back at maximum tension, began to glow red.

"*Shahaaaa!!*"

With an unearthly screech, Morte unleashed the two-strike one-handed ax skill Double Cleave.

At nearly invisible speed, the ax rotated twice, striking my chest and stomach at nearly the same time. I blew backward like a pile of rags from what felt like an explosion within my body, slammed into a large boulder, and fell to the ground.

The stun icon flashed, and my field of vision blinked and blacked out in spots. My HP bar began to drop precipitously, stopping only just before the halfway mark.

The stun effect itself lasted only three seconds, but I still couldn't stand. A freezing chill stole into me from the two spots where I'd been hit, both glowing red with damage effects. Even my fingers and toes felt numb.

As I crawled on all fours, a pair of fish-scale-patterned boots lazily approached. The owner of those boots stopped just six feet away, and I looked up to see, within the dim shadow of the coif, the glint of his eyes for the first time.

"Oooh," came his voice, slick and derisive. "That's a shocker. Still not yellow after all of that? You're good. This ax is upgraded to be plus six to Heaviness, you know that? It can even slice through plate armor."

As Morte continued on in his smarmy but venomous tone, my fingers began to regain their strength, and I gripped the hilt of my sword again.

"Aren't you going to finish me?"

"Oh, now, you're not going to get me with that one. I skip on over and you break out your best counter to surprise me! Besides, just a simple love tap at the end would be a really unfitting end to a duel with you, wouldn't it? I'll wait here for you to stand up. Take your time!"

So he could sense my plan to aim for his legs. Resigned, I put a hand against the boulder behind me to get to my feet.

In a duel, six feet might as well have been point-blank range. But even at this close distance, Morte held his round shield and hatchet loosely, carelessly at his sides, with not a concern in the world. It was not the laziness of a superior position, but the confidence of experience.

Thinking back, even before the duel, Morte had me outclassed in every respect. Battlefield position, use of the countdown timer, first strike, battle placement and tactics, and hidden tricks up the sleeve: everything. He understood the way of the duel in the retail version of *SAO* far, far better than I did. He might have even chosen his character build for the express purpose of excelling in duels. Otherwise he wouldn't waste a skill slot so he could use a redundant weapon type.

"...!"

At that point, my mind passed through its current deep, narrow valley, and my breath caught in my throat.

If Morte was a dueling specialist, could it be that leaving my HP just a tick above halfway was not a coincidence, but an intentional move on his part?

A half-strength duel ended as soon as either combatant's HP dropped below 50 percent. Within the safe zone of a city, any attack that occurred after the results screen popped up would be automatically nullified, and outside of town, extra damage would be classified a crime, turning the attacker's cursor orange.

But according to my hazy memory, the exact moment a duel ended was not when the HP reached half. It was at the point that the normal attacks or sword skills' damage had taken over half of the opponent's HP.

Meaning that if I had 510 out of 1000 HP remaining, and I suffered a single attack worth 600 damage...the duel would be over, but my HP would go to 0, killing me, and leaving the opponent a legal green player.

If Morte had left me just a bit of health on purpose...

He was not hoping to win this duel and force me to leave my quest for another day.

He was planning, here and now...

To kill me.

A chill colder than any ice ran up my back, and for just a moment, I shivered.

Sensing this, Morte's lips twisted upward, and he exhaled a chuckle.

"Aha!"

It wasn't the first time another player had wanted to kill me.

On the first night in this game of death, I had formed a brief pickup party with another player, who attempted to murder me.

His plan was not to swing his sword at me, but to have me killed by a summoned crowd of monsters: an MPK, or monster player-kill. And before he used his Hiding skill to disappear, he told me he was sorry.

Of course, an apology did not excuse the act of murder. But at the very least, that partner of mine had made his choice bitterly, to ensure that he received the Anneal Blade that would help him survive, as soon as humanly possible.

But Morte had no tangible benefit to gain by killing me. If I lost in the duel, I was simply going to leave the infiltration quest for tomorrow, and even if I didn't believe his promise, whether I completed the quest or not had no actual effect on Morte.

Which meant he was a PKer in the truest sense: He killed for the sake of killing.

It was impossible. *SAO* was an inescapable, deadly trap. Morte was stuck in this digital prison just like the rest of us. If he killed another player in the group of clearers advancing our progress in the game, he only delayed the possibility that we beat the game and earned our freedom. Under that simple fact, the act of knowingly murdering another player meant that he did not actually seek to be free of this place.

"...You can't..." I murmured, but Morte cut me off with another cackle.

"Aha! Let's not have this conversation. Not when the going's so good! Show me something, Kirito. This isn't the end of the strongest man in the game, is it?"

He held up his ax and deftly spun it around with three fingers. Even with that cocky show, there were no weak points to attack. If I rushed him at once, he would hold up his shield and finish me with a counter. If that counter happened to be a sword skill powerful enough to deal over half of my HP in damage, I would die.

There was a way to avoid the worst-case scenario—if I resigned right away. I would lose the duel, but at least Morte wouldn't be able to avoid turning into an orange criminal if he hit me. He was involved with the DKB with some kind of plot in mind, and surely he couldn't stand for his cursor to change color. That was all wishful thinking, I knew.

I could acknowledge my lack of power and surrender in order to survive, or I could aim for a come-from-behind victory, find out what Morte was after, continue the quest, and salvage some measure of pride.

Sadly, if I chose the latter, I had no stock of plans or secret weapons to make use of. If anything, it was Morte who was likely to have more up his sleeve. The overlooked one-handed ax actually became a bonus in a PvP battle. I knew that I could recognize any longsword, scimitar, dagger, rapier, greataxe, or greatsword skill just based on the initiating motion, but there were some one-handed ax or one-handed hammer skills I didn't even know the name of. In fact, since we'd started pushing forward from the start of the game, I couldn't name a single player on the frontier who used a simple ax…

Something prickled in the back of my brain.

The way he flipped the ax around with his fingers.

I'd seen someone doing the same thing before, and recently—here on the third floor.

It wasn't during the strategy meeting in town. It was before that…when Asuna, Kizmel, and I hid in the corridor of the queen spider's cave, as a group passed by.

Ax in his right hand, round shield in the left. And a gray metal coif on his head.

That description fit Morte to a T. It had to be the same person.

But this was impossible. The man I'd seen flipping his ax around...*was traveling with Kibaou and the ALS.*

Just seven or eight hours later, I saw Morte in the midst of Lind's DKB. He did have the coif on, but no shield, and his weapon was a longsword. That's why I hadn't considered he might be the same person I'd seen with Kibaou. The thought never occurred to me.

That was because I—and many others in *SAO*—saw a player's main weapon as his defining feature. I was a swordsman. Asuna was a fencer. Agil was a double-handed axman. And Morte was both a swordsman and an axman.

Morte was using this dual nature to moonlight in both the DKB and ALS. He switched his weapons back and forth, helping with Lind and Kibaou's quests at the same time.

But why? Was it sheer altruism, an attempt to make good on his beta experience? If that was the case, was I just imagining the cold bloodlust I felt from him?

Or was he hiding some true motive, even deeper, vaster, and darker than I could imagine?

"...What...what are you...?" I whispered in a voice so quiet even I couldn't hear it. Morte tilted his head in confusion.

"Hmm? Hmm? Feeling more up to it now? Don't worry, we've got all the time in the world."

"...That's true. And the fight isn't over yet," I said, this time at an audible volume.

It was perilous to keep fighting without a plan for victory. If Morte wasn't a good person at heart, it was quite likely that he would actually kill me.

But my instincts told me that surrendering and leaving was an even more dangerous choice. If I didn't get to the bottom of Morte's hidden intentions and discover his connections, something irreparably awful could happen in the near future...or so I felt.

He smiled gleefully at my response. "That's right, that's the spirit. You never know how your hand's going to play until you turn over that river card. So shall we get down to it? Flippety-flip!"

"...Time for the showdown, then?" I asked, brandishing my Anneal Blade in front of me.

"Aha! Very nice. Too bad we don't have an audience, though. It's...showtiiiime!" Morte blurted, raising his shield and holding his ax behind his body. We were only standing six feet apart, so the tip of my sword nearly touched his shield.

The will of battle rose in the two metal objects, like an electric charge, until virtual sparks snapped into life—and I moved.

I leaped off my right foot, circling toward his dominant hand, against the theory of shield combat. Morte spun to his right, trying to keep the shield facing me.

I expected that response. In order to land a major sword skill, the foe needed to be knocked off balance, staggered. The quickest way to do that was with a normal attack with a high staggering effect, but Morte couldn't use that. Even a minor hit would knock my HP below half, ending the duel. If he wanted to knock me into an open position, he had to deflect my attack with his shield.

If anything, the fact that he'd met my flanking maneuver with his shield rather than his ax proved that he was trying to use the duel as a method of legal PK-ing. The knowledge that any mistake could literally prove fatal was like a needle of ice in my brain, but there was no turning back now. If I didn't make use of all my experience and ability, the worst would come true.

"R-raah!" I howled, raising the Anneal Blade high overhead.

It was the exact same upper-right slash I attempted to no benefit right after Morte used his Quick Change trick, and with an added yell to boot.

Morte confidently raised his shield in a defensive position. The two-foot-wide wall of steel hid the venomous leer he wore.

In order to ensure that a shield guard inflicted a delay effect on the opponent, you couldn't just hold it up—it had to be thrust out in a parrying motion, just as the enemy attack struck. With his shield held before his face, Morte couldn't see my upper half, but he could see the top of my sword.

Morte's every sense must be focused on my blade, timing the exact moment the slash began.

If even a tenth of his attention was anywhere other than my sword, if he wasn't planning on a perfectly timed guard, if he happened to notice the red glow suffusing my left fist...

I would die.

Showdown.

I thrust forward at the shield, not with my sword, but my clenched left fist—the quickest of all martial arts skills, Flash Blow.

At this moment, Morte's left arm would be relaxed, waiting for the right time to guard against my sword.

The brief, red uppercut hit the round shield along its lower left edge. A metallic shock echoed through the clearing, and the wall of steel disappeared.

In battle, there were three bad things that could happen to weapons or shields: Destruction, in which the item disappeared entirely; Snatching, in which the enemy stole it away; and Dropping, in which the item fell to the ground. Attempting to cause any of these negative effects was known as a "disarm" attempt.

In general, these attacks came from monsters. The lakeside Swamp Kobold Trappers halfway through the first floor killed more than a few players by knocking weapons loose into the sinking mud, then preying on their victims when they rushed to pick the weapons up.

Players could attempt to disarm as well, but it was very difficult to pull off. You could either aim at the hand holding the weapon or attempt to hit the weapon directly on its side. But in either case, it would not work unless the weapon was held loosely. And the only time a player didn't have a death grip on his weapon was just before initiating an attack.

Assisted by sheer luck, my Flash Blow caught that precise moment perfectly. The shield was ripped from Morte's left hand and went flying into the night air. The smile beneath that dangling coif was gone, and one of his canines glinted in anger.

My shield disarm was successful, but I couldn't stop there. His HP bar was still at over 90 percent.

My experience in man-on-man combat was far inferior to Morte's. But I was certain that based on his Quick Change settings, he had two basic combat patterns: longsword with no shield and ax with shield. I hoped that pushing him into an ax with no shield helped close that experience gap. I had to start an attack that would take a little over 40 percent of his health away. If I couldn't do that, I probably wouldn't last long enough to win.

But winning and losing, living and dying—these concepts were nothing more than distractions.

Just move forward!

"Rahhh!"

With a true roar of triumph, I swung my sword down at his left shoulder. Morte leaned backward in an attempt to evade, but the end of my augmented blade caught his black scale mail, leaving behind a glowing red sign of damage. His HP was down to 85 percent.

"Shah!" he hissed, lashing back with his Harsh Hatchet. But all one-handed ax attacks swung in a wide arc and weren't very handy at such close range. I ducked to avoid the howling swipe. The name "hatchet" made the ax sound small, but its thick blade felt deadly as it brushed my hair overhead. Still in my crouch, I swiped at his legs. The tip of the sword smashed against the shins of his boots, two quick whacks. It wasn't nearly enough damage to cause localized effects, but it was another 5 percent of his health. Even better, the blow to his feet caused Morte to stumble.

Now!

I jumped up and assumed a sword skill premotion.

Morte's ax momentum was still to the right. If he attempted another horizontal swipe, my skill would fire off first...

But wait. Morte had overturned things I took for granted, again and again. Perhaps my assumption that the heavy swings of an ax weren't meant for ultra-tight range fell into that pattern, too.

I held my sword back from its position over my left shoulder. At the same moment, Morte's eyes gleamed from the shadows over his face.

"*Shaiiii!*"

With a scream, his ax flew directly for my face. But not blade-first. It was a square-based spike, embedded in the pommel of the ax. The vicious backhand thrust came much faster than the horizontal swing had.

"Hnng!!"

I gritted my teeth and pulled my head back desperately. The spike grazed my forehead and trailed to the left. Beyond the crimson light trailed by that attack, I fixed my sight on Morte's defenseless body.

By pulling my sword just an inch farther over my left shoulder, the system recognized the initiation of a skill, and the blade kicked into a high-pitched whine, glowing silver.

"...Raaaah!"

The Anneal Blade came down nearly vertical, hitting Morte on his right breast. The blade instantly shot back into a high position and sliced vertically again, this time catching him deep on the left. Then it leaped once again, and—deeper and heavier than before—buried itself in the dead center of his chest with a satisfying *wham!* It was a three-part sword skill I'd just learned two days before: Sharp Nail.

Three vertical slashes glowed red in Morte's chest, like the claw marks of some gigantic beast. Just as when I'd been hit by his Double Cleave, his body shot through the air to land on the surface of the water, back first.

The HP bar over his head rapidly fell, only to halt just a tick above 50 percent.

I knew that if I chased him down and just grazed him with the tip of my sword, I'd win the duel, but I couldn't move from my current position. I'd concentrated so hard on this attack that my brain buzzed with a high-pitched whine, and my heart raced in my chest.

Even Morte lay prone in the water for a good three seconds, but he quickly jumped to his feet with an enormous splash and inspected his body.

The three damage marks silently spit out little red blobs of light. Within moments, the spots disappeared, and he looked up at me, thirty feet away. His mouth twisted, and I caught a glimpse of gnashing teeth before the familiar leer returned.

"...Well, well, well, I can see why everyone says you're the best. When you knocked my shield off, was that the martial arts skill people talked about in the beta?"

"...Good question," I replied, straight-faced. I didn't want to give him any extra information. Morte's grin widened, and he spun the ax in his fingers again.

"By the way, if I asked where to learn that skill, would you actually tell me?"

"..."

I was tempted to tell him the location of the bearded master hidden in the mountains of the second floor, just to see if he would go and get the facial markings that didn't disappear until the quest was completed, but thought better of it.

"As long as you tell me who you practiced dueling with."

Morte's grin turned sour.

Unlike martial arts, the ways of the duel couldn't be taught by an NPC. For Morte to have gained this much knowledge and experience with dueling, he had to have conducted an astonishing number of duels with another player since the opening of the retail version of *SAO*. And if I had to guess, that player probably shared the same scheme as Morte, who was splitting time between both the DKB and ALS.

"Why, of *course* I'd love to tell you," he said, wriggling like a snake in the midst of the river, "but the truth is, I practice on the creatures of the forest. I only know the basics, see."

"Seemed like Lind really took a shine to you."

I decided not to mention Kibaou's name as well. The ends of Morte's mouth curled upward, and he whispered, "That's not entirely true, but I do like him quite a bit...Anywho, we've only got a hot minute left in our duel. What's the plan, boss? Shall we wrap this one up?"

"I think so. Our HP are about even, anyway," I growled.

I mentioned remaining HP as a means to remind him that he wasn't the only one who could attempt a PK through the duel, though it was a bluff, of course. Morte probably did mean to murder me, but I didn't have the conviction to kill another player, knowing it would be fatal, even against someone who intended me harm.

As if seeing right through my bluff, the ax wielder shook his head, rattling the hanging chains on his headgear, and grinned even wider.

"Very good, very good. I really admire that about you, Kirito. Besides, it's not a true fight until you go best of three. So here goes the tiebreaker!"

He spun his Harsh Hatchet around a few times and held it at a diagonal, still standing in eight inches of water. Was he calling my bluff or continuing the fight even with the threat of death over his head? In either case, there was no turning back. I lifted my Anneal Blade up again and into my customary mid-level stance.

Directly top and center in my view was the duel countdown, which read forty seconds left. As far as I could tell, our HP bars were at equal amounts. If time ran out, the victory would go to whoever had more HP left, but it rounded to increments of 5 percent, so that would probably result in a draw. Morte certainly wouldn't like that outcome—he was going to come after me at some point in the next forty seconds.

I wrung the last of my exhausted concentration out to focus on Morte. Now that I had played my martial arts hand, there was nothing left up my sleeve, but I had no idea if the same was true of him. Would he dart in at once or inch closer bit by bit?

In the next instant, Morte betrayed my expectations once again.

He leaned backward and held his ax high in the air. The crude blade took on a turquoise glow—a sword skill. But we were over thirty feet apart. Even Sonic Leap, the longest-range skill I was aware of, could not close that gap. Was there some ultra-long leaping attack available to the one-handed ax that I didn't know about?

I could dodge, defend, or move forward. For half a second, I couldn't decide—a half second that could have resulted in the loss of my life.

But the duel was ended in the most surprising of ways.

Just as he was about to activate his sword skill, Morte's head spun to the left, as though drawn by a sudden noise. He lowered the ax, automatically disengaging the skill, and the turquoise glow dissipated into the air off the blade.

"…"

I stood still, sword at the ready, while Morte held his hand up and waved it around.

"Well, dreadfully sorry, but it looks like I'm a bit out of time prematurely."

"…We still have thirty seconds left."

"Actually, you'd be surprised how long thirty seconds can be. I mean, if you counted one for every second, it would take you thirty seconds to finish, ah-ha-haaa," he blathered, then crouched and plunged a hand into the water at his feet. When it emerged, it was holding the Anneal Blade he'd abandoned near the start of the duel. He calmly straightened up and returned the sword to its sheath, as if he had known it would be in that precise spot in the water. Next he walked a few yards upstream and picked up the round shield where it lay at the waterside.

"Well, I've got to be off. That was fun; we should definitely try it again sometime."

As he walked away, I managed to find my voice. "I assume that if we draw, you'll let me do the quest at the camp."

Morte lifted his left hand without turning back and said, "Be my guest. You might find it a bit difficult, however. Ah-ha-ha-ha-haaa."

The duel counter hit zero, and Morte's retreating form was blocked by a large purple window announcing the results. As I expected, it was a draw. By the time the window vanished, the ax warrior was gone.

After a few more moments with my sword raised, I finally stretched and relaxed. My first step was to pull a recovery potion from my waistpouch, pop the cork, and drink it down. Its flavor, like acerola cherry juice spiked with tea, was not something I particularly savored, but that was a small price to pay for being able to recover full HP from a single bottle.

Next, I trained my ears but heard only the burbling of the river, the rustling of the trees, chirping insects, and a far-off wolf howl. There was nothing out of place that might have suggested why Morte called the duel off.

And what did he mean that completing the quest would be "a bit difficult"? Was he pretending to leave the duel only to sabotage my quest attempt after all? And why was Morte so insistent on keeping me away from the forest elf camp, going to the trouble of hiding and challenging me to a duel?

Now that it had ended in a tie, I couldn't get the answers to his plot out of him. On the other hand, at least I hadn't been killed. Ultimately, I couldn't decide what he was after. The result was a draw, but a fair observer probably had to admit that I'd lost.

"...I need to work harder," I muttered, putting my sword in the sheath over my back. But the truth was, I felt a resistance to training for PvP duels. As I'd learned today, even the half-finish setting could have fatal consequences. Whether it was legal or not, now that our lives were *our lives*, being experienced in PvP simply meant being skilled at murdering...

I shook my head and let out the breath I'd been holding in my lungs, sucking in the fresh night air. I could decide what to do about Morte's apparent duplicity with the DKB and ALS once I returned to the dark elf base and talked with Asuna. I couldn't completely rule out the possibility that he might simply be helping both groups out of a feeling of duty—yet.

With one last glance upstream in the direction Morte left, I spun the other way. A tall cliff loomed on the right side downstream, on top of which could be seen the flickering campfires of the elves.

Absent any unexpected intrusions, it wasn't a very hard quest. I just had to climb the cliff, sneak into the leader's tent, grab the orders off the table, then descend the cliff.

Wary of any followers behind me, I approached the cliff again. The slope at my side grew taller and taller as I neared, until it eclipsed my own height, when suddenly—

"Who are all of you?!" a voice bellowed, and I froze in alarm.

Did one of the night guards spot me? Even when I'm dozens of yards from the camp?

I instinctively leaped to my right to hide against the bottom of the cliff. I looked around wildly but didn't see any red enemy cursors.

Next, I realized that the voice had come from quite a long way away. Besides, I was alone—why would he say "all of you"? So... what did it mean?

I slowly rose, popping my head just a bit over the lip of the rising cliffside and staring at the foot of the circular hill.

On the opposite end of where I was hiding, at the entrance of the path that wound up the hill from the south, I noticed a number of silhouettes. There was a series of shouts that I couldn't make out. It seemed like two groups of five or six were facing off.

It was probably teams of dark elves and forest elves—perhaps another battle event, like the one that started the "Jade Key" quest. But as far as I knew, the "Infiltration" quest didn't involve anything of the sort.

Curious, I stared harder at the grouped figures. My Search skill kicked in and brought the distant sight into sharper detail, as well as summoning a number of color cursors, barely thicker than tiny strings.

A groan left my throat when I recognized the color of the cursors.

"Wha...?"

They were all green.

Both groups were players.

8

THE LARGE FOREST ELF CAMP AT THE TOP OF THE hill was not an instanced map generated only for players in the middle of a quest, so it was perfectly plausible for multiple parties to find themselves there at the same time. In addition to that, it was also possible for them to get into a fight over who was allowed to finish their quest first.

But with only a few dozen players this far ahead in the game, the odds of that happening were slim, and as far as I knew, Asuna and I and the DKB were the only people following the Elf War questline at the moment. Was this some kind of internal squabble in the DKB?

I didn't want to get any closer, but even in the few seconds I watched, the two groups were getting visibly heated. If they raised any more noise, the elf warriors atop the hill would notice and be on alert. Reluctantly, I climbed over the lip of the cliff, feeling it necessary to get a better idea of what was happening.

I was at the western edge of the hill, a semicircle protruding to the south. The dozen or so players were congregated at the southern end. There were only a few bushes at best for cover in the straight line between us, so I couldn't approach directly. My best bet was to head into the forest surrounding the hill and swing to the southeast, avoiding the gnarled roots and shrubs along the way.

Thanks to my recent life in the forest, I managed to circle

around to my destination in less than a minute without tripping over any roots. The massive trees at the lip of the hill were ideal for hiding, so I hugged the back of a particularly thick trunk and activated my Hiding skill before peering around.

A small path ran east and west at the foot of the hill, and branched north to climb toward the camp. At that T-intersection—actually an upside-down T from my perspective—the two groups glared at each other. There were six on the east side, while on the west side there were over ten. If this was DKB infighting, this had to represent about the entire guild.

Based on what I could see by the dim moonlight, they hadn't drawn their swords yet. But some of the members did have hands on the hilts of their weapons, and there was raw anger in the open air. The furious shouts and insults from before had stopped, but the mood seemed even more tense because of it.

One of the players from the east side of the intersection stepped forward. His long hair was tied behind his head, and a slender scimitar was strapped to his waist—this was clearly Lind, leader of the Dragon Knights Brigade. I could only see his silhouette from my position, but it seemed like the angular outline of his face was even more tense than usual.

Lind stared at the opposing party and spoke quietly. "There's no use continuing to argue about this. We reached this point first. As the rules state, we have the right to proceed with this quest before you."

It felt like a very stuffy, formal statement for an internal argument. And sure enough, another man leaped out from the other group, jabbing an accusatory finger at Lind.

"First? Ya only beat us by a couple seconds at best!"

—!!

I nearly gasped in astonishment but closed my mouth just in time.

That morningstar-like spiked hair, longsword on his back, and aggressive Kansai dialect. It could be none other than Kibaou, leader of the Aincrad Liberation Squad.

Which meant the dozen or so players across from Lind's half dozen were the ALS. But why were they here?

Kibaou's next outraged bellow halfway answered that question.

"And whaddaya mean, rules? If you made 'em up yourself, we don't gotta play along! We've got ta beat this assault quest, too, no matter what it takes!"

Beat this assault quest.

The words were loud and clear. So the ALS were on the Elf War campaign, too—and on the dark elf side, to boot. But during the field boss battle that day—well, the day before—the ALS members had seemed disinterested in the campaign when I'd asked around about it.

That left two possibilities. Either all members of the guild were ordered to keep quiet about it, or they'd started the campaign yesterday afternoon and reached the sixth chapter already in just twelve hours.

I couldn't believe the latter. The "Jade Key" quest was over in the span of a single battle, but "Vanquishing the Spiders," "The Flower Offering," "Emergency Orders," and "The Missing Soldier" couldn't *all* be completed in half a day without the presence of someone who truly knew what they were doing...perhaps a former beta tester taking the lead...

Which they had.

Yes, the ALS had a member who fit that profile, too.

Morte, the coif-wearing man, who'd traded blows with me just minutes before, a little ways down the river. He'd hidden his face and switched his weapons in order to slip into both guilds. If he was the guide for the DKB, nothing said he couldn't do the same for the ALS.

So had Kibaou beseeched Morte for assistance in order to blaze through all the quests in the campaign up to this point? But he was steadfast in his stance not to associate with former testers. Why would he ignore that philosophy so suddenly?

Confused, I watched the two leaders face off. Now it was Lind's turn to lose his cool.

"Whether it's quests or hunting grounds, first come, first served is the obvious way of things! If you're going to be the leader of a guild, you've got to follow your good conscience, Kibaou!"

At this haughty, sweeping statement by Lind's standards, Kibaou flashed his canines in a snarl.

"Conscience? You're gonna talk ta me about conscience, Lind?" He crossed his thick arms and leaned back, staring up at Lind's face with menace in his eyes. "Well, I got a bone to pick about that. Ever since we got here, you been hidin' the fact that this elf quest is crucial ta beatin' the floor boss!"

Wha—?!

I clamped my mouth shut before the startled exclamation could burst out of it and into the virtual night air.

Certainly, proceeding through the campaign carried its own rewards, such as money, experience, and loot, but it certainly wasn't necessary to beat the boss. The chamber door in the labyrinth tower would open whether the quest was active or not, the boss was available to fight, and if defeated, the way to the fourth floor was open. At least, that's how it was in the beta...but it was also that way on the first two floors in the retail game. And even if it had been changed for the third floor, nobody here could possibly know that for a fact yet.

But Kibaou continued his rant, full of the righteous anger of one absolutely convinced of his facts.

"You remember what happened five days ago. The raid nearly got wiped out 'cos we didn't know the boss cow had turned inta three. That same trap's been laid here on the third floor. Some trap that's gonna do us in if we ain't cleared the elf quest and got whatever items it gives out. You knew it was true, and ya didn't say a word of it during that strategy meeting! So where's your conscience now, huh?"

"...N..."

No! I had to prevent myself from screaming, right along with Lind.

At the very least, none of the quests in the campaign I completed on the third floor in the beta had any bearing on the floor boss. It was possible that the rewards had been altered since then, but the only ones who could confirm it were those who'd completed all ten chapters available on this floor, and it was unthinkable that anyone could have done that much in just four days. It was one thing to rush through the early quests, but the ninth and tenth were long affairs that required an entire day to complete.

Which meant this hypothetical life-saving item Kibaou was talking about was probably false info someone had maliciously fed him. And I had a bad feeling I knew who would do that...

"No! I don't know what you're talking about!" Lind shouted, breaking me out of my thoughts. I focused on the scene ahead of me, and even from this distance, I could make out the folds on his brow as he glared back at Kibaou. "The DKB have only been doing the campaign quest for the experience and rewards! I didn't mention it because there was no reason to bring it up!"

"Hah! And the *rewards* are items we'll need to beat the boss, no doubt!" Kibaou shot back, leaning forward and meeting Lind's gaze furiously. "You just wanna call the shots for all the frontline players, that's all! Well, I ain't gonna let *you* tell me the rules. We're goin' first, so wait here like good lil' boys!"

Kibaou turned forcefully toward the hill, but Lind's hand caught his shoulder. Instantly, the guild members behind both men bristled.

"Wait, don't do this! Maybe you're not aware of this, but these key spots disappear once someone completes the quest, only to reappear elsewhere at random. If we wait here, we won't be able to finish the quest after you!"

At this, Kibaou reached out and grabbed Lind's shirt at the chest. "This is what I mean about you not sharin' details! What you're sayin' is that if *you* do the quest first, we don't get to do it!"

"As is our right for being the first to the camp!"

"And I'm tellin' you, I ain't followin' your rules! If you want, we can set up some rules that make this whole kit and caboodle *real* simple!"

"...And what do you mean by that?"

...Oh no.

They were both absolutely furious. Shivata in the DKB might be able to step in before things got truly dangerous, but there was no officer with a similarly cool head on the ALS side.

I certainly couldn't improve the situation by trying to interfere now. But what options were available to defuse this perilous situation? I gritted my teeth hard.

Suddenly, Lind's words from just moments ago replayed within my head.

These key spots disappear once someone completes the quest.

From what I heard later, Kibaou and Lind stood there holding the other, neither backing down an inch, and all eighteen players present nearly ended up in a footrace up the hill to see who could ransack the forest elf camp first.

As allies of the forest elves, the DKB were supposed to deliver supplies from the home base to the captain in charge of the camp. But the ALS, working the dark elf story line, needed to steal the commander's orders, the same as me.

Meaning that if both guilds charged in at once, the dozen-plus forest elf warriors in the camp would be friendly NPCs to the DKCB but powerful (yet not as much as elite types like Kizmel) monsters to the ALS. If that happened, Lind's party of six would witness an open battle between Kibaou's dozen and the forest elves.

How would the DKB react?

The most sensible reaction would be to ignore the allied NPCs and deliver the supplies to the captain, thus completing the quest. It wasn't clear if the camp would simply vanish on the spot as soon as the quest ended, or if the captain would even be able to accept the supplies if he was stuck in combat, but at least that would do as little damage as possible to the frontline group as a whole.

But depending on the mental state of Lind and the DKB, the worst was also possible: siding with the forest elves and turning their swords on the ALS.

If the six DKB members joined with the dozen or so forest elves, their power would be about equal to the twelve ALS warriors. Since they weren't going to calmly challenge each other through the duel system, players on either side would turn into orange criminal players. At that point, there would be no stopping the infighting. We might be on the verge of the first top player killed since the first-floor boss battle...and at the hands of another player. If that happened, the frontline clearers would never again be a unified group.

Fortunately, that dire outcome for the state of our advancement in the game was avoided at the last moment.

Just as Kibaou and Lind began to climb the hill, each trying to push the other back, the elf camp simply disappeared, as though by magic—though according to *SAO*'s story, it probably *was* elven magic.

The two guild leaders and their sixteen followers, all comically locked in place in sprinting poses, stared dumbfounded at the top of the hill.

Eventually, a single player came trotting down the moonlit path. The moment they saw the face of the player who'd just beaten both guilds to the punch and completed the quest in the camp, no doubt that all present had one thought on their minds.

Not him again.

Faced with eighteen pairs of eyes, I was much less comfortable than I let on.

As soon as I made up my mind to beat them to the quest, I took the following actions.

I ran back through the forest the way I'd come, only several times faster, then sped along the river until I was directly beneath the camp. From there, I scrambled up the twenty-foot cliff. Once inside the camp, I made my way around the preset guard routines and snuck into the captain's tent. Careful not to wake the sleeping leader in the back, I snatched the sheet of orders off the table in the center of the tent. Once out in the open again, I retraced my steps around the guards and descended the cliff behind the camp.

It sounded simple when put like that, but if I hadn't learned the details from someone else during the beta test, I would certainly have been spotted in the process. Once I set foot back down on the riverside mud and the quest log updated, I nearly fell to the ground with relief.

A part of me wanted to just slip away and return to the base. But if I was going to help avert disaster between the DKB and ALS, I couldn't just spirit the camp away and leave. It had to be made clear to all that someone had completed the quest—or as good as completed, since it wasn't official until I reported to the dark elf commander.

So I climbed back up the cliff again, where the entire camp was vanishing in a poof of green light. Anyone else who wanted to finish the "Infiltration" quest or deliver supplies to the forest elf captain would have to find the camp in its new, randomized location, following the new marker on their maps. No matter where it appeared, there would be a way to sneak in the rear, but this cliff-climbing location was the only one I knew well. Even Argo the Rat would have a difficult time providing detailed maps for this part of her strategy guide series.

I crossed the hilltop, now bare of even a single fence, and descended the path to the foot of the hill.

Stopping a slight distance away from the stunned looks of the two guilds, I opened my window to check the time. It had taken just under five minutes to steal the commander's orders, traversal time included. Meaning that Lind and Kibaou had spent at least that much extra time trying to convince the other of his logic since I left the scene. Sadly for them, that effort had gone to waste.

Window closed and my hands in my pockets, I tried to put on as casual an attitude as I could.

"Sorry, I just finished this quest. You'll have to look for the camp elsewhere."

Lind's face went pale, while Kibaou's only grew darker. By the light of the moon, it was hard to tell which of them was angrier.

As I might have suspected, the first to speak was Kibaou, he of the blinding rage against all former beta testers.

"...No wonder I ain't seen ya around. The little beater boy was busy with the campaign. And just like this fool with the topknot, you knew we needed a quest reward ta beat the boss and didn't see fit ta tell anyone." Kibaou elbowed one of his DKB cohorts out of the way and glared back and forth at me and Lind. "In the end, y'all don't give a fig for rescuin' all eight thousand folks trapped in this game; that's all secondary to ya. Yer only among the top players so y'all can get your weapons and items and lord it over the rest of us, nothin' more. Yer just like all the other beaters what up an' vanished from the Town of Beginnings on the very first day. You ain't got the right to pretend yer inheritin' Diavel's lead!"

He'd been keeping his volume low prior to this, but now that the camp was gone, all restraint went out the window. As Kibaou's torrent of rage spilled forth, the ALS members at his back shouted encouragement and called Lind a cosplay freak.

The taunts about Diavel's will and cosplay were aimed squarely at Lind, who had dyed his hair blue in honor of the late knight. Even after I'd snuck in and nicked the quest from under their noses, their rage was still focused on the DKB.

Lind's face was clearly pale, even under the moonlight. His slender eyes were burning with anger, and his teeth were gritted hard.

But he did not explode in kind. He held out his hand to stifle any return shouts from the DKB team. Perhaps he felt ashamed of his attempt to force their way ahead to the camp. In any case, he showed great restraint in holding back, but the internal tension must have been unbelievably high.

He sucked in a deep breath, held it for several seconds, and let it out, then spoke, his voice tense but low.

"Kibaou. I will repeat myself: None of the DKB members, including me, had any idea that the rewards from the campaign quest would be crucial to defeating the boss. Where did you get this information?"

But Kibaou, still in the midst of his outburst of rage, ignored that question.

"Nice try, but I ain't fallin' for it! You're just thinkin' you can monopolize all that info for yerselves!"

"I just told you, that is not the case!"

They headed into a fresh round of angry shouts. I watched the back-and-forth, frustrated by this turn of events.

The "clearers" might be a handy shorthand term for those players who were active in advancing our progress in the game, but they were not a unified force.

There were the DKB, a group of handpicked elites; the ALS, who focused on expanding their group; Agil's neutral team; and then me, the outcast beater, and my partner, Asuna. On top of that, there was Morte, who for reasons unknown, was moonlighting in both guilds to get them to advance in the campaign, and the person (or people) acting as his dueling partner.

Ironically, I recalled Kizmel's story about the background of this world and how the humans had split into nine different nations.

"Lind, Kibaou," I said. They stopped butting heads long enough to glare at me.

There were no magic words that would heal the wounds between these two groups—they were too far apart for that. And all magic had been lost from this castle since the Great Separation of old. All the foolish remnants of humanity could do was make use of what they could.

"You both know I'm a beater. So I know what the rewards of the Elf War quest are and what effects they have. But I'm not rushing through the campaign for the rewards. I'm doing it to level up and strengthen my equipment so I can beat the floor boss. I'm sure you didn't go through the trouble of the guild quest just so you could squabble like this."

As soon as I stopped speaking, Kibaou jabbed an index finger at me. "Don't talk down ta me, just after ya slipped in and stole this quest like some kinda sneak thief! How you gonna prove yer not after the item rewards?! Even as we stand here, I know that deep down, yer just dyin' to get on with the next quest!"

"I'm stopping the campaign at this point," I said flatly. Kibaou growled a wordless question, and Lind squinted at me, his brow furrowing. I removed my hand from my coat pocket and jabbed a thumb behind me—up the gentle hill and far into the distance, where the dark silhouette of the labyrinth tower loomed.

"I'm about to start tackling the labyrinth. And while you're stuck in the campaign quagmire, bickering every step of the way, I'll be ransacking all the chests and ores in the tower. Remember, I'm a beater—don't expect me to leave any of the good stuff. And if you don't catch up by the boss chamber, I'll gather my own group of players to take him down. I'm a beater and a front-runner, and I'll do things however I please."

I stopped talking and put my hand down, but no one spoke up. The silence that covered the hill had to be 20 percent surprise, 30 percent anger, and 50 percent exasperation. Even I felt like I was overdoing it with this speech, but it was necessary to bring this tension under control.

Again, it was Kibaou who reacted first.

"...Ya got to the sixth chapter of the quest, and now yer gonna abandon it?"

"That's right," I confirmed, feeling a guilty throb deep in my chest.

It was heartbreaking to leave in the middle of this lengthy quest sequence—there were ten on this floor, and dozens if you counted everything up to its finale on the ninth floor. The system would allow me to come back and resume after finishing the labyrinth, but I expected Kibaou to demand that I destroy the commander's orders I'd just stolen to prove that I wasn't secretly after the rewards. Once that story item was gone, I could never complete the "Infiltration" quest.

That wasn't the only thing. Giving up on the campaign quest here meant leaving Kizmel behind. Her help in our activities the last few days was predicated upon our assistance of the dark elf advance force in their fight against the forest elves. If we abandoned that mission, she would have no cause to help us anymore.

But that was just how big campaign questlines worked.

If a single quest was a book, then a campaign was a series that spanned several volumes. As long as we were in the process of reading that series, we were within the story. But close the book, and the setting and characters were out of reach. The items and experience were just window dressing. The true value of the campaign quest was how it gave flesh and blood to the virtual setting and turned it into a story…

As I hung my head, feeling gloomy, a high-pitched cry stabbed my ears.

"That's impossible!"

I looked up and saw a man in the midst of the ALS crowd, waving a fist around as he screamed. His skinny torso was clothed in the moss-green tunic of the guild and dark studded leather, and he wore a leather mask of the same color, which covered his face except for the eyes and mouth. He was obscured by the other members, so I couldn't see his weapon.

The man's screech was strangely familiar. "He's full of it! You can't get to the boss chamber on your own! He's just pretending to go to the labyrinth so he can finish the campaign behind our backs!"

The other ALS members, and some of the DKB, started to rustle uneasily. From what I could make out of their voices, most were skeptical of my statement.

The skinny man screeched again. "Don't let that beater lie to you! He's the reason Diavel died! Ignore him and focus on the campaign..."

"Shut up, Joe," Kibaou grumbled, and the masked man named Joe grudgingly lowered his arm. This opening gave Lind a chance to speak.

"...I'm well aware of your skill, Kirito, but even you cannot conquer the labyrinth on your own. I'm not in total agreement with the ALS, but I do find it hard to believe that you have given up on the campaign. As a former tester, you certainly understand the benefit of completing an extended quest series. Besides"—his sharp eyes scanned the area—"where is your partner? What if she took the story item and ran off to complete the quest while you're occupying our attention here?"

It was completely off the mark but difficult to deny. My partner—temporary party member, technically—was back at the dark elf base, sleeping in the tent next to Kizmel. There was no way to spirit her here to prove my innocence.

I had no choice but to stay silent as both guilds hurled accusations in my direction. As the volume grew louder and louder, I was struck by faint déjà vu. It was the same kind of massive public condemnation that surrounded Nezha of the Legend Braves after admitting to his upgrading scam just after the second-floor boss battle.

Back then, the cries had eventually demanded his life as payment. If the other Braves hadn't gone down on hands and knees to apologize with him, someone might actually have drawn their sword on Nezha.

Now that I thought about it, one of the reasons that terrible, tense scene had come about was the mysterious man in the black poncho who taught the Braves about the trick to swindling others through the upgrade system. His presence seemed eerily similar to that of Morte's in this case.

Was it possible that they were the same person?

If that was the case, Morte's motivations were definitely evil. He'd convinced both guilds to take part in the elf quest on opposite sides and got them to collide at that hill. And that meant he was hiding at the riverside hoping to prevent anyone—meaning me—from completing the quest and causing the camp to disappear.

But...

What did he possibly stand to gain by pitting the DKB and ALS against each other?

While we weren't a unified group, the frontline players had successfully beaten the first and second floors and were just about to reach the third labyrinth. Weakening the group with infighting would only delay our ability to beat this game and escape. It would have a much wider effect than just PK-ing me.

Did Morte...not want to escape this digital prison?

Could *anyone* really think that way?

"Say something!" came the high-pitched screech again. I raised my head. The man Kibaou had called Joe was shouting, his eyes blazing through the holes in the mask. "Where is she? I bet she's rushing ahead, finishing all the quests before anyone else! And if not, bring her out here to prove it!"

It was not me who answered that challenge, or Kibaou, or Lind.

A voice, quiet but strong willed, carried through the night air of the forest from the back of the group.

"If it's me you want, I'm right here."

Later—much, much later—Asuna told me, "If someone had drawn their sword, I might have gone orange," with a grin on her face.

Fortunately, it did not rain blood, but there was a fresh, different kind of tension that gripped the scene.

Both guilds were quite shocked, of course. But that was nothing compared to me. For an instant, I thought I had to be imagining that voice.

I stood dumbfounded on the path halfway up the hill, staring at the wall of players ahead. Eventually, the ALS members moved right, and the DKB members moved left, as though pushed by some invisible force.

The open path split east and west at the foot of the hill, and there was thick forest beyond that. Right across from the T-intersection was a particularly wide and ancient tree that dwarfed the others. From around the rear of that tree, whose trunk I had just been hiding behind as I spied on the group only minutes ago, a single figure emerged.

A red hooded cape tinged with gray. A dark crimson tunic and leather skirt. And at her waist, a silver rapier that glinted and shone bright, even in the dim light of the moon.

If she was hiding behind that same tree, then she couldn't have been there all along, but only during the ten minutes I snuck around into the camp, I speculated, to little benefit or point.

Lind and Kibaou joined the others in stepping back. With the path entirely clear, the intruder coolly stepped forward. Underneath her rippling hood, the light brown eyes were firm and resolute. There was no way to read the emotions within.

Asuna the fencer, sole woman of the frontline population and my current partner, stopped at my right side and spun around theatrically, then spoke to the crowd, her voice crisp and clear.

"As his partner, I too will be heading for the labyrinth. Once there, we will be looking for the boss chamber. As I recall, whoever finds it first gets to be raid leader."

At that, both Lind and Kibaou went pale, and the other sixteen stirred and muttered. In a way, her statement was even more grandiose than mine, but no one stepped up with accusations this time, partly because of the surprise of her sudden entrance, and partly because of the sheer presence of that glittering Chivalric Rapier on her belt. The knight's sword, far better than even my Anneal Blade +8, unleashed a ghostly pressure in the bluish light of the moon.

This reminded me that I was planning to inform the group that the elf base camps were capable of forging weapons just as good during the meeting four days ago, but didn't get the chance after Lind's demand that we join guilds separately. Of course, if I had done that, all the guild forces would have immediately set upon the campaign quest, and this exact scene might have played out the same way, only with twice the people involved.

Just as I started to distract myself by planning to study the strange, unfriendly blacksmith more before revealing my findings to the group, it happened.

"I…I know the truth!! In the first and second floors, they didn't bother to help map the tower, they just went around opening all the leftover chests! There's no way that going from one to two will make a difference in getting them to the boss room!!"

Again, the screech belonged to Joe from the ALS. Now that the group had shifted right, I could see his entire form. Hanging from his skinny waist was a sharply curved dagger. I recognized it as a Numb Dagger, a rare drop from the minotaurs of the second-floor labyrinth that had an occasional chance to stun upon hitting an enemy.

Now that I knew him as a dagger user, the memory came back to me. Joe was the one who claimed that Nezha's upgrade scam had caused someone to die…as well as the one who accused me of being a former beta tester back on the first floor. Sadly, I couldn't put his face to memory because of the mask, but based on his open antagonism, that was a name I needed to know. I felt slightly ashamed that it had taken me this long.

My worst habit and weakness was my tendency not to look at others' faces or bother to remember their names. Someday that was going to put me in danger. I focused on skinny, short Joe, burning his image into my mind.

Once I was certain that I would remember him the next time I saw him, I finally opened my mouth to speak for the first time in two minutes.

"If you think we can't reach the boss chamber on our own, Joe, then why don't you just let us go? We're going to the labyrinth, just as we announced."

"I am gonna let you go! C'mon, Kiba, let's stop wasting time and move on to the next—"

The obnoxious shriek was cut off by a stern glare from his guild leader.

"Don't make me repeat myself, Joe. Shut yer damn mouth," Kibaou growled, then turned to me and Asuna. He scratched at his cactus hair and grumbled, "I jus' don't know what's what anymore. You really think you can handle the boss without the campaign quest rewards? If there's any chance at all that we need 'em to tackle the boss, it ain't too late to wait and find out."

"You have a point," I agreed and stared appraisingly at each leader in turn. "But if testing out the reward loot is truly your aim, then either the DKB or ALS should abandon the quest. If you attempt to complete the dark elf and forest elf factions at the same time, you will clash again, like tonight. If you can discuss the matter and determine which of the two will step down, I'm willing to wait until we've done our homework."

Once again, the two guild leaders and their cohorts went pale. Joe was obliviously ready to screech another accusation, but the greatsword user next to him yanked on his arm to shut him up.

In truth, I wanted to announce that one man had successfully convinced both guilds to start on the campaign, but alas, I had no proof that the swordsman Morte who had just joined the DKB was the same person as the ax warrior I saw among Kibaou's party in the cave. If I made accusations on uncertain evidence, it would only complicate the situation.

I watched the two leaders closely, hiding my desperate prayer behind a carefully crafted sour expression. If Morte's aim was to pit the guilds against each other, then I needed to prevent the group of clearers from breaking apart. It wasn't out of some great desire for justice—I just knew that Morte was my sworn enemy. This was a continuation of our duel, playing out on a very different battleground.

Kibaou and Lind shared a look for about two seconds, then snorted simultaneously. The ALS leader looked away in a huff, and the DKB boss turned to me and shook his head.

"I'm afraid that will be impossible, Kirito. Perhaps if we were just starting, but we've both reached the sixth chapter of the questline. We would be losing out on too much to stop now."

I resisted the urge to drop my shoulders in disappointment and nodded with the same stoic look on my face. "I see. Then while you are butting heads, we will be racing through the labyrinth."

"It is a shame, but I have to assume you are bluffing. The game's labyrinths are not so easy that a party of two can reach the boss—even if they happen to be you two. I realize this is not the best timing to ask, but have you considered giving up on your stubborn refusal yet? Perhaps the time is right to stop insisting on your solo play and join a guild. As I stated the other day, however, you cannot both join the same guild, in the interest of balance."

You're going to bring that up now? Seriously?

I went pale—*separate guilds* was just the magic phrase that would set Asuna off. As I feared, the moment he said that, the silent fencer took a menacing step forward. But what she said took me by surprise.

"It's not just the two of us."

Before I even had time to wonder, the space just left of me, dyed in the pale blue moonlight, silently split open.

I'd seen this phenomenon, of the space turning inside out, four nights earlier in the forest outside of Zumfut. Well, technically, I only heard the rustling of the cape from behind me, but it was clearly the same ability at work.

Only one person could successfully hide in full moonlight, in the middle of an empty field, with the watchful eyes of nearly twenty players, for several minutes, without being spotted.

The cloak with the invisibility charm parted left and right, and a sheer, shiny head of pale purple hair like fine silk caught the moonlight. Next came an elegant breastplate of black metal with purple inlay. In her left hand and at her left hip were a kite shield and longsword, both with the rich shine of mithril. The bare skin of her arms and legs appeared to be deep navy blue in the darkness.

When she raised her head triumphantly, her side bangs rustled lightly, revealing a stunning beauty and long, narrow ears. Her onyx eyes stared down the speechless group, and the *third* member of our party spoke in a sharp voice.

"I am Kizmel, a royal knight of the Pagoda Knights Brigade in the service of the kingdom of Lyusula!"

She extended her right arm from the cape in the direction of me and Asuna.

"I have pledged my support to the human warriors Kirito and Asuna as they venture forth to the Pillar of the Heavens! Even the stoutest guardians within the tower shall be as helpless as the morning dew before my blade!"

If they were at the sixth quest of the campaign, both the DKB and ALS must have recognized the name Kizmel mentioned as the nation beneath the dark elf queen's rule. The "Pillar of the Heavens" was descriptive enough to be an obvious term for the labyrinth tower.

What I couldn't tell was exactly why every guild member present was stunned into silence—whether it was Kizmel's beauty, the fact that an NPC knew our names, or the overwhelming power of the level-16 elite monster.

Probably all of the above, I decided. Lind staggered back a step or two, his face as pale as ice.

"A...are you sure you want to stand there, Kirito?"

"Huh? Why wouldn't I?"

"That dark elf's cursor is pitch-black...She must be a higher level than even the elite mob from the very first quest..."

Now I understood. To me and Asuna and the ALS members on the dark elf side of the campaign, Kizmel's color cursor was the yellow shade that signified an NPC. But Lind and the DKB were on the forest elf side, so it would be the red of an enemy monster. Depending on the level difference between the player and target, a red cursor would change shades all the way from light pink to dark crimson. Now that the elite knight had leveled up during our time together, she must have seemed nearly black to the level-15 Lind.

Kibaou glanced back and forth from the retreating Lind to Kizmel, cloak rippling in the night breeze. He took a few steps backward himself and hissed at his rival.

"Hey! Is it true her cursor's black?"

"Yes...I doubt we could defeat her as an entire party."

"That's crazy...How'd they get such a whopper ta work with 'em?" he moaned.

Kizmel must have heard him, because she turned to me and whispered, "Your human language is even more complex than I knew."

That was probably a comment on Kibaou's Kansai dialect. Whatever language engine Kizmel's AI used must only work with standard Japanese, so half of Kibaou's words had to be indecipherable to her.

I chuckled briefly, then realized something.

The group had been throwing around technical terms about the game: quests, campaigns, story items, and so on. These all pointed to the truth of the matter—that this was a virtual world existing only within a server in the real world. They suggested that the floating castle Aincrad was not a slice of the world set adrift into the sky by the Great Separation, but was merely the setting of this VRMMO game called *Sword Art Online*.

Of course, Kizmel had no knowledge of any of this. She was

born and raised in this world as a dark elf and fought her way to knighthood. Who knew how she interpreted the words of the game's players? Could we be certain that her interpretation did not do any damage to the AI controlling her?

Lind and Kibaou stepped down the hill to rejoin their partners, coming together for a deep discussion.

Now was the time to say to Kizmel what I hadn't been able to say—assuming I really thought of her not as an NPC assistant, but a partner...a friend.

"Kizmel," I muttered. There must have been something telling in my voice, for the dark elf knight and the fencer both turned to look at me. "Listen...Neither Asuna nor I were born in this castle. We were brought here from a far-off place, and we're fighting to get back home to our world."

Asuna sucked in a sharp breath. I reached out to brush the back of Kizmel's hand, facing her directly.

The elf knight stared back at me, slightly puzzled. There was no way to know what kind of information processing was happening behind those onyx-black pools.

Maybe I shouldn't have said that. Perhaps the GM will show up out of nowhere, pull her away, and reinitialize her.

After an eternity of silent seconds, Kizmel's luscious lips parted.

"Of course I know that."

"...Huh...?"

"I chose not to ask you about it until now. It is the last great charm that humanity has, is it not? To summon warriors from a foreign land and have them fight to unify all of the Pillars of the Heavens as one...We dark elves are much the same—we carry on a long battle to protect all of the secret keys from the forest elves and preserve the seal on the Sanctuary..."

"...Um...I...guess so...?"

Kizmel's description was a simple interpretation of the *SAO* incident in terms that made sense to the setting of the game, but I didn't see any reason to go overturning her understanding in order to make it clearer to her. Instead, I agreed with her explanation, and she smiled.

"We have teleportation charms that allow us to travel between floors, so we have no use for the Pillars of the Heavens that you humans are so fixated upon. However, if you wish, I will assist you in your quest. But only for a price." Her smile grew wider, and she looked back and forth at both of us. "Tell me of the land where you were born someday. What your families were like and how you were raised."

"...Yeah, sure. I promise," I said, struck by a sudden thought. What was the point of stressing that Aincrad was only a virtual world and a game? To Kizmel, and to Asuna and me, this world *was* the only reality. The game lingo "quest" was merely a human-language term for duty. What was wrong with that?

"And we'll also teach you all about our human language. If we go fighting in the labyrinth—that's what we call the Pillar of the Heavens—you're going to need to know our terms."

"I would very much like that," Kizmel replied, and I could sense Asuna smiling.

"Sorry about the wait. We've come to a decision," Lind announced, and the three of us looked back down the hill. The scimitar user clearly did not wish to get any closer to Kizmel, but he overcame his hesitation to climb a few steps up the slope.

"To get right to the point...the Dragon Knights Brigade and Aincrad Liberation Squad have both decided to abandon the campaign quest."

What?

I was mildly—no, significantly—surprised, but I made sure not to let that show on my face.

"However, it is still necessary to investigate whether or not the benefits of the campaign might be crucial to defeating the floor boss. We would like for your group to handle that duty."

What?

Again, I kept my face straight. In return, I asked him, "That's fine with me, but what are you going to do now?"

Lind looked uncomfortable, and Kibaou filled the awkward silence with an angry, resigned bellow. "That's obvious! We're gonna go map out the labyrinth! If we left it to y'all and someone died in an accident, I wouldn't sleep well at night!"

"...I see," I said, finally breaking my stoic expression with a wry smile. Asuna sighed and muttered, "That's one way of putting it."

But it was probably the best choice. The mysterious Morte did not show up, but he was probably still registered with the DKB while maintaining connections to the ALS. If both guilds continued with the campaign, it only left Morte with more opportunities to fan the flames of their rivalry. I had to get proof of Morte's plot so that I could expose him publicly and force the truth out of him.

Speaking of antagonistic characters, I looked around for Joe, wondering how he was taking this decision. I spotted him at the edge of the ALS group, back turned and hands folded behind his head in an obvious sulking pose. Once again, I couldn't help but be impressed at Kibaou's leadership that he could manage a handful like him in the guild.

Rather than actually saying that aloud, I took a deep breath and turned to Lind. "All right. Today's the nineteenth, and we were planning to tackle the boss on the twenty-first. We'll aim to finish the campaign by the evening of the twentieth and report the results. You'll have to trust our information, of course."

Now it was Lind's turn to give an awkward, stiff smile. "I'm not going to quibble about that at this point. Kirito, earlier you said that you were going to do what needed to be done as a front-runner. It pains me to admit it, but...you reminded me of Diavel."

He bit his lip several times before finally continuing. "In the very first strategy meeting down in Tolbana on the first floor, Diavel said that we had to beat the boss and get to the second floor to show everyone that the game could be beaten. That it was our duty as the best players. I...I thought I was carrying out his will. To create the guild he would have started and raise it to be the best...That was my duty..."

The other DKB members like Hafner and Shivata, and even the ALS, listened in silence to Lind's rare confession of his innermost feelings. When he raised his head again, there was a new light of determination in his eyes as he stared at me. The question that followed caught me by surprise.

"I think this is a good time to ask. You were the one who heard Diavel's dying words. What did he say...at the very end?"

I couldn't answer right away.

It wasn't because I'd forgotten, of course. But it was such a short and obvious message that I couldn't tell if it contained what Lind was hoping to hear.

Obviously, I couldn't make something up or refuse to tell him. I closed my eyes for a moment and summoned a mental image of the self-styled knight's face before answering.

"You have to take it from here. Kill the boss...That's what Diavel said."

Lind's face immediately scrunched up, and he hung his head again.

Eventually, his trembling voice traveled along the night breeze to my ears.

"...We will. On this floor...and the next, and the next after that. That's why the Dragon Knights were formed."

He turned back to his five comrades, head still hung, and held out a clenched fist. Hafner, the subleader of the group, joined him, then Shivata the swordsman, Naga with his flail, and two more whose names I didn't know yet, all thrusting their fists forward in a salute.

When Lind turned around again, back properly straight, his face held that familiar lofty, elite expression. He looked at me, then Kibaou, and announced stiffly, "The DKB will begin tackling the labyrinth in the morning. We will meet next at the assembly place in Zumfut on the twentieth, seventeen hundred hours. Good evening."

Even Kibaou watched without his usual sarcastic comments

as the six Dragon Knights marched over the grass to the east. Finally, he summoned all of his scorn and spat.

"Keh! Stupid brat, always lookin' down on us like he's so high an' mighty! As if I ain't got a heapin' helpin' of Diavel's will myself! C'mon, let's go! We ain't gonna stand around and let them get the jump on us. Let's go find that damn boss chamber!"

The other members of the ALS roared in approval, and the dozen headed off to the west. Apparently they had already set up base in the next town.

Kibaou, walking at the rear of his team, proceeded about five yards down the slope of the hill before stopping and turning back in our direction.

"Hey, kid…" He stopped briefly and made a face like he was drinking an antidote potion. "…Mr.…Kirito…"

My eyes went wide, and Asuna gurgled a sound that went something like "Frb!" Fortunately, Kibaou didn't seem to be paying attention to our reactions. He scratched at his cactus hair.

"I ain't gonna thank ya, 'cos ya stole the quest out from under my nose. But…I'm startin' to get the feelin' that it ain't the worst thing in the world ta have a guy like you—just one!—among the group. That's all."

He turned back to catch up with his group, and I managed to get out one final sentence.

"No need to 'mister' me next time."

With a wave of his hand in response, the leader of the Aincrad Liberation Squad descended behind the slope of the hill and disappeared.

Once the sound of their footsteps died out and there were no more color cursors in view, Asuna let out a deep, long breath.

I glanced over at her and she looked up to catch my eye. I realized that I still hadn't said anything to her about the fact that I'd left to complete the quest on my own while she was sleeping. She didn't appear to be angry, but it could also be her normal-looking next-level rage mode, so I knew I had to bring up the topic gingerly.

"Umm…I'm certain you have many things to say…"

"Of course."

"R-right."

"But I'm willing to wait until we get back to base."

"R-right."

With a secret sigh of relief, I turned to Kizmel this time. The dark elf knight was staring at the direction of the ALS in silence, then noticed my gaze and smiled.

"Your human knight brigades are not so bad after all, but they are a far cry from my Pagoda Tree Knights."

"W-well, naturally. We just call them guilds, though."

"I shall remember that. But, Kirito…I do not approve of this recklessness. If I had not woken and found you missing, we would not have been able to race here in time."

"S-sorry. And…thanks."

So it was Kizmel who had noticed first, not Asuna. My partner must have sensed what I was thinking, because she pouted and said, "It was my idea to chase after you, just so you know. I figured you were up to another one of your insane schemes. And I was right…Just after you told me not to go antagonizing the guilds, too."

"S-sorry. And thanks."

I bowed to them deeply and removed a sheaf of parchment from my coat pocket—the commander's orders I'd stolen from the forest elf camp.

"Well, let's leave the labyrinth up to them and deliver this bad boy to our dear commander."

9

HAVING ANNOUNCED THAT WE WOULD HAVE THE ten quests of the campaign available on this floor completed by five o'clock on December twentieth—just forty hours from then—we returned to the dark elf base, delivered the item to the commander to finish the "Infiltration" quest, and immediately left for our next mission.

The seventh chapter, "Butterfly Collection," was a brief breather of a quest that simply involved finding and defeating a giant butterfly released by the forest elves for reconnaissance. It would have been even easier with a decent Throwing Knives skill, but I didn't have the open slot at this point, so we had to go racing after the butterfly in the night forest, picking up stones to throw at it.

In the eighth chapter, "The Western Spirit Tree," the dark elf commander had read and digested the top-secret forest elf orders we brought back and was prepared to lead an attack on the forest elf base. He wanted to have the Jade Key secretly transported to their outpost on the fourth floor. Asuna, Kizmel, and I, accompanied by three dark elf soldiers, headed for the spirit tree the elves used to travel between floors.

Of course, these transport missions never ended uneventfully, and as we made our way toward the tree at the western edge of the forest, a mysterious band dressed in black ambushed us. Out of the four masked attackers—labeled UNKNOWN MARAUDERS in the game—we handily dispatched three. Both Asuna and I were well over the expected level at this point, and we had the services of the elite knight Kizmel. But the fourth marauder threw a smoke bomb and stole the key from the confused elven soldiers.

Naturally, I knew this ambush was coming, and I was ready to attempt defeating all four of them, but it was indeed an unwinnable fight. The other three bodies immediately blackened and melted away, so there was no way to tell who they were.

In the ninth quest, "Pursuit," we had to chase the thief through the forest. In the beta, I remembered this single quest lasting nearly from morning until night. It took that long because finding the "Shining Signal"—a small bottle of glowing liquid one of the elf soldiers hit the thief with—was incredibly hard in the midst of the deep forest.

We started the ninth chapter after noon on the nineteenth, and I was prepared for it to last well into the night. To my surprise—though at this point, I should have expected it—Kizmel's help proved invaluable. She stood at the lead and immediately pointed out the direction of the glowing light at every turn, so we discovered the thief's hideout cave by two o'clock.

The next step was to report to the commander, so we went back to base for food and rest, and by the evening, we were ready for the tenth and final quest of the campaign on the third floor, "Retrieving the Key." It was a difficult task that involved exploring a large dungeon, though not as large as the labyrinth. This was too much to complete before the end of the day, especially since our day had begun well before dawn, so we had to turn back after defeating the enormous whip spider boss of the dungeon's first level.

At eleven o'clock that night, we returned to the base and took turns bathing. This time, Kizmel decided to barge in during Asuna's turn, and sadly, there was no way to tell exactly what was happening beyond the tent flap based on the brief shrieks, splashes, and occasional laughing. After a late dinner, we went to bed and woke up in the early morning of December twentieth. After a quick tune-up with the blacksmith and some supply refills at the item shop, we briskly headed to conquer the second floor of the large underground dungeon.

Since we had returned to camp, the extra soldiers no longer accompanied us, but it was actually easier to coordinate high-level combat maneuvers with just the three of us. We powered our way through the insect and animal monsters, and finally came across the masked thief's hideout at the bottom of the dungeon.

We snuck up and peered through the window of their dining-room-like space, spotting five more thieves without masks on. They weren't forest elves, and certainly not dark elves. They were an entirely different race with skin dark purple, as though rotting away, and somehow demonic features.

The information on their cursors identified them as Fallen Elf Warriors. Kizmel looked nervous, but there wasn't time to stop and ask her about it. We proceeded onward and won several inescapable battles, finally arriving at the final boss of the dungeon and quest, the Fallen Elf Commander.

He was a difficult foe with a number of minions, but with our levels at the realistic limit for this floor, he posed no true threat to us. When Asuna's Chivalric Rapier delivered the killing blow, the commander hurled a final curse at us and melted away.

At the back of the room was a mountain of treasure, along with the Jade Key. This time, we managed to transport the key all the way to the spirit tree, signaling the end (at least on the third floor) of the long, long campaign.

But just as Asuna and I were about to high-five each other on a job well done, Kizmel interrupted with a surprising statement.

"Asuna…and Kirito," she said slowly and carefully, the light playing over her beautiful purple hair. "Now that it is clear the Fallen are in league with the forest elves, we must deliver this key to the fortress on the next floor above with haste. I believe that this task will fall upon me to complete…"

"Huh?"

Asuna's eyes went wide, and she took a step forward. Her face had the nervous smile of one who suspected what was coming. "Th-then we'll go with you. Just in case there's another ambush."

"Thank you, Asuna. Your offer is very kind."

Kizmel stopped there. She moved over to Asuna's side and looked upward.

We were close to the outer perimeter of Aincrad, and the pure blue expanse stretched out before us. The knotted trunk of the spirit tree stood in stark contrast to the cobalt sky behind it.

Near the roots of the fifteen-foot-wide tree was a large, gaping knot that led to a hollowed interior, but unlike the trees of Zumfut, this was not carved out by human hands. In the darkness within the hole, a blue light pulsed. Around the tree, mossy rocks formed a solid wall, and the only gate that accessed the tree was guarded by a quartet of dark elf sentries.

This tree was a teleporter for elves, and the forest elves had their own on the other side of the floor. As you might expect, there was much debate during the beta regarding whether or not these trees could be used to bypass the labyrinth. One guild even pulled together a thirty-man raid party to assault the tree, but the four guards easily quashed the attempt. My guess was that even if they'd succeeded, nothing would happen inside the tree.

As she stared up at the tree, Kizmel's next statement confirmed that months-old expectation.

"...Sadly, only the people of Lyusula are permitted to pass through the spirit tree's gate..."

Asuna was expecting this. After several long moments of silence, she nodded. "I see..."

"Yes," Kizmel returned solemnly. The elf shut her lips tight for a while, then turned and circled her arms around Asuna's back. The fencer's eyes widened briefly in surprise, but she returned the knight's embrace just as quickly.

With her mouth right at Asuna's ear, Kizmel whispered just loud enough for me to hear, "After I lost my sister a month ago, I was waiting to find my place to die. When I crossed blades with the white knight of Kales'Oh, I thought I was going to see my sister again. But...you and Kirito appeared and saved me. She must have guided you to my side..."

I didn't know Tilnel the herbalist had ever really existed in Aincrad. There was no way to know if the dark elves and forest elves had really carried out a major battle if there were no players around to see it. Those memories, including Tilnel, might have simply been implanted into Kizmel's programming as a story background, a backbone to her character.

But I could have sworn I saw a pale shimmer in the air beside Kizmel and Asuna. Perhaps it was just the light engine shining through the branches of the spirit tree. Or perhaps...

"...We'll see you again, won't we?" Asuna murmured into Kizmel's hair. The elf nodded vigorously.

"Absolutely. The Holy Tree will guide us together."

She squeezed harder, then released her hold. Kizmel shared one last smile with Asuna before looking at me.

I was expecting a handshake, perhaps a high five...but Kizmel strode forward with no hesitation and enveloped me in her arms as well. The cool, smooth metal of her armor and fresh piney scent made me feel like I was deep in a forest.

"The next time we meet, Kirito, I will tell you more of my dreams," she whispered. I put my hands on her back.

"Yeah, sounds good."

"It is a promise, then."

And with a last squeeze of her arms, Kizmel let go. She took a step back, then another, and raised her right fist to her left breast in salute. Asuna and I automatically returned it.

"And now...this is farewell. I am sorry not to accompany you to the Pillar of the Heavens, but I believe that you have the skill to dispatch its guardians. Be done with them and ascend. I will be waiting for you on the fourth floor."

"Take care, Kizmel," Asuna said. The knight smiled, then spun on her heel. Long cloak flapping, she strode off for the gate.

The guards stepped aside, she passed through, and they closed behind her.

Kizmel stepped through the knothole of the spirit tree without a backward glance and disappeared into its darkness. A few seconds later, the faint blue light flashed much brighter.

On the left side of my vision, the third HP bar that had been displayed for the last week vanished with a breezy jingle.

In the end, the reward for completing the third-floor portion of the Elf War campaign did not contain anything useful for defeating the boss.

When the commander back at the base thanked us for our service, the list of items we were able to choose from included half a dozen pieces of gear. But no matter how many times I pored over their specs, effects, and flavor text, there wasn't a single word that suggested any particular connection to the floor boss.

I ended up choosing a pair of leather boots with extra resistance to Tumbling and some extra jumping power (after having slipped during my duel with Morte), and Asuna picked out a new hooded cape made of the same material as Kizmel's favorite cloak. The faintly glowing pale purple cape gave a solid bonus to hiding and increased agility, though not to the extent of the original.

Until this point, our interactions with the dark elf commander had been very perfunctory—absolutely NPC-like. When we had chosen our rewards, he rose from his chair, and with concern on his face, said, "We elves are long-lived, but we can be hurt with blades as much as anyone else, and a deep-enough wound will kill. We are not gifted with the hardiness of the dwarves and humans. The Fallen Elves you fought in the underground maze are the descendants of those who sought to use the Holy Tree's magic to forge themselves bodies impervious to blades. This happened before the Great Separation, and they were banished for it. They are numerous throughout this castle, and their cooperation with the forest elves in search of the keys is troubling in the extreme. As the advance troop, we will remain here for now, surveying for traces of the Fallen before returning to our fortress on the fourth floor. Your continued assistance will be greatly appreciated."

Asuna and I shared a brief look and nodded together.

"W-we'd be happy to."

"Anything we can do."

"Good. Your help is a boon...I suspect the general at the fortress will treat you magnanimously. Take this commendation with you."

The commander picked a tightly rolled piece of parchment off his desk and offered it to me. We thanked him for this extra reward and were preparing to leave when the commander spoke again.

"You are going to climb the Pillar of the Heavens to the fourth floor?"

"Y...yes, that's the plan."

"In that case, be wary of the guardian beast's poisonous attack. You ought to prepare yourselves with plenty of poison-counteracting potions while you are in camp."

"Th-thank you very much for the advice," I said, bowing and leaving the tent.

As soon as I ventured outside, a horn sounded, signaling the passage of noon. I took a dozen steps toward the inviting scent of the dining tent before looking over to Asuna.

"...I'm not going to say I wasn't grateful for the advice, but..."

"Now it's harder to say that the quest rewards helping with the boss wasn't true..."

Over the past day, I'd explained to Asuna about my riverside duel with the swordsman/axman Morte and his suspicious activities.

Morte had joined the Dragon Knights Brigade and was helping them with the campaign—that much had been confirmed by Argo. And it was also certainly true that he was moonlighting with the Aincrad Liberation Squad, using a different class of weapon.

However, I suspected that Kibaou's sudden interest in the campaign, and his firm belief that the rewards were crucial to defeating the boss, were based on info Morte fed to him. If that source was a total lie, I was hoping to use that fact to get Kibaou to fess up about where he'd learned it. And yet...

"None of the items we could earn for finishing the quest had any special effect against the floor boss. Since Kibaou said the items you earned from the elf quest were necessary to avoid big trouble against the boss...then you could say that his information was a lie..."

"Right...But if someone claimed that the hint about poison antidotes *was* that reward, it's a lot harder to write it off entirely," Asuna responded almost immediately, her quick wit in keeping with her agility-first build. "All you can do now is just explain the truth exactly as it happened at the meeting tonight. If we watch Morte's reaction closely, maybe he'll give something away. At any rate, let's eat and take a break before we go. I hope they let us use Kizmel's tent."

"...G-good point."

Even if it was available to use, now that the owner was away on the fourth floor, it would just be the two of us sleeping under the same canopy. I chose not to bring that up and trotted after Asuna to the dining tent.

Thankfully, when Asuna did notice that the two of us would be sharing a tent alone, there was no fruit for her to throw, so I got a faceful of soft cushion instead.

Five in the evening.

The second strategy meeting was about to begin in the meeting grounds of Zumfut.

Lind's DKB and Kibaou's ALS had finished mapping the labyrinth tower up to the boss chamber on the top floor. The DKB had just barely beaten them to the door, so for the second floor in a row, the MC of the strategy meeting and the leader of the raid would be Lind.

What threw Asuna and me for a loop was Morte's absence from the meeting grounds. Perhaps he had changed his entire gear setup—in the safety of town, he could feel free to put on weapons whose skills he didn't have—taken off his coif, and slipped among the crowd in a form I didn't recognize, but Asuna said that as far as she could tell, both guilds had the same lineup as the second-floor boss battle.

The meeting began with the schedule of tomorrow morning's battle, then moved into actual strategy. Argo had already released her strategy guide on the boss, and based upon that beta test information, we split up the parties into separate roles.

Once the questions and answers were out of the way, Lind asked me to speak. Naturally, he wanted a report on the campaign quest rewards. I stood up and started off with a basic quest outline. When I reached the part about the Fallen Elves, the crowd started to stir. Some of them wanted more details about that, but I chose to keep it brief, knowing that Argo would soon be releasing the second volume of her Elf War guide.

"First things first: Nothing in the items themselves had any unique relation to the floor boss. However, after we received our loot, the elf commander gave us one piece of advice about the boss."

The entire crowd was silent, not wanting to miss this information.

"Umm...He said, bring plenty of antidote pots, because the boss uses poison attacks...That's it."

Now the silence turned awkward. It was such an obvious, basic piece of advice—who *wouldn't* bring a stock of antidotes to a major fight? I cleared my throat and added a piece of information for the sake of the commander's honor.

"Just so you know, the boss in the beta test didn't have a crazy poison attack. Since that might be the thing that was altered in this fight, it's probably a good idea to bring as many potions as you can. I'll leave it up to Lind and Kibaou to decide if this info counts as a 'quest reward crucial to defeating the boss' or not."

I sat back down, and the meeting grounds erupted into chatter. Some thought it was a letdown that there were no secret weapons against the boss, while others claimed that this knowledge was far more useful than an item. Foremost among the latter opinion was Joe from the ALS, who screeched that if we all tried the campaign now, we might learn something even more important.

Once again, Kibaou shut him up with a single command, and when the group had quieted down, Lind rounded up the discussion with his ever-solidifying leadership.

"We will visit every item shop tonight, even on the lower floors, and procure more than enough potions for tomorrow. As planned, we will begin our operation at nine o'clock tomorrow morning. Meet at the north gate of Zumfut. We will then travel to Dessel, the closest town to the labyrinth. After a short break, we will enter the tower. If all goes according to plan, we will defeat the floor boss by two in the afternoon."

He paused and surveyed the forty-some members gathered from left to right, then raised a bracing call. "Tomorrow night, we will celebrate in the main town of the fourth floor! C'mon, everyone...Let's win this fight!"

During the last meeting, I'd watched Lind deliver a speech on stage and thought, *You've got a long way to go to replace Diavel.*

But even if he did not become Diavel himself, Lind had a role to play that was his and his alone. Something much more crucial than mine, as I kept running from the truly important things. A role that someone had to take on, if we were actually going to reach that far-off hundredth floor.

Meanwhile, some were trying to fulfill roles that *no one* ought to touch. Morte was attempting to get the DKB and ALS to clash. The man in the black poncho had lured the Legend Braves into swindling other players. Whatever their intentions were, they surely would not stop now. I had to continue playing my role so that I could deal with their future machinations. Even the outcast of the front-runners could help in his own way.

I joined the others in raising my right hand toward the flat expanse of rock and steel a hundred yards above, and clutched my newfound determination deep within my chest.

At 1:12 PM the next day—Wednesday, December 21, 2022—Nerius the Evil Treant, boss of the third floor of Aincrad, was defeated by a forty-two-man raid built from seven parties.

The large tree monster liberally used a wide-area poison skill that hadn't been there in the beta, but our stock of antidotes did not run dry. As I expected, Asuna's Chivalric Rapier easily outclassed any other weapon present in damage, and the rest of the group was left in awe.

The battle took fifty-three minutes. As on the second floor, there were no fatalities.

Morte the ax warrior was not among the raid.

10

"...I WAS REALLY TRYING TO GET IT," ASUNA SULKED as we climbed the spiral staircase to the fourth floor.

"Huh? Get what?" I asked. She pouted even harder.

"The Last Attack bonus, obviously."

"Ah...r-right..."

"Your sword skill and mine hit at the exact same moment at the end. They were both two-part combos, and my rapier has more attack power than your sword, doesn't it?"

"Y-yes..."

"So how did you wind up with it? Logic states I should have gotten the LA."

"Um, well...I'm guessing that maybe my attack hit just a teensy-tiny bit faster than yours maybe?"

"No! It was *simultaneous!!*"

She turned her head away in a huff and sped faster up the stairs. I hurried after her and tried to change the subject.

"Besides, remember when we were talking on the last staircase? I was mentioning how combat in *SAO* is like an, um...what was the word again?"

"A concerto!" she snapped, not bothering to turn around.

I pointed at her cape. "Yeah, that! The concerto is the thing where one instrument plays the lead, while the rest form the backing orchestra. I assumed that it was a reference to one versus many in combat, but maybe I was wrong..."

"...Oh?" Asuna replied, slowing down so she could look sidelong at me. "What does it mean, then?"

"Umm...well, you're always alone, even when you're in a party or raid...but when you're in trouble, there are people around you to help you out..."

"...That's about the last thing I'd expect you to come up with," she said honestly. I had to agree. I must have still been a bit loopy from the adrenaline of my first boss fight in a week.

Asuna glanced exasperatedly at me, let out a brief sigh, and smiled.

"In that case, the lead player in the third-floor concerto wasn't you or me."

"...Huh? Who was it?"

"Kizmel, of course."

I had to agree. In nearly every battle during the ten quests of the campaign, Kizmel's overwhelming strength was the primary factor. She supported our endeavors at every turn. The concerto of the third floor, played on the stage of that deep, deep forest, undoubtedly featured the dark elf knight as its star.

"...We'll see her again, won't we?" Asuna mumbled. I had no answer at first. A chalk-colored door appeared ahead in the distance.

The DKB and ALS were still down in the boss chamber, conducting a dice-rolling tournament to see who would receive which piece of loot. Once again, it was our job to be the first to open the door to the next floor and to send Argo a message notifying her of the boss's defeat.

With thoughts of the next floor in my mind, untrod upon by the foot of any player, but somewhere containing our dear friend, I said...

"We will. I'm sure of it."

AFTERWORD

Hello, this is Reki Kawahara. Thanks for reading *Sword Art Online Progressive 2*.

Since we're safely under way by now, I think it's time to admit that this insane concept of following the conquest of Aincrad from the very first floor onward did not actually begin in this exact form.

As viewers of the *SAO* anime series from July to December 2012 know, the anime reordered the events of Aincrad into a more cohesive timeline. But in my original novel, the early parts of Aincrad were basically skipped over entirely. It starts with the first day of the game in December 2022, then jumps ahead six months to April 2023, when Kirito meets the Moonlit Black Cats.

This would be so much of a gap between the first and second episode, it was suggested that I write a plot that at least covers the conquering of the first floor. So I ended up producing a novella from Kirito and Asuna's first meeting to the boss. I fondly (?) remember the pale look on the producers' faces when I brought back twice the pages they needed, but at any rate, that was the genesis of "Aria of a Starless Night" from the first volume.

In essence, that was the end of my job, but once I finished "Aria," I was still left wondering what had happened to Kirito and Asuna after that. As I wrote in the last volume's afterword, I just wanted to see what our two heroes (and Argo, and Agil, and Kibaou) would do on the second floor. Of course, if I started on that, it would cause all kinds of contradictions with the main series, and I wasn't sure what to do for a while.

But it's the author's nature not to be able to stop once he's found something to write...so I scrawled the "Rondo of a Fragile Blade" in a dazed trance, and it too ended up far longer than I expected. Soon I learned that I'd be able to put out both "Aria" and "Rondo" in a single book, in October 2012. So in many ways, the *Progressive* series was the product of some unplanned circumstances. There's no other way I would have found the determination to write about all hundred floors of Aincrad from the start—no matter how much that desire might have existed within me.

Of course, now that I've started, there's no turning back to the Town of Beginnings! So at long last, here is the third-floor story, "Concerto of Black and White." As I announced last volume, this story's theme was campaign quests, but I'm sad to admit that I became so focused on Kizmel the NPC that the latter part of the quest had to be very quickly wrapped up.

While writing it, I was struck by how strange MMORPG quests really are. In a single-player RPG, at least your character is born into that universe and goes on an adventure, so challenging these various quests makes a kind of sense. But the player-characters in MMOs always have a bit of a stranger-in-a-strange-land vibe to them. They seem to take on more of the player's personality...I do get that feeling from actual MMOs, but in *SAO*, this fictional VRMMO, the characters *are* the players. Kirito and Asuna are visitors from the "foreign" realm of the real world and can tackle the quests of Aincrad as such. I wrote "Concerto" while pondering what they would feel and think. As a natural consequence of that, I had to write a little bit about how Aincrad itself came to be, and I'll reveal more of that backstory as we go along. After all, that campaign still has a long way to go.

The story of the fourth floor will probably come next year, but

I still intend to follow Kirito and the gang all the way to the hundredth floor, so I hope you tag along. The next volume of *SAO* proper is the fourteenth, which starts with the result of Kirito's duel with the Integrity Knight Eugeo. Hope you check it out!

Once again, I must extend super-thanks to my illustrator abec for providing super-cool, super-exciting illustrations despite her super-tough schedule, Mr. Kurusu for turning my nonsense scribbles into that super-beautiful map, and as usual, my beleaguered editors, Mr. Miki and Mr. Tsuchiya. And to all of you readers, for picking up my thirtieth published book, a truly heartfelt thanks!! I'll see you again next year!!

Reki Kawahara—October 2013